LINDA HOWARD

says that whether she's reading them or writing them, books have long played a profound role in her life. She cut her teeth on Margaret Mitchell and from then on continued to read widely and eagerly. In recent years her interest has settled on romance fiction, because she's "easily bored by murder, mayhem and politics." After twenty-one years of penning stories for her own enjoyment, Ms. Howard finally worked up the courage to submit a novel for publication—and met with success! Happily, the Alabama author has been steadily publishing ever since.

MERLINE LOVELACE

spent twenty-three years as an air force officer, serving tours at the Pentagon and at bases all over the world before she began a new career as a novelist. When she's not tied to her keyboard, she and her own handsome hero, her husband of thirty years, Al, enjoy traveling, golf and long lively dinners with friends and family. Merline enjoys hearing from readers and can be reached by e-mail via Internet through Harlequin's Web site at www.eHarlequin.com.

Overload
LINDA HOWARD

If a Man Answers
MERLINE LOVELACE

Silhouette Books

Published by Silhouette Books
America's Publisher of Contemporary Romance

SILHOUETTE BOOKS

Copyright in the collection:
© 2002 by Harlequin Books S.A.

ISBN 0-373-48477-1

The publisher acknowledges the copyright holders of the individual works as follows:

OVERLOAD
Copyright © 1993 by Linda Howington

IF A MAN ANSWERS
Copyright © 1998 by Merline Lovelace

OVERLOAD
Linda Howard

Dear Reader,

I have to be a little warped, but I've always kind of wanted to be trapped in an elevator. It seems like a fairly safe, small adventure, one you can tell your grandchildren about. Now, I wouldn't want to be trapped in an elevator packed with people, or with someone who has a bad case of body odor, or with…well, you get the idea. But getting trapped in an elevator with, say, a handsome man—that's something else entirely. That's a nice little adventure, right? So that's the situation in which I put my heroine in *Overload*. Elizabeth didn't get trapped in an elevator with just any man; nope, this was an ex-lover, whom she had been trying to avoid. He, of course, used the situation to his own advantage, because Elizabeth wasn't a woman a man could easily give up, not when he knew the answers to all the questions she had about him and their relationship, if he could only get her to listen.

I hope you enjoy it.

Linda Howard

Chapter One

It was hot, even for Dallas.

The scorching heat of the pavement seared through the thin leather of Elizabeth Major's shoes, forcing her to hurry even though it was an effort to move at all in the suffocating heat. The sleek office building where she worked didn't have its own underground parking garage, the builders having thought it unnecessary, since a parking deck was situated right across the street. Every time Elizabeth crossed the street in the rain, and every time she had risked being broiled by crossing it since this heat wave had begun, she swore that she would start looking for other office space. She always changed her mind as soon as she got inside, but it made her feel better to know she had the option of relocating.

Except for the parking situation, the building was perfect. It was only two years old, and managed to be both charming and convenient. The color scheme in the lobby was a soothing mixture of gray, dark mauve and white, striking the precise balance between masculine and feminine, so both genders felt comfortable. The lush greenery so carefully tended by a professional service added to the sense of freshness and spaciousness. The elevators were both numerous and fast and, so far, reliable. Her office having previously been in an older building where the elevator service had been cramped and erratic, Elizabeth doubly appreciated that last quality.

A private guard service handled the security, with a man stationed at a desk in the lobby for two shifts, from six in the morning until ten at night, as none of the businesses located in the building currently worked a third shift. Anyone wanting to come in earlier than six or stay later than ten had to let the guard service know. There was a rumor that the data processing firm on the tenth floor was considering going to three full shifts, and if that happened there would be a guard on duty around the clock. Until then, the building was locked down tight at 10:00 p.m. on weekdays and at 6:00 p.m. on weekends.

She pushed open the first set of doors and sighed with relief as the cool air rushed to greet her, washing over her hot face, evaporating the uncomfortable sweat that had formed in the time it had taken her to park her car and cross the street. When she entered the lobby itself through the second set of heavy glass doors, the full benefit of air conditioning swirled around her, making her shiver uncontrollably for just a second. Her panty hose had been clinging uncomfortably to her damp legs, and now the clammy feel made her grimace. For all that, however, she was jubilant as she crossed the lobby to the bank of elevators.

A big, unkempt man, a biker from the looks of him, entered the elevator just ahead of her. Immediately alert and wary, Elizabeth shifted her shoulder bag to her left shoulder, leaving her right hand unencumbered, as she stepped in and immediately turned to punch the button for the fifth floor, only to see a big, callused hand already pressing it. She aimed a vague smile, the kind people give each other in elevators, at the big man, then resolutely kept her gaze on the doors in front of her as they were whisked silently and rapidly to the fifth floor. But she relaxed somewhat, for if he was going to the fifth floor, he was undoubtedly involved, in some way, with Quinlan Securities.

She stepped out, and he was right on her heels as she

marched down the hallway. Her offices were on the left, the chic interior revealed by the huge windows, and she saw that her secretary, Chickie, was back from lunch on time. Not only that, Chickie looked up and watched her coming down the hall. Or rather, she watched the man behind her. Elizabeth could see Chickie's big dark eyes fasten on the big man and widen with fascination.

Elizabeth opened her office door. The biker, without pausing, opened the door to Quinlan Securities, directly across the hall from her. Quinlan Securities didn't have any windows into the hallway, only a discreet sign on a solid-looking door. She had been glad, on more than one occasion, that there were no windows for more than one reason. The people who went through that door were...*interesting*, to say the least.

"Wow," Chickie said, her gaze now fastened on the closed door across the hall. "Did you see that?"

"I saw it," Elizabeth said dryly.

Chickie's taste in men, regrettably, tended toward the unpolished variety. "He wore an earring," she said dreamily. "And did you see his hair?"

"Yes. It was long and uncombed."

"What a *mane!* I wonder why he's going into Quinlan's." Chickie's eyes brightened. "Maybe he's a new staffer!"

Elizabeth shuddered at the thought, but it was possible. Unfortunately the "Securities" in Quinlan Securities didn't refer to the financial kind but the physical sort. Chickie, who didn't have a shy bone in her body, had investigated when they had first moved into the building and cheerfully reported that Quinlan handled security of all types, from security systems to bodyguards. To Elizabeth's way of thinking, that didn't explain the type of people they saw coming and going from the Quinlan offices. The clientele, or maybe it was the *staff*, had a decidedly rough edge. If they were the former, she couldn't imagine them having enough money to afford security services. If they were the latter, she likewise couldn't imagine a client feeling comfortable around bodyguards who looked like mass murderers.

She had dated Tom Quinlan, the owner, for a while last winter, but he had been very closemouthed about his business, and she had been wary about asking. In fact, everything about Tom had made her wary. He was a big, macho, take-charge type of man, effortlessly overwhelming in both personality and body. When she had realized how he was taking over her life, she had swiftly ended the relationship and since then gone out of her way to avoid him. She would *not* lose control of her life again, and Tom Quinlan had overstepped the bounds in a big way.

Chickie dragged her attention away from the closed door across the hall and looked expectantly at Elizabeth. "Well?"

Elizabeth couldn't hold back the grin that slowly widened as her triumph glowed through. "She loved it."

"She did? You *got* it?" Chickie shrieked, jumping up and sending her chair spinning.

"I got it. We'll start next month." Her lunch meeting had been with Sandra Eiland, possessor of one of the oldest fortunes in Dallas. Sandra had decided to renovate her lavish hacienda-style house, and Elizabeth had just landed the interior-design account. She had owned her own firm for five years now, and this was the biggest job she had gotten, as well as being the most visible one. Sandra Eiland loved parties and entertained often; Elizabeth couldn't have paid for better advertising. This one account lifted her onto a completely different level of success.

Chickie's enthusiasm was immediate and obvious; she danced around the reception area, her long black hair flying. "Look out, Dallas, we are cooking now!" she crowed. "Today the Eiland account, tomorrow—tomorrow you'll do something else. We are going to be *busy*."

"I hope," Elizabeth said as she passed through into her office.

"No hoping to it." Chickie followed, still dancing. "It's guaranteed. The phone will be ringing so much I'll have to have an assistant. Yeah, I like the idea of that. Someone else can answer the phone, and I'll chase around town finding the stuff you'll need for all the jobs that will be pouring in."

"If you're chasing around town, you won't be able to watch the comings and goings across the hall," Elizabeth pointed out in a casual tone, hiding her amusement.

Chickie stopped dancing and looked thoughtful. She considered Quinlan's to be her own secret treasure trove of interesting, potential men, far more productive than a singles' bar.

"So maybe I'll have *two* assistants," she finally said. "One to answer the phone, and one to chase around town while I stay here and keep things organized."

Elizabeth laughed aloud. Chickie was such an exuberant person that it was a joy to be around her. Their styles complemented each other, Elizabeth's dry, sometimes acerbic wit balanced by Chickie's unwavering good nature. Where Elizabeth was tall and slim, Chickie was short and voluptuous. Chickie tended toward the dramatic in clothing, so Elizabeth toned down her own choices. Clients didn't like to be overwhelmed or restrained. It was subtle, but the contrast between Elizabeth and Chickie in some way relaxed her clients, reassured them that they wouldn't be pressured into a style they weren't comfortable with. Of course, sometimes Elizabeth wasn't comfortable with her own style of dress, such as today, when the heat was so miserable and she would have been much happier in shorts and a cotton T-shirt, but she had mentally, and perhaps literally, girded her loins with panty hose. If it hadn't been for the invention of air conditioning, she never would have made it; just crossing the street in this incredible heat was a feat of endurance.

Chickie's bangle bracelets made a tinkling noise as she seated herself across from Elizabeth's desk. "What time are you leaving?"

"Leaving?" Sometimes Chickie's conversational jumps were a little hard to follow. "I just got back."

"Don't you ever listen to the radio? The heat is *hazardous*. The health department, or maybe it's the weather bureau, is warning everyone to stay inside during the hottest part of the day, drink plenty of water, stuff like that. Most businesses are opening only in the mornings, then letting their people go home early so they won't get caught in traffic. I checked around. Just about everyone in the building is closing up by two this afternoon."

Elizabeth looked at the Eiland folder she had just placed on her desk. She could barely wait to get started. "You can go home anytime you want," she said. "I had some ideas about the Eiland house that I want to work on while they're still fresh in my mind."

"I don't have any plans," Chickie said immediately. "I'll stay."

Elizabeth settled down to work and, as usual, soon became lost in the job. She loved interior design, loved the challenge of making a home both beautiful and functional, as well as suited to the owner's character. For Sandra Eiland, she wanted something that kept the flavor of the old Southwest, with an air of light and spaciousness, but also conveyed Sandra's sleek sophistication.

The ringing of the telephone finally disrupted her concentration, and she glanced at the clock, surprised to find that it was already after three o'clock. Chickie answered the call, listened for a moment, then said, "I'll find out. Hold on." She swiveled in her chair to look through the open door into Elizabeth's office. "It's the guard downstairs. He's a substitute, not our regular guard, and he's checking the offices, since he doesn't know anyone's routine. He says that almost everyone else has already gone, and he wants to know how late we'll be here."

"Why don't you go on home now," Elizabeth suggested. "There's no point in your staying later. And tell the guard I'll leave within the hour. I want to finish this sketch, but it won't take long."

"I'll stay with you," Chickie said yet again.

"No, there's no need. Just switch on the answering machine. I promise I won't be here much longer."

"Well, all right." Chickie relayed the message to the guard, then hung up and retrieved her purse from the bottom desk drawer. "I dread going out there," she said. "It might be worth it to wait until after sundown, when it cools down to the nineties."

"It's over five hours until sundown. This is July, remember."

"On the other hand, I could spend those five hours beguiling the cute guy who moved in across the hall last week."

"Sounds more productive."

"And more fun." Chickie flashed her quick grin. "He won't have a chance. See you tomorrow."

"Yes. Good luck." By the time Chickie sashayed out of the office, scarlet skirt swinging, Elizabeth had already become engrossed in the sketch taking shape beneath her talented fingers. She always did the best she could with any design, but she particularly wanted this one to be perfect, not just for the benefit to her career, but because that wonderful old house deserved it.

Her fingers finally cramped, and she stopped for a moment, noticing at the same time how tight her shoulders were, though they usually got that way only when she had been sitting hunched over a sketch pad for several hours. Absently she flexed them and was reaching for the pencil again when she realized what that tightness meant. She made a sound of annoyance when a glance at the clock said that it was 5:20, far later than she had meant to stay. Now she would have to deal with the traffic she had wanted to avoid, with this murderous heat wave making everyone ill-tempered and aggressive.

She stood and stretched, then got her bag and turned off the lights. The searing afternoon sun was blocked by the tall building next door, but there was still plenty of light coming through the tinted windows, and the office was far from dark. As she stepped out into the hall and turned to lock her door, Tom Quinlan exited his office and did the same. Elizabeth carefully didn't look at him, but she felt his gaze on her and automatically tensed. Quinlan had that effect on her, always had. It was one of the reasons she had stopped dating him, though not the biggie.

She had the uncomfortable feeling that he'd been waiting for her, somehow, and she glanced around uneasily, but no one else was around. Usually the building was full of people at this hour, as the workday wound down, but she was acutely aware of the silence around them. Surely they weren't the only two people left! But common sense told her that they were, that everyone else had sensibly gone home early; she wouldn't have any buffer between herself and Quinlan.

He fell into step beside her as she strode down the hall to the elevators. "Don't I even rate a hello these days?"

"Hello," she said.

"You're working late. Everyone else left hours ago."

"You didn't."

"No." He changed the subject abruptly. "Have dinner

with me." His tone made it more of an order than an invitation.

"No, thank you," she replied as they reached the elevators. She punched the Down button and silently prayed for the elevator to hurry. The sooner she was away from this man, the safer she would feel.

"Why not?"

"Because I don't want to."

A soft chime signaled the arrival of a car; the elevator doors slid open, and she stepped inside. Quinlan followed, and the doors closed, sealing her inside with him. She reached out to punch the ground-floor button, but he caught her hand, moving so that his big body was between her and the control panel.

"You do want to, you're just afraid."

Elizabeth considered that statement, then squared her shoulders and looked up at his grim face. "You're right. I'm afraid. And I don't go out with men who scare me."

He didn't like that at all, even though he had brought up the subject. "Are you afraid I'll hurt you?" he demanded in a disbelieving tone.

"Of course not!" she scoffed, and his expression relaxed. She knew she hadn't quite told the truth, but that was her business, not his, a concept he had trouble grasping. Deftly she tugged her hand free. "It's just that you'd be a big complication, and I don't have time for that. I'm afraid you'd really mess up my schedule."

His eyes widened incredulously, then he exploded. "Hellfire, woman!" he roared, the sound deafening in the small enclosure. "You've been giving me the cold shoulder for over six months because you don't want me to interfere with your *schedule?*"

She lifted one shoulder in a shrug. "What can I say? We all have our priorities." Deftly she leaned past him and punched the button, and the elevator began sliding smoothly downward.

Three seconds later it lurched to a violent stop. Hurled off balance, Elizabeth crashed into Quinlan; his hard arms wrapped around her as they fell, and he twisted his muscular body to cushion the impact for her. Simultaneously the lights went off, plunging them into complete darkness.

Chapter Two

The red emergency lights blinked on almost immediately, bathing them in a dim, unearthly glow. She didn't, couldn't move, not just yet; she was paralyzed by a strange mixture of alarm and pleasure. She lay sprawled on top of Quinlan, her arms instinctively latched around his neck while his own arms cradled her to him. She could feel the heat of his body even through the layers of their clothing, and the musky man-scent of his skin called up potent memories of a night when there had been no clothing to shield her from his heat. Her flesh quickened, but her spirit rebelled, and she pushed subtly against him in an effort to free herself. For a second his arms tightened, forcing her closer, flattening her breasts against the hard muscularity of his chest. The red half-light darkened his blue eyes to black, but even so, she could read the determination and desire revealed in them.

The desire tempted her to relax, to sink bonelessly into his embrace, but the determination had her pulling back. Almost immediately he released her, though she sensed his reluctance, and rolled to his feet with a lithe, powerful movement. He caught her arms and lifted her with ridiculous ease. "Are you all right? Any bruises?"

She smoothed down her skirt. "No, I'm fine. You?"

He grunted in reply, already opening the panel that hid the emergency phone. He lifted the receiver and punched the button that would alert Maintenance. Elizabeth waited, but he didn't say anything. His dark brows drew together, and finally he slammed the receiver down. "No answer. The maintenance crew must have gone home early, like everyone else."

She looked at the telephone. There was no dial on it, no buttons other than that one. It was connected only to Maintenance, meaning they couldn't call out on it.

Then she noticed something else, and her head lifted. "The air has stopped." She lifted her hand to check, but there was no cool air blowing from the vents. The lack of noise had alerted her.

"The power must be off," he said, turning his attention to the door.

The still air in the small enclosure was already becoming stuffy. She didn't like the feeling, but she refused to let herself get panicky. "It probably won't be long before it comes back on."

"Normally I'd agree with you, if we weren't having a heat wave, but the odds are too strong that it's a system overload, and if that's the case, it can take hours to repair. We have to get out. These lights are battery operated and won't stay on long. Not only that, the heat will build up, and we don't have water or enough oxygen in here." Even as he spoke, he was attacking the elevator doors with his strong fingers, forcing them open inch by inch. Elizabeth added her strength to his, though she was aware that he could handle it perfectly well by himself. It was just that she couldn't tolerate the way he had of taking over and making her feel so useless.

They were stuck between floors, with about three feet of the outer doors visible at the bottom of the elevator car. She helped him force open those doors, too. Before she could say anything, he had lowered himself through the opening and swung lithely to the floor below.

He turned around and reached up for her. "Just slide out. I'll catch you."

She sniffed, though she was a little apprehensive about what she was going to try. It had been a long time since she had done anything that athletic. "Thanks, but I don't need any help. I took gymnastics in college.'' She took a deep, preparatory breath, then swung out of the elevator every bit as gracefully as he had, even encumbered as she was with her shoulder bag and handicapped by her high heels. His dark brows arched, and he silently applauded. She bowed. One of the things that she had found most irresistible about Quinlan was the way she had been able to joke with him. Actually there was a lot about him that she'd found irresistible, so much so that she had ignored his forcefulness and penchant for control, at least until she had found that report in his apartment. She hadn't been able to ignore that.

''I'm impressed,'' he said.

Wryly she said, ''So am I. It's been years.''

''You were on the college gymnastics team, huh? You never told me that before.''

''Nothing to tell, because I *wasn't* on the college team. I'm too tall to be really good. But I took classes, for conditioning and relaxation.''

''From what I remember,'' he said lazily, ''you're still in great shape.''

Elizabeth wheeled away and began walking briskly to the stairs, turning her back on the intimacy of that remark. She could feel him right behind her, like a great beast stalking its prey. She pushed open the door and stopped in her tracks. ''Uh-oh.''

The stairwell was completely dark. It wasn't on an outside wall, but it would have been windowless in any case. The hallway was dim, with only one office on that floor having interior windows, but the stairwell was stygian. Stepping into it would be like stepping into a well, and she felt a sudden primal instinct against it.

''No problem,'' Quinlan said, so close that his breath stirred her hair and she could feel his chest brush against her back with each inhalation. ''Unless you have claustrophobia?''

"No, but I might develop a case any minute now."

He chuckled. "It won't take that long to get down. We're on the third floor, so it's four short flights and out. I'll hold the door until you get your hand on the rail."

Since the only alternative was waiting there until the power came back on, Elizabeth shrugged, took a deep breath as if she were diving and stepped into the dark hole. Quinlan was so big that he blocked most of the light, but she grasped the rail and went down the first step. "Okay, stay right there until I'm with you," he said, and let the door close behind him as he stepped forward.

She had the immediate impression of being enclosed in a tomb, but in about one second he was beside her, his arm stretched behind her back with that hand holding the rail, while he held her other arm with his free hand. In the warm, airless darkness she felt utterly surrounded by his strength. "I'm not going to fall," she said, unable to keep the bite from her voice.

"You're sure as hell not," he replied calmly. He didn't release her.

"Quinlan—"

"Walk."

Because it was the fastest way to get out of his grasp, she walked. The complete darkness was disorienting at first, but she pictured the stairs in her mind, found the rhythm of their placement, and managed to go down at almost normal speed. Four short flights, as he had said. Two flights separated by a landing constituted one floor. At the end of the fourth flight he released her, stepped forward a few steps and found the door that opened onto the first floor. Gratefully Elizabeth hurried into the sunlit lobby. She knew it was all in her imagination, but she felt as if she could breathe easier with space around her.

Quinlan crossed rapidly to the guard's desk, which was unoccupied. Elizabeth frowned. The guard was always there—or rather, he had always been there before, because he certainly wasn't *now*.

When he reached the desk, Quinlan immediately began trying to open the drawers. They were all locked. He straightened and yelled, "Hello?" His deep voice echoed in the eerily silent lobby.

Elizabeth groaned as she realized what had happened. "The guard must have gone home early, too."

"He's supposed to stay until everyone is out."

"He was a substitute. When he called the office, Chickie told him that I would leave before four. If there were other stragglers, he must have assumed that I was among them. What about you?"

"Me?" Quinlan shrugged, his eyes hooded. "Same thing."

She didn't quite believe him, but she didn't pursue it. Instead she walked over to the inner set of doors that led to the outside and tugged at them. They didn't budge. Well, great. They were locked in. "There has to be some way out of here," she muttered.

"There isn't," he said flatly.

She stopped and stared at him. "What do you mean, 'there isn't'?"

"I mean the building is sealed. Security. Keeps looters out during a power outage. The glass is reinforced, shatter-proof. Even if we called the guard service and they sent someone over, they couldn't unlock the doors until the electricity was restored. It's like the vault mechanisms in banks."

"Well, you're the security expert. Get us out. Override the system somehow."

"Can't be done."

"Of course it can. Or are you admitting there's something you can't do?"

He crossed his arms over his chest and smiled benignly.

"I mean that I designed the security system in this building, and it can't be breached. At least, not until the power comes back on. Until then, I can't get into the system. No one can."

Elizabeth caught her breath on a surge of fury, more at his attitude than the circumstances. He just looked so damn *smug*.

"So we call 911," she said.

"Why?"

"What do you mean, why? We're stuck in this building!"

"Is either of us ill? Hurt? Are we in any danger? This isn't an emergency, it's an inconvenience, and believe me, they have their hands full with real emergencies right now. And they can't get into the building, either. The only possible way out is to climb to the roof and be lifted off by helicopter, but that's an awful lot of expense and trouble for someone who isn't in any danger. We have food and water in the building. The sensible thing is to stay right here."

Put that way, she grudgingly accepted that she had no choice. "I know," she said with a sigh. "It's just that I feel so...trapped." In more ways than one.

"It'll be fun. We'll get to raid the snack machines—"

"They operate on electricity, too."

"I didn't say we'd use money," he replied, and winked at her. "Under the circumstances, no one will mind."

She would mind. She dreaded every minute of this, and it could last for *hours*. The last thing she wanted to do was spend any time alone with Quinlan, but it looked as if she had no choice. If only she could relax in his company, she wouldn't mind, but that was beyond her ability. She felt acutely uncomfortable with him, her tension compounded of several different things: uppermost was anger that he had dared to pry into her life the way he had; a fair amount of guilt, for she knew she owed him at least an explanation, and the truth was still both painful and embarrassing; a sort of wistfulness, because she had enjoyed so much about him; and desire—God, yes, a frustrated desire that had been feeding for months on the memory of that one night they had spent together.

"We don't have to worry about the air," he said, looking around at the two-story lobby. "It'll get considerably warmer in here, but the insulation and thermal-glazed windows will keep it from getting critically hot. We'll be okay."

She forced herself to stop fretting and think sensibly. There was no way out of this situation, so she might as well make the best of it, and that meant staying as comfortable as they could. In this case, comfortable meant cool. She began looking around; as he'd said, they had food and water, though they would have to scrounge for it, and there was enough furniture here in the lobby to furnish several living rooms, so they had plenty of cushions to fashion beds. Her mind skittered away from that last thought. Her gaze fell on the stairway doors, and the old saying "hot air rises" came to mind. "If we open the bottom stairway doors, that'll create a chimney effect to carry the heat upward," she said.

"Good idea. I'm going to go back up to my office to get a flashlight and raid the snack machine. Is there anything you want from your office while I'm up there?"

Mentally she ransacked her office, coming up with several items that might prove handy. "Quite a bit, actually. I'll go with you."

"No point in both of us climbing the stairs in the dark," he said casually. "Just tell me what you want."

That was just like him, she thought irritably, wanting to do everything himself and not involve her. "It makes more sense if we both go. You can pilfer your office for survival stuff, and I'll pilfer mine. I think I have a flashlight, too, but I'm not certain where it is."

"It's eight flights, climbing, this time, instead of going down," he warned her, looking down at her high heels.

In answer, she stepped out of her shoes and lifted her eyebrows expectantly. He gave her a thoughtful look, then gave in without more argument, gesturing her ahead of him. He relocated a large potted tree to hold the stairway door propped open, handling it as casually as if the big pot didn't weigh over a hundred pounds. Elizabeth had a good idea how heavy it was, however, for she loved potted plants and her condo was always full of greenery. She wondered how it would feel to have such strength, to possess Quinlan's basic self-confidence that he could handle any situation or difficulty. With him, it was even more than mere confidence; there was a certain arrogance, subtle but unmistakably there, the quiet arrogance of a man who knew his own strengths and skills. Though he had adroitly sidestepped giving out any personal information about his past, she sensed that some of those skills were deadly.

She entered the stairwell with less uneasiness this time, for there was enough light coming in through the open door to make the first two flights perfectly visible. Above that, however, they proceeded in thick, all-encompassing darkness. As he had before, Quinlan passed an arm behind her back to grip the rail, and his free hand held her elbow. His hand had always been there whenever they had gone up or down steps, she remembered. At first it had been pleasurable, but soon she had felt a little smothered, and then downright alarmed. Quinlan's possessiveness had made her uneasy, rather than secure. She knew too well how such an attitude could get out of hand.

Just to break the silence she quipped, "If either of us smoked, we'd have a cigarette lighter to light our path."

"If either of us smoked," he came back dryly, "we wouldn't have the breath to climb the stairs."

She chuckled, then saved her energy to concentrate on

the steps. Climbing five floors wasn't beyond her capabilities, but it was still an effort. She was breathing hard by the time they reached the fifth floor, and the darkness was becoming unnerving. Quinlan stepped forward and opened the door, letting in a sweet spill of light.

They parted ways at their respective offices, Quinlan disappearing into his while Elizabeth unlocked hers. The late-afternoon light was still spilling brightly through the windows, reminding her that, in actuality, very little time had passed since the elevator had lurched to a halt. A disbelieving glance at her wristwatch said that it had been less than half an hour.

The flashlight was the most important item, and she searched the file cabinets until she found it. Praying that the batteries weren't dead, she thumbed the switch and was rewarded by a beam of light. She switched it off and placed it on Chickie's desk. She and Chickie made their own coffee, as it was both more convenient and better tasting than the vending machine kind, so she got their cups and put them on the desk next to the flashlight. Drinking from them would be easier than splashing water into their mouths with their hands, and she knew Chickie wouldn't mind if Quinlan used her cup. Quite the contrary.

Knowing that her secretary had an active sweet tooth, Elizabeth began rifling the desk drawers, smiling in appreciation when she found a six-pack of chocolate bars with only one missing, a new pack of fig bars, chewing gum, a honey bun and a huge blueberry muffin. Granted, it was junk food, but at least they wouldn't be hungry. Finally she got two of the soft pillows that decorated the chairs in her office, thinking that they would be more comfortable for sleeping than the upholstered cushions downstairs.

Quinlan opened the door, and she glanced at him. He had removed his suit jacket and was carrying a small black leather bag. He looked at her loot and laughed softly. "Were you a scout, by any chance?"

"I can't take the credit for most of it. Chickie's the one with a sweet tooth."

"Remind me to give her a big hug the next time I see her."

"She'd rather have you set her up on a date with that biker who came in after lunch."

He laughed again. "Feeling adventurous, is she?"

"Chickie's *always* adventurous. Was he a client?"

"No."

She sensed that that was all the information he was going to give out about the "biker." As always, Quinlan was extremely closemouthed about his business, both clients and staff. On their dates, he had always wanted to talk about *her,* showing interest in every little detail of her life, while at the same time gently stonewalling her tentative efforts to find out more about him. It hadn't been long before that focused interest, coupled with his refusal to talk about himself, had begun making her extremely uncomfortable. She could understand not wanting to talk about certain things; there was a certain period that she couldn't bring herself to talk about, either, but Quinlan's secretiveness had been so absolute that she didn't even know if he had any family. On the other hand, he had noticed the gap in her own life and had already started asking probing little questions when she had broken off the relationship.

There was a silk paisley shawl draped across a chair, and Elizabeth spread it across the desk to use as an upscale version of a hobo's pouch. As she began piling her collection in the middle of the shawl, Quinlan casually flicked at the fringe with one finger. "Do people actually buy shawls just because they look good draped across chairs?"

"Of course. Why not?"

"It's kind of silly, isn't it?"

"I guess it depends on your viewpoint. Do you think it's silly when people spend hundreds of dollars on mag wheels for their cars or trucks, just because they look good?"

"Cars and trucks are useful."

"So are chairs," she said dryly. She gathered the four corners of the shawl together and tied them in a knot. "Ready."

"While we're up here, we need to raid the snack machines, rather than rely on what you have there. There's no point in making extra trips upstairs to get more food when we can get it now."

She gave him a dubious look. "Do you think we'll be here so long that we'll need that much food?"

"Probably not, but I'd rather have too much than too little. We can always return what we don't eat."

"Logical," she admitted.

He turned to open the door for her, and Elizabeth stared in shock at the lethal black pistol tucked into his waistband at the small of his back. "Good God," she blurted. "What are you going to do with that?"

Chapter Three

He raised his eyebrows. "Whatever needs doing," he said mildly.

"Thank you so much for the reassurance! Are you expecting any kind of trouble? I thought you said the building was sealed."

"The building *is* sealed, and no, I'm not expecting any trouble. That doesn't mean I'm going to be caught unprepared if I'm wrong. Don't worry about it. I'm always armed, in one way or another. It's just that this is the first time you've noticed."

She stared at him. "You don't usually carry a pistol."

"Yes, I do. You wouldn't have noticed it now if I hadn't taken my coat off."

"You didn't have one the night we—" She cut off the rest of the sentence.

"Made love?" He finished it for her. His blue eyes were steady, watchful. "Not that night, no. I knew I was going to make love to you, and I didn't want to scare you in any way, so I locked the pistol in the glove compartment before I picked you up. But I had a knife in my boot. Just like I do now."

It was difficult to breathe. She fought to suck in a deep breath as she bypassed the issue of the pistol and latched on to the most shocking part of what he'd just said. "You *knew* we were going to make love?"

He gave her another of those thoughtful looks. "You don't want to talk about that right now. Let's get finished here and get settled in the lobby before dark so we can save the batteries in the flashlights."

It was another logical suggestion, except for the fact that night wouldn't arrive until about nine o'clock, giving them plenty of time. She leaned back against the desk and crossed her arms. "Why don't I want to talk about it now?"

"Just an assumption I made. You've spent over half a year avoiding me, so I didn't think you would suddenly want to start an in-depth discussion. If I'm wrong, by all means let's talk." A sudden dangerous glitter lit his eyes. "Was I too rough? Was five times too many? I don't think so, because I could feel your climaxes squeezing me," he said bluntly. "Not to mention the way you had your legs locked around me so tight I could barely move. And I know damn good and well I don't snore or talk in my sleep, so just what in hell happened to send you running?"

His voice was low and hard, and he had moved closer so that he loomed over her. She had never seen him lose control, but as she saw the rage in his eyes she knew that he was closer to doing so now than she had ever imagined. It shook her a little. Not because she was afraid of him—at least, not in that way—but because she hadn't imagined it would have mattered so much to him.

Then she squared her shoulders, determined not to let him take charge of the conversation and turn it back on her the way he had so many times. "What do you mean, you *knew* we would make love that night?" she demanded, getting back to the original subject.

"Just what I said."

"How could you have been so sure? *I* certainly hadn't planned on it happening."

"No. But I knew you wouldn't turn me down."

"You know a damn lot, don't you?" she snapped, incensed by that unshakable self-confidence of his.

"Yeah. But I don't know why you ran afterward. So why don't you tell me? Then we can get the problem straightened out and pick up where we left off."

She glared at him, not budging. He ran his hand through his dark hair, which he kept in a short, almost military cut. He was so controlled, it was one of the few gestures of irritation she could ever remember him making. "All right," he muttered. "I knew you were hiding things from me, maybe because you didn't trust what was between us. I thought that once we'd made love, once you knew you belonged to me, you'd trust me and stop holding back."

She forgot to glare. Her arms dropped to her sides, and she gaped at him. "I *belong* to you? I beg your pardon! Do you have a bill of sale that I don't know about?"

"Yes, belong!" he barked. "I had planned on marriage, kids, the whole bit, but you kept edging away from me. And I didn't know why. I still don't."

"Marriage? Kids?" She could barely speak, she was so astounded. The words came out in a squeak. "I don't suppose it ever occurred to you to let me in on all of this planning you were doing, did it? No, don't bother to answer. You made up your mind, and that was it, regardless of how *I* felt."

"I knew how you felt. You were in love with me. You still are. That's why it doesn't make sense that you ran."

"Maybe not to you, but it's crystal clear to me." She looked away, her face burning. She hadn't realized her feelings had been so obvious to him, though she had known fairly early in their relationship that she loved him. The more uneasy she had become, however, the more she had tried to hide the intensity of her feelings.

"Then why don't you let me in on the secret? I'm tired of this. Whatever it is I did, I apologize for it. We've wasted enough time."

His arrogance was astonishing, even though she had recognized that part of his character from the beginning. Quinlan was generally a quiet man, but it was the quietness of someone who had nothing to prove, to himself or anyone else. He had decided to put an end to the situation, and that was that, at least from his viewpoint.

But not from hers.

"You listen to me, Tom Quinlan," she said furiously. "I don't care what plans you've made, you can just write me out of them. I don't want—"

"I can't do that," he interrupted.

"Why not?"

"Because of this."

She saw the glitter in his eyes and immediately bolted away from the desk, intent on escape. She was quick, but he was quicker. He seized her wrists and folded her arms behind her back, effectively wrapping her in his embrace at the same time. The pressure of his iron-muscled arms forced her against the hard planes of his body. Having seen him naked, she knew that his clothing disguised his true strength and muscularity, knew that she didn't have a prayer of escaping until he decided to release her. She declined to struggle, contenting herself with a furious glare.

"Cat eyes," he murmured. "The first time I saw you, I knew you were no lady. Your eyes give you away. And I was right, thank God. The night we spent together proved that you don't give a damn about what's proper or ladylike. You're wild and hot, and we wrecked my bed. You should have known there's no way in hell I'd let you go."

He was aroused. She could feel his hardness thrusting against her, his hips moving ever so slightly in a nestling motion, wordlessly trying to tempt her into opening her thighs to cradle him. It *was* tempting. Damn tempting. She couldn't deny wanting him, had never tried to, but he was right: she didn't trust him.

"It won't work," she said hoarsely.

"It already has." The words were soft, almost crooning, and his warm breath washed over her mouth a second before his lips were there, firm and hot, his head slanting to deepen

the kiss and open her mouth to him. She hadn't meant to
do so, but she found herself helpless to prevent it. Right
from the beginning, his kisses had made her dizzy with
delight. His self-confidence was manifested even in this;
there was no hesitancy, no awkwardness. He simply took
her mouth as if it were his right, his tongue probing deep,
and a deep shudder of pleasure made her quake.

Held against him as she was, she could feel the tension
in his body, feel his sex throbbing with arousal. He had
never made any effort to disguise his response to her.
Though it had been obvious even on their first date, he
hadn't pressured her in any way. Maybe she had started
falling in love with him then, because he had been both
amused and matter-of-fact about his frequent arousal, his
attitude being that it was a natural result of being in her
company. She hadn't felt threatened in any way; in fact,
looking back, she realized that Quinlan had gone out of his
way to keep from alarming her. He had been remarkably
unaggressive, sexually speaking, despite the persistent evidence of his attraction. She had never felt that she might
have to face a wrestling match at the end of an evening.
Even the night they had made love, she hadn't fully realized
the seriousness of his kisses until she had somehow found
herself naked in bed with him, her body on fire with need.
Then she had discovered that he was very serious, indeed.

The memory made her panic, and she tore her mouth
away from his. She had no doubt that if she didn't stop him
now, within five minutes he would be making love to her.
The hot sensuality of his kisses was deceptive, arousing her
more and faster than she'd expected. It had been the same
way that one night. He had just been kissing her; then, before she knew it, she had been wild for him. She hadn't
known such intense heat and pleasure had existed, until
then.

"What's wrong?" he murmured, reclaiming her mouth

with a series of swift, light kisses that nevertheless burned. "Don't you like it? Or do you like it too much?"

His perceptiveness alarmed her even more, and despite herself she began to struggle. To her surprise, he released her immediately, though he didn't step back.

"Tell me what went wrong, babe." His tone was dark and gentle. "I can't make it right if I don't know what it is."

She put her hands on his chest to force him away and was instantly, achingly aware of his hard, warm flesh covered only by a thin layer of cotton. She could even feel the roughness of his hair, the strong, heavy beat of his heart pulsing beneath her fingers. "Quinlan—"

"Tell me," he cajoled, kissing her again.

Desperately she slipped sideways, away from him. Her body felt overheated and slightly achy. If she didn't tell him, he would persist in his seductive cajoling, and she didn't know how long she could resist him. "All right." She owed him that much. She didn't intend to change her mind about dating him, but at least he deserved an explanation. She should have told him before, but at the time all she had wanted was to stay as far away from him as possible. "But...later. Not right now. We need to get everything gathered up and get settled in the lobby."

He straightened, amusement in his eyes. "Where have I heard that before?"

"It isn't polite to gloat."

"Maybe not, but it's sure as hell satisfying."

She was nervous. Quinlan was surprised at the depth of her uneasiness, because that wasn't a trait he associated with Elizabeth. He wondered at the cause of it, just as he had wondered for the past six months why she had run from him so abruptly after spending the night in his arms. She wasn't afraid of him; that was one of the things he liked best about her. For him to find women attractive, they had to be intelligent, but unfortunately that intelligence tended to go hand in glove with a perceptiveness that made them shy away from him.

He couldn't do anything about his aura of dangerousness, because he couldn't lose the characteristics, the habits or the instincts that made him dangerous. He didn't even want to. It was as much a part of him as his bones, and went as deep. He had made do with shallow relationships for the sake of physical gratification, but inside he had been waiting and watching. Though the life he had led sometimes made him feel as if only a few people in this world really *saw* what went on around them, that most people went through life wearing blinders, now that he was mostly out of the action he wanted the normalcy that the average person took for granted. He wanted a wife and family, a secure, settled life; as soon as he had met Elizabeth, he had known that she was the one he wanted.

It wasn't just her looks, though God knew he broke out in a sweat at the sight of her. She was a little over average height, as slim as a reed, with sleek dark hair usually pulled back in a classic chignon. She had the fast lines of a thoroughbred, and until he had met her, he hadn't known how sexy that was. But it was her eyes that had gotten him. Cat eyes, he'd told her, and it was true, but though they were green, it was more the expression in them than the color that made them look so feline. Elizabeth's nature shone in her eyes. She had given him a warning look that had said she wasn't intimidated by him at all, underlaid by a cool disdain that was certainly catlike.

Excitement and arousal had raced through him. The more he'd learned about her, the more determined he had been to have her. She was sharply intelligent, witty, sarcastic at times and had a robust sense of humor that sometimes caught him off guard, though it always delighted him. And she burned with an inner intensity that drew him as inexorably as a magnet draws steel.

The intensity of his attraction had caught him off guard. He wanted to know everything there was to know about her, even her childhood memories, because that was a time in her life that would be forever closed to him. He wanted to have children with her and was fascinated by the possibility of a daughter in Elizabeth's image, a small, strong-willed, sharp-tongued, dimpled cherub. Talking about Elizabeth's own childhood made that possibility seem tantalizingly real.

At first Elizabeth had talked openly, with that faint arrogance of hers that said she had nothing to hide and he could like it or lump it. But then he had begun to sense that she *was* hiding something. It wasn't anything he could put his finger on; it was more of a withdrawal from him, as if she had built an inner wall and had no intention of letting him progress past that point.

Both his training and his nature made it impossible for him just to let it pass. Her withdrawal didn't make sense, because he *knew*, knew with every animal instinct in him that she felt the same way he did. She wanted him. She loved him. If she were truly hiding something, he wanted to know about it, and he had both the skill and the resources to find out just about anything in a person's life. His inquiries had turned up the fact that she had been married before, but the marriage had seemed to be fairly typical, and fairly brief, the sort of thing a lot of college graduates drifted into, quickly finding out they didn't suit. He'd had his own short fling with marriage at that age, so he knew how it happened. But the more he'd thought about it, the more he'd noticed that the period of her marriage was the one period she didn't talk about, not even mentioning that she'd ever been married at all. He was too good at what he did not to realize the significance of that, and he had begun to probe for answers about those two missing years. At the same time, feeling her slipping away from him, he had made a bold move to cement their relationship and taken her to bed, trusting in the bonds of the flesh to both break down the barriers and hold her to him until she learned to trust him completely.

It hadn't worked.

She had fled the next morning while he was still in the shower, and this was the first time he'd gotten her alone since then.

Over half a year wasted. Almost seven long damn months, endless nights spent in burning frustration, both physical and mental.

But he had her now, all alone, and before they left this building he intended to know just what the hell happened and have her back where she belonged, with him.

Chapter Four

"Let's get those snack machines raided," she muttered, grabbing up her ditty bag of goodies and heading for the door. Quinlan had been standing there, staring at her for what seemed like several minutes but had probably been less than thirty seconds. There was a hooded, predatory expression in his gleaming blue eyes, and she just couldn't stand there, like a tethered goat, for another second.

He sauntered out in her wake, and she relocked the office door, then looked up and down the dim hallway. "Just where *are* these snack machines?" she finally asked. "I'm not a junk food junkie, so I've never used them."

"There's a soft drink machine at this end of the hallway," he said, pointing, "but there are snack machines in the insurance offices. They have a break room for their employees, but they let us use them." He set off down the long hallway, away from the bank of elevators, and Elizabeth trailed after him.

"How are we going to get in?" she asked caustically. "Shoot the lock off?"

"If I have to," he replied, lazy good humor in his voice. "But I don't think it will come to that."

She hoped not. From what she could tell, insurance companies tended to be rather humorless about such things. She could well imagine receiving a bill for damages, which she could certainly do without.

Quinlan knelt in front of the insurance company's locked door and unzipped the leather bag, taking from it a small case resembling the one in which she kept her makeup brushes. He flipped it open, though, and the resemblance ended. Instead of plush brushes, there was an assortment of oddly shaped metal tools. He took two of them out, inserted the long, thin, bent one into the keyhole, then slid the other instrument in beside it and jiggled it with small, delicate movements.

Elizabeth sidled closer, bending down to get a better look. "Can you teach me how to do that?" she asked in an absent tone, fascinated with the process.

The corners of his mouth twitched as he continued to gingerly work at the lock. "Why? Have you just discovered a larcenous streak?"

"Do *you* have one?" she shot back. "It just seems like a handy skill to have, since you never know when you'll accidentally lock yourself out."

"And you're going to start carrying a set of locksmith's tools in your purse?"

"Why not?" She nudged the black leather bag with her toe. "Evidently you carry one in yours."

"That isn't a purse. Ah," he said with satisfaction, as he felt the lock open. He withdrew the slender tools, stored them in their proper places in the case and replaced the case in the bag. Then he calmly opened the door.

"Explain the difference between my purse and yours," she said as she entered the dim, silent insurance office.

"It isn't a purse. The difference is the things that are in them."

"I see. So if I emptied the contents of my purse into your leather bag, it would then become a purse?"

"I give up," he said mildly. "Okay, it's a purse. Only men don't call them purses. We call them satchels or just plain leather bags."

"A rose by any other name," she murmured with gentle triumph.

He chuckled. "That's one of the things I like best about

you. You're such a gracious winner. You never hesitate at all to gloat.''

"Some people just ask for it more than others." She looked around, seeing nothing but empty desks and blank computer screens. "Where's the break room?"

"This way." He led her down a dark interior hallway and opened the last door on the right.

The room had two windows, so it wasn't dark. A variety of vending machines lined one wall, offering soft drinks, coffee, juice and snacks. A microwave oven sat on a counter, and a silent refrigerator stood at another wall. There was a vinyl sofa with splits in the cushions that allowed the stuffing to show, and a number of folding chairs shoved haphazardly around two cafeteria tables.

"Check the refrigerator while I open the machines," Quinlan said. "See if there's any ice. We don't need it now, but it would be nice to know that it's there just in case. Do it as fast as you can, to keep the cold air in."

"I do know about refrigerators and power failures," she said pointedly. Swiftly she opened the freezer compartment, and vapor poured out as cold air met warm. There were six ice trays there, all of them full. She shut the door just as fast as she had opened it. "We have ice."

"Good." He had the snack machine open and was removing packs of crackers.

Elizabeth opened the main refrigerator door but was disappointed with the contents. A brown paper bag sat in lone splendor, with several translucent greasy spots decorating it. She had no interest in investigating its contents. There was an apple, though, and she took it. The shelves in the door were lined with various condiments, nothing that tempted her. The thought of putting ketchup on the honey bun was revolting.

"Just an apple here," she said.

He finished loading his booty into the leather bag. "Okay,

we have cakes, crackers and candy bars, plus the stuff you got from Chickie's desk. My best guess is we'll get out of here sometime tomorrow morning, so this should be more than enough. Do you want a soft drink, or juice? There's water downstairs, so we don't need to raid the drink machines. It's strictly a matter of preference.''

She thought about it, then shook her head. "Water will be enough.''

He zipped the bag. "That's it, then. Let's make ourselves comfy downstairs.''

"Should we leave a note?'' she asked.

"No need. I'll take care of things when the power comes on and everything gets back to normal.''

The trip downstairs was considerably easier with the aid of one of the flashlights, and soon they reentered the lobby, which was noticeably cooler because of the two-story ceiling. She looked out through the dark glass of the double entrance; the street was oddly deserted, with only the occasional car passing by. A patrol car crawled past as she watched. "It looks weird,'' she murmured. "As if everyone has been evacuated.''

"If the power doesn't come back on,'' Quinlan said in a grim tone, "it will probably get a lot busier once the sun goes down and things cool off a little. By the way, I tried to call out from my office, just to see what was going on and let someone know where we were, but I couldn't get a call to go through. If there's a city-wide blackout, which I suspect, the circuits will be jammed with calls. But I did find a battery-operated radio, so we'll be able to listen to the news.''

"Turn it on now,'' she suggested, walking over to a sofa to dump her load on it. "Let's find out what's going on.''

He opened the leather bag and took out a small radio, not even as big as her hand. After switching it on and getting only static, he began running through the frequencies, looking for a station. Abruptly a voice jumped out at them, astonishingly clear for such a small radio. ''—the National Guard has been called out in several states to help prevent looting—''

''Damn,'' Quinlan muttered. ''This sounds bad.''

''Information is sketchy,'' the announcer continued, ''but more reports are coming in, and it looks as if there has been a massive loss of electrical power across the Southeast and most of Texas.''

''I'm not an expert,'' a second voice said, ''but the southern tier of the country has been suffering under this heat wave for two weeks, and I imagine the demands for electricity overloaded the system. Have we had any word yet from the governor?''

''Nothing yet, but the phone lines are tied up. Please, people, don't use the telephones unless it's an emergency. Folks can't get through to 911 if you're on the phone to your friends telling them that your power's out, too. Believe me, they *know*.''

The second announcer chimed in, ''Remember the safety precautions the Health Department has been telling us for two weeks. It's especially critical without electricity for air conditioning and fans. Stay out of the sun if possible. With the power off, open your windows for ventilation, and drink plenty of liquids. Don't move around any more than you have to. Conserve your energy.''

''We'll be on the air all night long,'' said the first announcer, ''operating on emergency power. If anything happens you'll hear it first here on—''

Quinlan switched off the radio. ''Well, now we know what happened,'' he said calmly. ''We'll save the batteries as much as we can.''

She gave him a mock incredulous look. ''What? You mean you don't have replacement batteries?''

''It isn't my radio.''

It wasn't necessary for him to add that if it had been, of course he would have had extra batteries. She wished it *were* his radio. And while she was wishing, she wished she had left the building on time, though she wasn't certain she wouldn't be in a worse situation at her condo. Certainly she was safer here, inside a sealed building.

The magnitude of the problem was stunning. This wasn't something that was going to be corrected in a couple of hours. It was possible they would still be locked in at this time tomorrow.

She looked at Quinlan. "Are you *sure* it won't get dangerously hot in here?"

"Not absolutely positive, but reasonably sure. We'll be okay. We have water, and that's the most important thing. Actually, we're probably as comfortable as anyone in this city is, except for those places that have emergency generators. If we start getting too warm, we'll just take off some clothes."

Her heart literally jumped, sending her pulse rate soaring, and immediately she began to feel uncomfortably warm. Her stomach muscles clenched at the thought of lying naked in the darkness with him, but it was the tightness of desire. While her mind was wary, her body remembered the intense pleasure of his lovemaking. She turned back to the windows to keep him from reading her expression. Staring at the glass made her think of something else, and gratefully she seized on it.

"When it gets dark, will anyone on the outside be able to see us in here when we turn on a flashlight? Does the privacy glazing work at night?"

"Anyone who looked closely would be able to tell that there's a light in here, I suppose," he said thoughtfully. "But no one will be able to actually *see* us."

Just the possibility was enough. She had been about to arrange their supplies in the seating area closest to the entrance, but now she moved farther away. The lobby had several comfortable seating areas, and she chose one that was close to the middle. It was at least semiprivate, with a long, waist-high planter that created the sense of a small alcove. It was also closer to the bathrooms, making it a better choice all the way around.

She arranged their food supplies on a low table, while Quinlan shoved the chairs around to make more room. Then he collected cushions from the other chairs and stacked them close to hand, ready to make into beds when they decided to sleep. Elizabeth gave the cushions a sidelong glance. She wasn't sure she would be able to close her eyes with Quinlan so close by, or that it would be smart to sleep, even if she could.

She looked at him and started when she found him watching her. He didn't look away as he unknotted his tie and stripped it off, then unbuttoned his shirt down to his waist and rolled up his sleeves. His actions were practical, but the sight of his muscled, hairy chest and hard belly aroused a reaction in her that had nothing to do with common sense.

"Why don't you take off those panty hose?" he suggested in a low, silky voice. "They have to be damn hot."

They were. She hesitated, then decided wryly that it wasn't the thin nylon that would protect her from him. Only *she* could do that. Quinlan wasn't a rapist; if she said no, he wouldn't force himself on her. She had never been afraid of that; her only fear was that she wouldn't be able to say no. That was one reason why she had avoided him for the past six months. So leaving her panty hose on wouldn't keep him from making love to her if she couldn't say no, and taking them off wouldn't put her at risk if she did keep herself under control. It was, simply, a matter of comfort.

She got a flashlight and carried it into the public rest room, where she propped it on one of the basins. The small room felt stuffy and airless, so she hurriedly removed her panty hose and immediately felt much cooler. She turned on the cold water and held her wrists under the stream, using the time-proven method of cooling down, then dampened one of the paper towels and blotted her face. There. That was much better.

A few deep breaths, a silent pep talk and she felt ready to hold Tom Quinlan at arm's length for the duration. With her panty hose in one hand and the flashlight in the other, she returned to the lobby.

He was waiting for her, sprawled negligently in one of the chairs, but those blue eyes watched her as intently as a tiger watches its chosen prey. "Now," he said, "let's have our little talk."

Chapter Five

Her heart lurched in her chest. It strained her composure to walk over to the chairs and sit down, but she did it, even crossed her legs and leaned back as negligently as he. "All right," she said calmly.

He gave her that considering look again, as if he were trying to decide how to handle her. Mentally she bristled at the idea of being "handled," but she forced down her irritation. She knew how relentless Quinlan could be when crossed; she would need to keep her thoughts ordered, not let him trip her up with anger.

He remained silent, watching her, and she knew what he wanted. He had already asked the question; he was simply waiting for the answer.

Despite herself, Elizabeth felt a spurt of anger, even after all these months. She faced him and went straight to the heart of the matter. "I found the file you had on me," she said, every word clipped short. "You had me investigated."

"Ah." He steepled his fingers and studied her over them. "So that's it." He paused a few seconds, then said mildly, "Of course I did."

"There's no 'of course' to it. You invaded my privacy—"

"As you invaded mine," he interrupted smoothly. "That file wasn't lying out in the open."

"No, it wasn't. I looked in your desk," she admitted without hesitation.

"Why?"

"I felt uneasy about you. I was looking for some answers."

"So why didn't you ask *me?*" The words were as sharp as a stiletto.

She gave him a wry, humorless smile. "I did. Many times. You're a master at evasion, though. I've been to bed with you, but I don't know much more about you right now than I did the day we met."

He neatly sidestepped the charge by asking, "What made you feel uneasy? I never threatened you, never pushed you. You know I own and run my company, that I'm solvent and not on the run."

"You just did it again," she pointed out. "Your ability to evade is very good. It took me a while to catch on, but then I noticed that you didn't answer my questions. You always responded, so it wasn't obvious, but you'd just ask your own question and ignore mine."

He surveyed her silently for a moment before saying, "I'm not interested in talking about myself. I already know all the details."

"I'd say that the same holds true for me, wouldn't you?" she asked sweetly. "I wanted to know about *you,* and got nowhere. But I didn't have you investigated."

"I wouldn't have minded if you had." Not that she would have been able to find out much, he thought. Great chunks of his life after high school graduation weren't to be found in public records.

"Bully for you. *I* minded."

"And that's it? You walked out on me and broke off our relationship because you were angry that I had you investigated? Why didn't you just yell at me? Throw things at me? For God's sake, Elizabeth, don't you think you took it a little far?"

His tone was both angry and incredulous, making it plain

that he considered her reaction to be nothing short of hysteric, far out of proportion to the cause.

She froze inside, momentarily paralyzed by the familiar ploy of being made to feel that she was in the wrong, that no matter what happened it was her fault for not being good enough. But then she fought the memories back; she would never let anyone make her feel that way again. She had gotten herself back, and she knew her own worth. She knew she hadn't handled the matter well, but only in the way she had done it; the outcome itself had never been in question.

Her voice was cool when she replied. "No, I don't think I took it too far. I'd been feeling uneasy about you for quite a while. Finding that you had investigated me was the final factor, but certainly not all of it."

"Because I hadn't answered a few questions?" That incredulous note was still there.

"Among other things."

"Such as?"

In for a penny, in for a pound. "Such as your habit of taking over, of ignoring my objections or suggestions as if I hadn't even said anything."

"Objections to what?" Now the words were as sharp as a lash. His blue eyes were narrowed and vivid. A bit surprised, she realized that he was angry again.

She waved her hand in a vague gesture. "Any little thing. I didn't catalog them—"

"Surprises the hell out of me," he muttered.

"But you were constantly overriding me. If I told you I was going shopping, you insisted that I wait until you could go with me. If I wanted to wear a sweater when we were going out, you insisted that I wear a coat. Damn it, Quinlan, you even tried to make me change where I bank!"

His eyebrows rose. "The bank you use now is too far away. The one I suggested is much more convenient."

"For whom? If I'm perfectly happy with my bank, then it isn't inconvenient for me, is it?"

"So don't change your bank. What's the big deal?"

"The big deal," she said slowly, choosing her words, "is that you want to make all the decisions, handle everything yourself. You don't want a relationship, you want a dictatorship."

One moment he was lounging comfortably, long legs sprawled out in front of him; the next he was in front of her, bending over to plant his hands on the arms of her chair and trap her in place. Elizabeth stared up at him, blinking at the barely controlled rage in his face, but she refused to let herself shrink from him. Instead she lifted her chin and met him glare for glare.

"I don't believe it!" he half shouted. "You walked out on me because I wanted you to change banks? God in heaven." He shoved himself away from the chair and stalked several paces away, running his hand through his hair.

"No," she shouted back, "I walked out because I refuse to let you take over my life!" She was unable to sit still, either, and surged out of the chair. Instantly Quinlan whirled with those lightning-quick reactions of his, catching her arms and hauling her close to him, so close that she could see the white flecks in the deep blue of his irises and smell the hot, male scent of his body. Her nostrils flared delicately as she instinctively drank in the primal signal, even though she stiffened against his touch.

"Why didn't you tell me you were married before?"

The question was soft, and not even unexpected, but still she flinched. Of course he knew; it had been in that damn investigative report.

"It isn't on my list of conversational topics," she snapped. "But neither is it a state secret. *If* our relationship had ever progressed far enough, I would have told you then. What was I supposed to do, trot out my past life the minute we met?''

Quinlan watched her attentively. As close as they were, he could see every flicker of expression on her face, and he had noticed the telltale flinch even though she had replied readily enough. Ah, so there *was* something there.

''Just how far did our relationship have to go?'' he asked, still keeping his voice soft. ''We weren't seeing anyone else. We didn't actually have sex until that last night together, but things got pretty hot between us several times before that.''

''And I was having doubts about you even then,'' she replied just as softly.

''Maybe so, but that didn't stop you from wanting me, just like now.'' He bent his head and settled his mouth on hers, the pressure light and persuasive. She tried to pull away and found herself powerless against his strength, even though he was taking care not to hurt her. ''Be still,'' he said against her lips.

Desperately she wrenched her head away. He forced it back, but instead of kissing her again, he paused with his mouth only a fraction of an inch above hers. ''Why didn't you tell me about it?'' he murmured, his warm breath caressing her lips and making them tingle. With his typical relentlessness, he had fastened on an idea and wouldn't let it go until he was satisfied with the answer. The old blind fear rose in her, black wings beating, and in panic she started to struggle. He subdued her without effort, wrapping her in a warm, solid embrace from which there was no escape.

''What happened?'' he asked, brushing light kisses across her mouth between words. ''What made you flinch when I

mentioned it? Tell me about it now. I need to know. Did
he run around on you?''

''No.'' She hadn't meant to answer him, but somehow,
caught in those steely arms and cradled against his enticing
heat, the word slipped out in a whisper. She heard it and
shuddered. ''No!'' she said more forcefully, fighting for
control. ''He didn't cheat.'' If only he had, if only his de-
structive attention had been diluted in that way, it wouldn't
have been so bad. ''Stop it, Quinlan. Let me go.''

''Why did you start calling me Quinlan?'' His voice remained low and soothing, and his warm mouth kept pressing
against hers with quick, gentle touches. ''You called me
Tom before, and when we made love.''

She had started calling him Quinlan in an effort to distance herself from him. She didn't want to think of him as
Tom, because the name was forever linked in her mind with
that night when she had clung to his naked shoulders, her
body lifting feverishly to his forceful thrusts as she cried
out his name over and over, in ecstasy, in need, in completion. Tom was the name of her lover; Quinlan was the man
she had fled.

And Quinlan was the one she had to deal with now, the
man who never gave up. He held her helpless in his grasp,
taking kiss after kiss from her until she stopped trying to
evade his mouth and opened her lips to him with a tiny,
greedy sound. Instantly he took her with his tongue, and the
sheer pleasure of it made them both shudder.

His warm hand closed over her breast, gently kneading.
She groaned, the sound captured by his mouth, and desperately tried to marshal her resistance. He was seducing her
just as effortlessly as he had the first time, but even though
she realized what was happening she couldn't find the willpower to push him away. She loved him too much, savored

his kisses too much, desired him too strongly, found too much pleasure in the stroke of those hard hands.

The pressure of his fingers had hardened her nipple into a tight nub that stabbed his palm even through the layers of fabric protecting her. He deepened the kiss as he roughly opened the buttons of her blouse and shoved a hand inside the opening, then under the lacy cup of her bra to find the bare flesh he craved. She whimpered as his fingers found her sensitive nipple and lightly pinched at it, sending sharp waves of sensation down to her tightening loins. The sound she made was soft, more of a vibration than an actual noise, but he was so attuned to her that he felt it as sharply as an electrical shock.

She was limp as he bent her back over his arm and freed her breast from the lace that confined it, cupping the warm mound and lifting it up to his hungry mouth. He bent over her, sucking fiercely at her tender flesh, wild with the taste and scent and feel of her. He stabbed at her nipple with his tongue, excited and triumphant at the way she arched responsively at every lash of sensation. She wanted him. He had told himself that there had been no mistaking her fiery response that night, but the six months since then had weakened his assurance. Now he knew he hadn't been wrong. He barely had to touch her and she trembled with excitement, already needing him, ready for him.

He left her breast for more deeply voracious kisses taken from her sweetly swollen lips. God, he wanted her! No other woman had ever made him feel as Elizabeth did, so completely attuned with and lost within her.

He wanted to make love to her, *now,* but there were still too many unanswered questions. If he didn't get things settled while he had her marooned here, unable to get away from him, it might be another six months before he could corner her again. No, by God, it wouldn't be; he couldn't stand it again.

Reluctantly he left her mouth, every instinct in him wanting to take this to completion, knowing that he could if only he didn't give her a chance to surface from the drugging physical delight, but he still wanted answers and couldn't wait, didn't dare wait, to get them. "Tell me," he cajoled as he trailed his mouth down the side of her neck, nibbling on the taut tendon and feeling the response ripple through her. Finally—*finally*—he was on the right track. "Tell me what *he* did that made you run from *me*."

Chapter Six

Frantically Elizabeth tried to jerk away, but he controlled her so easily that her efforts were laughable. Nevertheless, she lodged her hands against his heavy shoulders and pushed as hard as she could. "Let me go!"

"No." His refusal was flat and calm. "Stop fighting and answer me."

She couldn't do either one, and she began to panic, not because she feared Quinlan, but because she didn't want to talk about her marriage to Eric Landers, didn't want to think about it, didn't want to revive that hell even in memory. But Quinlan, damn his stubborn temperament, had fastened on the subject and wouldn't drop it until he got what he wanted. She knew him, knew that he intended to drag every detail out of her, and she simply couldn't face it.

Sheer survival instinct made her suddenly relax in his arms, sinking against him, clutching his shoulders instead of pushing against them. She felt his entire body tighten convulsively at her abrupt capitulation; her own muscles quivered with acute relief, as if she had been forcing them to an unnatural action. Her breath caught jerkily as her hips settled against his and she felt the thick ridge of his sex. His arousal was so familiar, and unbearably seductive. The lure of his sexuality pulled her even closer, her loins growing heavy and taut with desire.

He felt the change in her, saw it mirrored almost instantly in her face. One moment she had been struggling against him, and the next she was shivering in carnal excitement, her body tense as she moved against him in a subtle demand. He cursed, his voice thick, as he tried to fight his own response. It was a losing battle; he had wanted her too intensely, for too long. Talking would have to wait; for now, she had won. All he could think about was that she was finally in his arms again, every small movement signaling eager compliance. He didn't know what had changed her mind, and at this moment he didn't particularly care. It was enough that she was once again clinging to him, as she had the one night they had spent together, the night that was burned into his memory. He had tossed restlessly through a lot of dark, sleepless hours since then, remembering how it had been and aching for the same release, needing her beneath him, bewildered by and angry at her sudden coldness.

There was nothing cold about her now. He could feel her heat, feel her vibrating under his hands. Her hips moved in an ancient search, and a low moan hummed in her throat as she found what she had sought, her legs parting slightly to nestle his hard sex between them.

Fiercely he thrust his hand into her hair and pulled her head back. "Do you want this?" he asked hoarsely, hanging on to his control with grim concentration. It had happened so abruptly that he wanted to make sure before another second had passed, before she moved again and launched him past the point of no return. He hadn't felt like this since he'd been a teenager, the tide of desire rising like floodwaters in his veins, drowning thought. God, he didn't care what had caused her to change; right now, all he wanted was to thrust into her.

For a second she didn't answer, and his teeth were already clenching against a curse when she dug her nails into his shoulder and said, "Yes."

Her senses whirled dizzily as he lowered her to the floor, right where they stood. "The sofa..." she murmured, but then his weight came down on top of her and she didn't care anymore. Her initial tactic had been a panicked effort to distract him, but her own desire had blindsided her, well-ing up and overwhelming her senses so swiftly that she had no defense against it. She had hungered for him for so long, lying awake during the long, dark nights with silent tears seeping from beneath her lids because she missed him so much, almost as much as she feared him—and herself. The relief of being in his arms again was almost painful, and she pushed away all the reasons why this shouldn't happen. She would face the inevitable later; for now, all she wanted was Tom Quinlan.

He was rough, his own hunger too intense, too long denied, for him to control it. He shoved her skirt up to her waist and dragged her panties down, and Elizabeth willingly opened her thighs to receive him. He dealt just as swiftly with his pants, then brought his loins to hers. His penetration was hard and stabbing, and she cried out at the force of it. Her hips arched, accepting, taking him deeper. A guttural sound vibrated in his wide chest; then he caught the backs of her thighs, pulling her legs higher, and he began thrusting hard and fast.

She loved it. She reveled in it. She sobbed aloud at the strong release that pulsed through her almost immediately, the staggering physical response that she had known only with this man and had thought she would never experience again. She had been willing to give up this physical ecstasy in order to protect her inner self from his dominance, but oh, how she had longed for it, and bitterly wondered why the most dangerous traps had the sweetest bait.

Blinded by the ferocity of his own need, he anchored her writhing hips with his big hands and pounded into her. Dazedly she became aware of the hard floor beneath her, bruising her shoulders, but even as her senses were recovering from their sensual battering and allowing her to take stock of her surroundings, he gripped her even harder and convulsed. Instinctively she held him, cradling him with arms and legs, and the gentle clasp of her inner warmth. His harsh, strained cries subsided to low, rhythmic moans, then finally to fast and uneven breathing as he relaxed on top of her, his heavy weight pressing her to the floor.

The silence in the huge, dim lobby was broken only by the erratic intake and release of their breathing. His slowing heartbeat thudded heavily against her breasts, and their heated bodies melded together everywhere that bare flesh touched bare flesh. She felt the moisture of sweat, and the inner wetness that forcibly awakened her to the realization that their frantic mating had been done without any means of protection.

Her own heart lurched in panic; then logic reasserted itself and she calmed down. She had just finished her monthly cycle; it was highly unlikely that she could conceive. Perversely, no sooner had she had that reassuring thought than she was seized by a sense of loss, even of mourning, as if that panicked moment had been truth rather than very remote possibility.

"Elizabeth?"

She didn't open her eyes. She didn't want to face reality just yet, didn't want to have to let him go, and that was something reality would force her to do.

He lifted himself on his elbows, and she could feel the penetrating blue gaze on her face, but still she clung to the safety of her closed eyes.

She felt his muscles gathering, and briefly she tried to hold him, but he lifted himself away from her, and she caught her breath at the slow withdrawal that separated his body from hers. Despite herself, the friction set off a lingering thrill of sensation, and her hips lifted in a small, uncontrollable, telltale movement. Because there was no sanctuary any longer, she opened her eyes and silently met his gaze. That curious, sleepy blankness of sexual satisfaction was on his face, as she knew it must also be on hers, but in his eyes was a predatory watchfulness, as if he knew his prey had been caught but not vanquished.

His astuteness was disturbing, as it had always been. Her own gaze dared him to try to make anything more of what had just happened than an unadorned act of sex, without cause or future.

His mouth twisted wryly as he knelt away from her and pulled his pants up, zipping them with a faint, raspy sound. Then he got to his feet and effortlessly lifted her to hers. Her skirt, which had been bunched around her waist, dropped to the correct position. Elizabeth instinctively clenched her thighs to hold the wetness between them.

Quinlan shrugged out of his shirt and handed it to her, then leaned down and retrieved her panties from the floor. Thrusting them into her hands, too, he said, "Take off those clothes and put on my shirt. It's getting warmer in here, and you'll be more comfortable in something loose."

Silently she turned, picked up the flashlight and went into the ladies' rest room. Her knees were shaking slightly in reaction, and her loins throbbed from the violence of his possession. He hadn't hurt her, but it was as if she could still feel him inside.

She stared at her reflection in the mirror, the image ghostly with only the flashlight for illumination, making her eyes look huge and dark. Her hair had come loose and tumbled around her shoulders; she pushed it back distractedly, still staring at herself, then buried her face in her hands.

How could she go back out there? God, how could she have been so *stupid?* Alone with him for little more than an hour, and she had had sex with him on the floor like an uncontrolled animal. She couldn't even blame it on him; no, *she* had made the big move, grabbing at him, pushing her hips at him, because she had panicked when he had tried to pull back and begin asking questions again. She had gotten exactly what she had asked for.

She felt confused, both ashamed and elated. She was ashamed that she had used sex as an evasion tactic…or maybe she was ashamed that she had used it as an *excuse* to do what she had been longing to do anyway. The physical desire she felt for him was sharp and strong, so urgently demanding that stopping felt unnatural, all of her instincts pushing her toward him.

Her body felt warm and weak with satiation, faintly trembling in the aftermath. But now that he was no longer touching her, the old wariness was creeping back, pulling her in two directions. She had thought the decision simple, though it had never been easy, but now she was finding that nothing about it, either Quinlan or her own emotions, was simple.

Dazedly she stripped off her disheveled clothing and used some wet paper towels to wash; the cool moisture was momentarily refreshing, but then the close heat of the rest room made sweat form almost as fast as she could wash it off. Ironically she admitted that, no matter how reluctant she was, she had no real choice but to face him again. If she remained in here, she would have heat stroke. It was a sad day when a woman couldn't even count on a rest room for sanctuary. Ah, well, she hadn't yet found any place that was truly safe from him, for her own memories worked against her.

Just as she pulled on her panties, the door was thrust open and Quinlan loomed in the opening, his big body blotting out most of the light from the lobby but allowing the welcome entrance of relatively cooler air. The subtle breeze washed around her body, making her nipples pucker slightly. Or was that an instinctive female reaction to the closeness of her mate? She didn't want to think of him in such primitive, possessive terms, but her body had different priorities.

He noticed, of course. His gaze became smoky with both desire and possessiveness as he openly admired her breasts.

But he didn't move toward her, holding himself very still as if he sensed her confusion. "Hiding?" he asked mildly.

"Delaying," she admitted, her tone soft. She didn't try to shield her body from him; such an action would seem silly, after what they had just done. It wasn't as if he hadn't seen her completely naked before, as if they hadn't made love before. Moreover, he had decided to remove his pants and stood before her wearing only a pair of short, dark boxers. Barefoot and mostly naked, his dark hair tousled and wet with both sweat and the water he had splashed on his face, he was stripped of most of the trappings of civilization. Despite the heat, a shiver ran up her spine in yet another feminine response to the primitiveness of his masculinity, and she looked away to keep him from seeing it in her face.

He came to her and took up his shirt, holding it for her to slip into; then, when she had done so, he turned her and began buttoning the garment as if she were a child being dressed. "You can't stay in here," he said. "Too damn hot."

"I know. I was coming out."

He shepherded her toward the door, his hand on her back. She wondered if the action was just his usual take-charge attitude, or if he was acting on some primitive instinct of his own, to keep the female from bolting. Probably a mixture of the two, she thought, and sighed.

He had been busy while she had been in the rest room, and she realized she had delayed in there much longer than she had intended. He had arranged the extra cushions on the floor—in the shape of a double bed, she noticed—and gotten some cool water from the fountain, the cups ready for them to drink. The water was welcome, but if he thought she was going to docilely stretch out on those cushions, he would shortly be disillusioned. She sat down in a chair and reached for a cup, sipping it without enthusiasm at first, then more eagerly as she rediscovered how good plain water was for quenching thirst. It was a delight of childhood that tended to be forgotten in the adult world of coffee, tea and wine spritzers.

"Are you hungry?" he asked.

"No." How could she be hungry? Her nerves were so tightly drawn that she didn't think she would be able to eat until they got out of here.

"Well, I am." He tore open the wrapping on the big blueberry muffin and began eating. "Tell me about your marriage."

She stiffened and glared at him. "It wasn't a good marriage," she said tightly. "It also isn't any of your business."

He glanced pointedly at the floor where they had so recently made love. "That's debatable. Okay, let's try it this way. I'll tell you about my marriage if you'll tell me about yours. No evasion tactics. I'll answer any question you ask."

She stared at him in shock. "*Your* marriage?"

He shrugged. "Sure. Hell, I'm thirty-seven years old. I haven't lived my entire life in a vacuum."

"You have your nerve!" she flared. "You jumped down my throat for not talking about my past marriage when you've only now mentioned your own?"

He rubbed the side of his nose and gave her a faintly sheepish look. "That occurred to me," he admitted.

"Well, let me put another thought in your dim Neanderthal brain! The time for heart-to-heart confidences was over a long time ago. We aren't involved any longer, so there's no point in 'sharing.'"

He took another bite of the muffin. "Don't kid yourself. What we just did felt pretty damn involved to me."

"That was just sex," she said dismissively. "It had been a while, and I needed it."

"I know exactly how long it had been." His blue gaze sharpened, and she knew he hadn't liked her comment.

"You haven't gone out with anyone else since you walked out on me."

She was enraged all over again. "Have you had me followed?"

He had, but he wasn't about to tell her that now. Instead he said, "Chickie worries because your social life, in her words, resembles Death Valley—nothing of interest moving around."

Elizabeth snorted, but she was mollified, because she had heard Chickie make that exact comment on a couple of occasions. Still, she would have to have a word with her about discretion.

"I've been busy," she said, not caring if he believed her or not, though it happened to be the truth. She had deliberately been as busy as she could manage in order to give herself less free time to think about him.

"I know. You've found a lot of lilies to gild."

Her teeth closed with a snap. "That's so people will have a reason to install your fancy security systems. I gild the lilies, and you protect them."

"I protect *people*," he clarified.

"Uh-huh. That's why you set up so many security systems for people who live in rough neighborhoods, where their lives are really in danger."

"I can see we aren't going to agree on this."

"You brought it up."

"My mistake. Let's get back to the original subject, namely our respective failed marriages. Go ahead, ask me anything you want."

The perfect response, of course, was that she wasn't interested. It would also be a lie, because she was not only interested, she was suddenly, violently jealous of that unknown, hitherto unsuspected woman who had been his wife, who had shared his name and his bed for a time, and who had been, in the eyes of the world, his mate. Elizabeth firmly kept her mouth closed, but she couldn't stop herself from glaring at him.

Quinlan sighed. "All right, I'll tell you the boring facts without making you ask. Her name was Amy. We dated during college. Then, when college was finished, it seemed like we should do adult things, so we got married. But I was away on my job a lot, and Amy found someone in the office where she worked who she liked a lot better. Within six months of getting married we knew it had been a mistake, but we held out for another year, trying to make it 'work,' before we both realized we were just wasting time. The divorce was a relief for both of us. End of story."

She was still glaring at him. "I don't even know where you went to college."

He sighed again. She was getting damn tired of that sigh, as if he were being so noble in his dealings with an irrational woman. "Cal Tech."

"Ah." Well, that explained his expertise with electronics and computers and things.

"No children," he added.

"I should hope not!" It was bad enough that he had, for some reason, concealed all the rest of the details of his life. "If you'd kept *children* hidden, I would never have forgiven you."

His eyes gleamed. "Does this mean you *have?*"

"No."

He gave a startled shout of laughter. "God, I've missed you. You don't dissemble at all. If you're grouchy, you don't feel any need at all to make nice and pretend to be sweetness and light, do you?"

She gave him a haughty look. "I'm not sweetness and light."

"Thank God," he said fervently. He leaned back and

spread his hands, then stretched his long, muscular legs out before him in a posture of complete relaxation. "Okay, it's your turn. Tell me all the deep, dark secrets about *your* marriage."

Chapter Seven

"Show-and-tell was your idea, not mine." Her throat tightened at the idea of rehashing the details, reliving the nightmare even in thought. She just couldn't do it.

"You asked questions."

"I asked where you went to college, hardly the same as prying into your private life." Agitated, she stood up and longingly looked through the huge windows to the world outside. Only two thin sheets of transparent material kept her prisoner here with him, but it would take a car ramming into the glass at respectable speed to break it. The glass looked fragile but wasn't, whereas she was the opposite. She looked calm and capable, but inside she hid a weakness that terrified her.

"Don't run away," Quinlan warned softly.

She barely glanced at him as she edged out of the semi-circle of sofa and chairs. "I'm not running," she denied, knowing that it wasn't the truth. "It's cooler moving around."

Silently Quinlan got to his feet and paced after her, big and virtually naked, the dark boxer shorts nothing more than the modern version of the loincloth. His muscled chest was hairy, the thick curls almost hiding his small nipples, and a silky line of hair ran down the center of his abdomen to his groin. His long legs were also covered with hair, finer and straighter, but he was undoubtedly a dominating male animal in his prime. Elizabeth gave him a distracted, vaguely alarmed look that suddenly focused on his loins, and her eyes widened.

He looked down at himself and shrugged, not pausing in

his slow, relentless pursuit. ''I know, at my age I shouldn't have recovered this fast. I usually don't,'' he said thoughtfully. ''It's just my reaction to you. Come here, sweetheart.'' His voice had turned soft and cajoling.

Wildly Elizabeth wondered if this was going to degenerate into the stereotypical chase around the furniture. On the heels of that thought came the certain knowledge that if she ran, Quinlan would definitely chase her, instinctively, the marauding male subduing the reluctant female. She could prevent that farce by not running, thereby giving him nothing to chase. On the other hand, if she stood still things would only reach the same conclusion at a faster pace. Evidently the only real choice she had was whether or not to hold on to her dignity. If she had felt differently about him she could have said ''no,'' but she had already faced that weakness in herself. For right now, in these circumstances, she couldn't resist him—and they both knew it.

He drew closer, his eyes gleaming. ''For tonight, you're mine,'' he murmured. ''Let me at least have that. You can't get away from me here. You don't even want to get away, not really. The circumstances aren't normal. When we get out of here you'll have options, but right now you're forced to be with me. Whatever happens won't be your fault. Just let go and forget about it.''

She drew a deep, shuddering breath. ''Pretty good psychologist, aren't you? But I'm not a coward. I'm responsible for whatever decisions I make, period.''

He had reached her now, one arm sliding around her back. Elizabeth looked up at him, at the tousled dark hair and intense blue eyes, and her heart squeezed. ''All right,'' she whispered. ''For tonight. For as long as we're locked in here.'' She closed her eyes, shivering with sensual anticipation. She would let herself have this, just for now; she would feast on him, drown herself in sensation, let the darkness of the night wrap protectively around them and hold off thought. The time would come all too soon when she would have to push him away again; why waste even one precious minute by fighting both him and herself?

"Anything," she heard herself say as he lifted her. Her voice sounded strange to her, thick, drugged with desire. "For tonight."

His low, rough laugh wasn't quite steady as he lowered her to the cushions. "Anything?" he asked. "You could be letting yourself in for an interesting night."

She put out her hand and touched his bare chest. "Yes," she purred. "I could be."

"Cat." His breathing was fast and unsteady as he swiftly stripped her panties down her legs and tossed them to the side. "You won't be needing those again tonight."

She pulled at the waistband of his shorts. "And you won't be needing these."

"Hell, I only kept them on because I figured you'd fight like a wildcat if I came after you stark naked." He dealt with his shorts as rapidly as he had her underwear.

She was already excited by the anticipation of his slow, thorough loveplay. Quinlan was a man who enjoyed the preliminaries and prolonged them, as she had learned during the one night she had spent with him. It didn't happen this time, though. He pushed her legs open, knelt between them and entered her with a heavy thrust that jarred her. The shock of it reverberated through her body; then her inner muscles clamped down in an effort to slow that inexorable invasion.

He pushed deeper, groaning at the tightness of her, until he was in her to the hilt. She writhed, reaching down to grasp his thighs and hold him there, but he slowly withdrew, then just as slowly pushed back into her.

"Did your husband make you feel like this?" he whispered.

Her head rolled on the cushions at the speed and intensity

of the sensations. It was an effort to concentrate on his words. "N-no," she finally sighed.

"Good." He couldn't keep the savage satisfaction out of his voice. He didn't like the thought of anyone else pleasing her. This was something she had known only with him; he had realized it immediately when they had first made love, but he had needed to hear her say it, admit that she had given her response to no one else.

He teased her with another slow withdrawal and thrust. "What did he do to you?" he murmured, and pulled completely away from her.

Her eyes opened in protest and she reached for him, moaning low in her throat as she tried to reestablish that delicious contact. Then comprehension made her eyes flare wider, and she jerked backward, away from him, trying to sit up. "You bastard!" she said in a strangled tone.

Quinlan caught her hips and dragged her back, slipping into her once again. "Tell me," he said relentlessly. "Did he mistreat you? Hurt you in any way? What in hell did he do that you're making me pay for?"

Elizabeth wrenched away from him again. She felt ill, all desire gone. How could he have done that to her? She fought to cover herself with his shirt, all the while calling herself several harsh names for her stupidity in thinking they could have this night, that she could give herself a block of time unattached to either past or present. She should have remembered that Quinlan never gave up.

No, he never gave up. So why didn't she tell him? It wouldn't be easy for her to relive it, but at least then he would know why she refused to allow him any authority in her life, why she had denied herself the love she so desperately wanted to give him.

She curled away from him, letting her head fall forward onto her knees so her hair hid her face. He tried to pull her back into his arms, into his lovemaking, but she resisted him, her body stiff in reaction to the memories already swamping her.

"Don't touch me!" she said hoarsely. "You wanted to know, so sit there and listen, but don't—don't touch me."

Quinlan frowned, feeling vaguely uneasy. He had deliberately pushed her, though he hadn't intended to push so hard that she withdrew from him, but that was what had happened. His body was still tight with desire, demanding release. He ground his teeth together, grimly reaching for control; if Elizabeth was ready to talk, after all these months, then he was damn well going to listen.

She didn't lift her head from her knees, but in the silent, darkening lobby, he could plainly hear every soft word.

"I met him when I was a senior in college. Eric. Eric Landers. But you already know his name, don't you? It was in your damn report. He owned an upscale decorating firm, and getting a part-time job there was a real plum."

She sighed. The little sound was sad, and a bit tired. "He was thirty-five. I was twenty-one. And he was handsome, sophisticated, self-assured, worldly, with quite a reputation as both a ladies' man and a well-known professional. I was more than flattered when he asked me out, I was absolutely giddy. Chickie would seem grim compared to the way I felt.

"We dated for about three months before he asked me to marry him, and for three months I felt like a princess. He took me everywhere, wined and dined me at the best places. He was interested in every minute of my day, in everything I did. A real princess couldn't have been more coddled. I was a virgin—a bit unusual, to stay that way through college, but I'd been studying hard and working part-time jobs, too, and I hadn't had time for much socializing. Eric didn't push me for sex. He said he could wait until our wedding night, that since I had remained a virgin that long, he wanted to give me all the traditional trappings."

"Let me guess," Quinlan said grimly. "He was gay."

She shook her head. "No. His ladies' man reputation was for real. Eric was very gentle with me on our wedding night. I'll give him that. He never mistreated me that way."

"If you don't mind," Quinlan interrupted, his teeth coming together with an audible snap, "I'd rather not hear about your sex life with him, if that wasn't the problem."

Elizabeth was surprised into lifting her head. "Are you jealous?" she asked warily.

He rubbed his hand over his jaw; as late in the day as it was, his five-o'clock shadow had become more substantial and made a rasping sound as his hand passed over it. "Not jealous, exactly," he muttered. "I just don't want to hear it, if you enjoyed making love with him. Hell, *yes,* I'm jealous!"

She gave a spurt of laughter, startling herself. She had never expected to be able to laugh while discussing Eric Landers, but Quinlan's frustration was so obvious that she couldn't help it.

"I don't mind giving the devil his due," she said in a generous tone. "You can pat yourself on the back, because you know you were the first to—umm—"

"Satisfy you," he supplied. A sheepish expression crossed his face.

"I'm not very experienced. You're the only man I've gone to bed with since my divorce. After Eric, I just didn't want to let anyone close to me."

She didn't continue, and the silence stretched between them. It was growing darker by the minute as the sun set completely, and she was comforted by the shield of night. "Why?" Quinlan finally asked.

It was easier to talk now, after that little bit of laughter and with the growing darkness concealing both their expressions. She felt herself relaxing, uncurling from her protective knot.

"It was odd," she said, "but I don't think he wanted me

to be sensual. He wanted me to be his perfect princess, his living, breathing Barbie doll. I had gotten used to his protectiveness while we were dating, so at first I didn't think anything of it when he wanted to be with me every time I set foot outside the door. Somehow he always came up with a reason why I shouldn't put in for this job, or that one, and why I couldn't continue working with him. He went shopping with me, picked out my clothes…at first, it all seemed so flattering. My friends were so impressed by the way he treated me.

"Then he began to find reasons why I shouldn't see my friends, why first this one and then that one wasn't 'good' for me. I couldn't invite them over, and he didn't want me visiting them, or meeting them anywhere for lunch. He began vetting my phone calls. It was all so gradual," she said in a faintly bewildered tone. "And he was so gentle. He seemed to have a good reason for everything he did, and he was always focused on me, giving me the kind of attention all women think they want. He only wanted what was best for me, he said."

Quinlan was beginning to feel uneasy. He shifted position, leaning his back against one of the chairs and stretching out in a relaxed position that belied his inner tension. "A control freak," he growled.

"I think we'd been married about six months before I really noticed how completely he'd cut me off from everyone and everything except him," she continued. "I began trying to shift the balance of power, to make a few decisions for myself, if only in minor things, such as where I got my hair cut."

"Let me make another guess. All of a sudden he wasn't so gentle, right?"

"He was furious that I'd gone to a different place. He took the car keys away from me. That was when I really became angry, for the first time. Until then, I'd made excuses, because he'd been so gentle and loving with me. I'd never defied him until then, but when he took the keys out of my purse I lost my temper and yelled at him. He knocked me down,'' she said briefly.

Quinlan surged to his feet, raw fury running through him so powerfully that he couldn't sit there any longer. To hell with trying to look relaxed. He paced the lobby like a tiger, naked and primitive, the powerful muscles in his body flexing with every movement.

Elizabeth kept on talking. Now that she had started, she wanted to tell it all. Funny, but reliving it wasn't as traumatic as she had expected, not as bad as it had been in her memories and nightmares. Maybe it was having someone else with her that blunted the pain, because always before she had been alone with it.

"I literally became his prisoner. Whenever I tried to assert myself in any way, he'd punish me. There was no pattern to it. Most of the time he would slap me, or even whip me, but sometimes he would just yell, and I never knew what to expect. It was as if he knew that yelling instead of hitting me made it even worse, because then the next time I *knew* he'd hit me, and I'd try, oh, I'd try so hard, not to do anything that would cause the next time. But I always did. I was so nervous that I always did something. Or he'd make up a reason.

"Looking back,'' she said slowly, "it's hard to believe I was so stupid. By the time I realized what he had done and started trying to fight back, he had me so isolated, so brainwashed, that I literally felt powerless. I had no money, no friends, no car. I was ashamed for anyone to know what was happening. That was what was so sick, that he could convince me it was my fault. I did try to run away once, but he'd paid the doorman to call him if I left, and he found me within half an hour. He didn't hit me that time. He just tied me to the bed and left me. The terror of waiting, helpless, for him to come back and punish me was so bad that hitting me would have been a relief, because that would have meant it was over. Instead he kept me tied for two days, and I nearly became hysterical every time he came into the room.''

Quinlan had stopped pacing. He was standing motionless, but she could feel the tension radiating from him.

''He put locks on the phone so I couldn't call out, or even answer it,'' she said. ''But one day he blacked my eye. I don't even remember why. It didn't take much to set him off. When I looked in the mirror the next morning, all of a sudden something clicked in my brain and I knew I had to either get away from him or kill him. I couldn't live like that another day, another hour.''

''I'd have opted for killing him,'' Quinlan said tonelessly. ''I may yet.''

''After that, it was all so easy,'' she murmured, ignoring him. ''I just packed my suitcases and walked out. The doorman saw me and reached for the phone...and then stopped. He looked at my eye and let the phone drop back into the cradle, and then he opened the door for me and asked if he could call a cab for me. When I told him I didn't have any money, he pulled out his wallet and gave me forty dollars.

''I went to a shelter for abused women. It was the hardest, most humiliating thing I've ever done. It's strange how the women are the ones who are so embarrassed,'' she said reflectively. ''Never the men who have beaten them, terrorized them. *They* seem to think it was their right, or that the women deserved it. But I understand how the women feel, because I was one of them. Its like standing up in public and letting everyone see how utterly stupid you are, what bad judgment you have, what horrible mistakes you've made. The women I met there could barely look anyone in the eye, and they were the victims!

''I got a divorce. It was that simple. With the photographs

taken at the shelter, I had evidence of abuse, and Eric would have done anything to preserve his reputation. Oh, he tried to talk me into coming back, he made all sorts of promises, he swore things would be different. I was even tempted," she admitted. "But I couldn't trust my own judgment any longer, so the safest thing, the only thing to do was stay away from romantic relationships in general and Eric Landers in particular."

God, it was so plain now. Quinlan could barely breathe with the realization of the mistakes he'd made in dealing with her. No wonder she had pulled away from him. Because he'd wanted her so much, he had tried to take over, tried to coddle and protect her. It was a normal male instinct, but nothing else could have been more calculated to set off her inner alarms. When she had needed space, he had crowded her, so determined to have her that he hadn't let anything stand in his way. Instead of binding her to him, he had made her run.

"I'm not like Landers," he said hoarsely. "I'll never abuse you, Elizabeth, I swear."

She was silent, and he could sense the sadness in her. "How can I trust you?" she finally asked. "How can I trust *myself*? What if I make the wrong decision about you, too? You're a much stronger man than Eric could ever hope to be, both physically and mentally. What if you *did* try to hurt me? How could I protect myself? You want to be in charge. You admit it. You're dominating and secretive. God, Quinlan, I love you, but you scare me to death."

His heart surged wildly in his chest at her words. He had known it, but this was the first time she had actually said so. She loved him! At the same time he was suddenly terrified, because he didn't see any way he could convince her to trust him. And that was what it was: a matter of trust. She had lost confidence in her own ability to read character. He didn't know what to do; for the first time in his life he had no plan of action, no viable option. All he had were his instincts, and he was afraid they were all wrong, at least as far as Elizabeth was concerned. He had certainly bungled it so far. He tried to think what his life would be like without her, if he never again could hold her, and the bleakness of the prospect shook him. Even during these past hellish months, when she had avoided him so totally, even refusing to speak to him on the phone, he hadn't felt this way, because he had still thought he would eventually be able to get her back.

He had to have her. No other woman would do. And he wanted her just as she was: elegant, acerbic, independent, wildly passionate in bed. That, at last, he had done right. She had burned bright and hot in his arms.

He suspected that if he asked for an affair, and only that, she would agree. It was the thought of a legal, binding relationship that had sent her running. She had acted outraged when he had mentioned marriage and kids, getting all huffy because he hadn't included her in the decision-making, but in truth it was that very thing that had so terrified her. Had she sensed he had been about to propose? Finding the file had made her furious, but what had sent her fleeing out the door had been the prospect that he wanted more than just a sexual relationship with her. She could handle being intimate with him; it was the thought of giving him legal rights that gave her nightmares.

He cleared his throat. He felt as if he were walking blindfolded through a mine field, but he couldn't just give up. "I have a reason for not talking about myself," he said hesitantly.

Her reply was an ironic, "I'm sure you do."

He stopped, shrugging helplessly. There was nothing he could tell her that wouldn't sound like an outrageous lie. Okay, that had been a dead end.

"I love you."

The words shook him. He'd admitted the truth of it to himself months ago, not long after meeting her, in fact, but it had been so long since he'd said them aloud that he was startled. Oh, he'd said them during his marriage, at first. It had been so easy, and so expected. Now he realized that the words had been easy because he hadn't meant them. When something really mattered, it was a lot harder to get out.

Elizabeth nodded her head. It had gotten so dark that all he could see was the movement, not her expression. "I believe you do," she replied.

"But you still can't trust me with your life."

"If I needed someone to protect me from true danger, I can't think of anyone I would trust more. But for the other times, the day-to-day normal times that make up a true lifetime, I'm terrified of letting someone close enough to ever have that kind of influence on me again."

Quinlan took another mental sidestep. "We could still see each other," he suggested cautiously. "I know I came on too strong. I'll hold it down. I won't pressure you to make any kind of commitment."

"That wouldn't be fair to you. Marriage is what you want."

"I want *you,*" he said bluntly. "With or without the legal trappings. We're great in bed together, and we enjoy each other's company. We have fun together. We can do that without being married, if that's all that's making you shy away from me."

"You want to have an affair?" she asked, needing to pin him down on his exact meaning.

"Hell, no. I want everything. The ring, the kids, all of it. But if an affair is all I can have, I'll take it. What do you say?"

She was silent a long time, thinking it over. At last she sighed and said, "I think I'd be a fool to make any decision right now. These aren't normal circumstances. When the power is back on and our lives are back to normal, then I'll decide.''

Quinlan had always had the knack of cutting his losses. He took a step toward her. ''But I still have tonight,'' he said in a low tone. ''And I don't intend to waste a minute of it.''

Chapter Eight

It was much as it had been that other night, and yet it was much more intense. Quinlan made love to her until she literally screamed with pleasure, and then loved her past her embarrassment. The darkness wrapped around them like a heated cocoon, suspending time and restrictions, allowing anything to be possible. The hours seemed endless, unmarked as they were by any clock or other means that civilized man had developed. The streets outside remained dark and mostly empty; he didn't turn on the radio again, because he didn't want the outside world to intrude, and neither did she.

It was too hot to sleep, despite the high ceiling in the lobby that carried the heat upward. They lay on the cushions and talked, their voices not much more than slow murmurs in the sultry heat. Quinlan's big hands never left her bare body, and Elizabeth suspended her thoughts for this one magic night. She became drowsy, but all inclination to sleep fled when he turned to her in the thick, heated darkness, pressing down on her, his callused hands stroking and probing until she writhed on the cushions. His lovemaking was as steamy as the night, as enveloping. In the darkness she had no inhibitions. She not only let him do as he wanted with her, she reveled in it. There wasn't an inch of her body that he didn't explore.

Daylight brought sunlight and steadily increasing temperatures, but the power remained off. Even though she knew it was impossible to see inside through the glazed windows, she was glad that they could remain snugly hidden in their own little lair. They drank water and ate, and Elizabeth insisted on washing off again in the smothering heat of the rest room, though she knew it wouldn't do any good to clean up with Quinlan waiting impatiently for her outside. Did the man never get tired?

She heard other voices and froze, panicking at the thought of being caught naked in the rest room. Had the power come back on? Impossible, because it was dark in the bathroom. Or had the guard cut off the lights in here before he'd left the day before? She hadn't even thought to check the switch.

Then she heard a familiar call sign and relaxed. The radio, of course. A bit irritated, with herself for being scared and with him because he'd caused it, she strode out of the rest room. "I nearly had a heart attack," she snapped. "I thought someone had come in and I was caught in the rest room."

Quinlan grinned. "What about me? I'm as naked as you are."

He was still sprawled on the cushions, but somehow he looked absolutely at home in his natural state. She looked down at herself and laughed. "I can't believe this is happening."

He stared to say, *It'll be something to tell our grandkids,* but bit the words back. She wouldn't want to hear it, and he'd promised he wouldn't push her. He held out his hand to her, and she crawled onto the cushions with him, sinking into his arms.

"What was on the news?"

"A relatively quiet night in Dallas, though there was some sporadic looting. The same elsewhere. It was just too damn hot to do anything very strenuous."

"Oh, yeah?" she asked, giving him a sidelong glance.

He laughed and deftly rolled her onto her back, mounting her with a total lack of haste that demonstrated how many times during the night he'd done the same thing. "The news?" she prompted.

He nuzzled her neck, breathing in the sweet woman scent. "Oh, that. The national guard has been mobilized from Texas to the East Coast. There were riots in Miami, but they're under control now."

"I thought you said things were relatively quiet?"

"That *is* quiet. With electricity off in almost a quarter of the country, that's amazingly quiet." He didn't want to talk about the blackout. Having Elizabeth naked under him went to his head faster than the most potent whiskey. He kissed her, acutely savoring her instant response, even as he positioned her for his penetration and smoothly slid within. He felt the delicious tightening of her inner muscles as she adjusted to him, the way her fingers dug into his shoulders as she tried to arch even closer to him. His feelings for her swamped him, and he found himself wishing the electricity would never come back on.

Afterward, she yawned and nestled down on his shoulder. "Did the radio announcers say when the power company officials thought the power would be back on?"

"Maybe by this afternoon," he said.

So soon? She felt a bit indignant, as if she had been promised a vacation and now it had been cut short. But this wasn't a vacation; for a lot of people, it was a crisis. Electricity could mean the difference between life and death for someone who was ill. If all they had was a few more hours, she meant to make the best of them.

It seemed that he did, too. Except for insisting that they regularly drink water, he kept her in his arms. Even when he finally tired and had to take a break from lovemaking, he remained nestled within her body. Elizabeth was too tired to think; all she could do was feel. Quinlan had so completely dominated her senses that she would have been alarmed, if she hadn't seen the same drugged expression in his eyes that she knew was in hers. This wasn't something he was doing to her; it was something they were sharing.

They dozed, their sweaty bodies pressed tightly together despite the heat.

It was the wash of cool air over her skin that woke her, shivering.

Quinlan sat up. "The power's back on," he said, squinting up at the overhead lights that seemed to be glaring after the long hours without them. He looked at his watch. "It's eleven o'clock."

"That's too soon," Elizabeth said grumpily. "They said it would be this afternoon."

"They probably gave themselves some extra time in case something went wrong."

Feeling incredibly exposed in the artificial light, Elizabeth scrambled into her clothing. She looked at her discarded panty hose in distaste and crumpled them up, then threw them into the trash.

"What do we do now?" she asked, pushing her hair back.

Quinlan zipped his pants. "Now we go home."

"How? Do we call the guard service?"

"Oh, I'll call them all right. Later. I have a few things to say. But now that the power's on, I can get us out of here."

While he tapped into the security system, Elizabeth hastily straightened the furniture, shoving it back into place and restoring all the cushions to their original sites. A blush was already heating her face at the possibility of anyone finding out about their love nest, literally in the middle of the lobby. She didn't know if she would ever be able to walk into this building again without blushing.

Quinlan grunted with satisfaction as he entered a manual override into the system that would allow him to open the side door. "Come on," he said, grabbing Elizabeth's hand.

She barely had time to snatch up her purse before he was hustling her out of there. She blinked in the blinding sunshine. The heat rising off the sidewalk was punishing. "We can't just leave the building unlocked," she protested.

"I didn't. It locked again as soon as the door closed." Taking her arm, he steered her around the corner and across the street to the parking deck.

Before she could react, he was practically stuffing her into his car. "I have my own car!" she said indignantly.

"I know. Don't worry, it isn't going anywhere. But we don't know that the electricity is on all over the city, and we don't know what kind of situation you'll find at your place. Until I know you're safe, I'm keeping you with me."

It was the sort of high-handed action that had always made her uneasy in the past, but now it didn't bother her. Maybe it was because she was so sleepy. Maybe it was because he was right. For whatever reason, she relaxed in the seat and let her eyes close.

He had to detour a couple of times to reach her apartment, but the traffic was surprisingly light, and it didn't take long, not even as long as normal. She didn't protest when he went inside with her. The electricity was on there, too, the central air conditioning humming as it tried to overcome the built-up heat.

"Into the shower," Quinlan commanded.

She blinked at him. "What?"

He put his arm around her, turning her toward her bedroom. "The shower. We're both going to take a nice, cool shower. We're in good shape, but this will make us feel better. Believe me, we're a little dehydrated."

Their bargain had been only for the night, but since it had already extended into the day, she supposed it wouldn't hurt to carry it a little further. She allowed him to strip her and wasn't at all surprised when he undressed and climbed in with her. The shower spray was cool enough to raise a chill, and it felt wonderful. She turned around to let it wash over her spine and tilted her head back so the water soaked through her sweat-matted hair.

"Feel good?" he murmured, running his hands over her. She would have thought that he was washing her, except that he wasn't using soap.

"Mmm." He bent his head and Elizabeth lifted hers. If only she could stay this way, she thought. Kissing him, being kissed by him. His hard arms locked around her. Feeling him so close, all worries pushed aside...

The cool shower was revitalizing in more ways than one. Abruptly he lifted her and braced her against the wall, and she gasped as he drove deep into her. There was nothing slow about it this time; he took her fiercely, as wild as he had been the day before on the floor of the lobby, as if all those times in between had never been.

Later they went to bed. She could barely hold her eyes open while he dried her hair, then carried her to the bed and placed her between the cool, smooth sheets. She sighed, every muscle relaxing, and immediately went to sleep, not knowing that he slipped into bed beside her.

Still, she wasn't surprised when she woke during the afternoon and he was there. Lazily she let her gaze drift over his strong-boned features. He needed to shave; the black beard lay on his skin like a dark shadow. His hair was tousled, and his closed eyelids looked as delicate as a child's. Odd, for she had never thought of Quinlan as delicate in any way, never associated any sort of softness with him. Yet he had been tender with her, even in his passion. It wasn't the same type of gentleness Eric had displayed; Eric had been gentle, she realized now, because he hadn't *wanted* any responding passion from her. He had wanted her to be nothing more than a doll, to be dressed and positioned and shown off for his own ego. Quinlan, on the other hand, had been as helpless in his passion as she had been in hers.

Her body quivered at his nearness. Still half asleep, she

pushed at him. His eyes opened immediately, and he rolled onto his back. "What's wrong?"

"Plenty," she said, slithering on top of him and feeling the immediate response between his legs. "It's been at least—" She paused to look at the clock, but it was blinking stupidly at her, not having been reset since the power had come back on. "It's been too damn long since I've had this." She reached between his legs, and he sucked in his breath, his back arching as she guided him into place.

"God, I'm sorry," he apologized fervently, and bit back a moan as she moved on him. This was the way he had always known his Elizabeth could be, hot with uncomplicated passion, a little bawdy, intriguingly earthy. She made him dizzy with delight.

Her eyes were sultry, her lips swollen and pouty from his kisses, her dark hair tumbling over her shoulders. He watched her expression tighten with desire as she moved slowly up and down on him, her eyes closing even more. "Just for that," she murmured, "I get to be on top."

He reached overhead and caught the headboard, his powerful biceps flexing as his fists locked around the brass bars. "No matter how I beg and plead?"

"No matter what you say," she assured him, and gasped herself as her movements wrenched another spasm of pleasure from her nerve endings.

"Good." Quinlan arched, almost lifting her off the bed. "Then I won't accidentally say something that will make you quit."

He didn't. When she collapsed, exhausted, on his chest, they were both numb with pleasure. He thrust his hand into her tangled hair and held her almost desperately close. She inhaled the hot, musky scent of his skin, and with the slightest of motions rubbed her cheek against the curly hair on his chest. She could feel his heart thudding under her ear, and the strong rhythm was reassuring. They slept again, and woke in the afternoon with the sun going down in a blaze of red and gold, to drowsily make love again.

He got up to turn on the television sitting on her dresser, then returned to bed to hold her while they watched the news, which was, predictably, all about the blackout. Elizabeth felt a little bemused, as if a national crisis had passed without her knowing about it, even though she had been intimately embroiled in this one. Intimately, she thought, in more ways than one. Perhaps that was why she felt so out of touch with reality. She hadn't spent the past twenty-four hours concentrating on the lack of electricity, she had been concentrating on Quinlan.

The Great Blackout, as the Dallas newscasters were calling it, had disrupted electrical services all over the Sun Belt. The heat wave, peak usage and solar flares had all combined to overload and blow circuits, wiping out entire power grids. Elizabeth felt as if her own circuits had been seriously damaged by Quinlan's high-voltage lovemaking.

He spent the night with her. He didn't ask if he could, and she didn't tell him that he couldn't. She knew that she was only postponing the inevitable, but she wanted this time with him. Telling him about Eric hadn't changed her mind, any more than knowing about Eric had changed Quinlan's basic character.

When morning came, they both knew that the time-out had ended. Reality couldn't be held at bay any longer.

"So what happens now?" he asked quietly.

She looked out the window as she sipped her coffee. It was Saturday; neither of them had to work, though Quinlan had already talked to a couple of his staffers, placing the calls almost as soon as he'd gotten out of bed. She knew that all she had to say was one word, "Stay," and they would spend the weekend in bed, too. It would be wonderful, but come Monday, it would make it just that much more difficult to handle.

"I don't see that the situation has changed," she finally said.

"Damn it, Elizabeth!" He got up, his big body coiled with tension. "Can you honestly say that I'm anything like Landers?"

"You're very dominating," she pointed out.

"You love me."

"At the time, I thought I loved him, too. What if I'm wrong again?" Her eyes were huge and stark as she stared at him. "There's no way you can know how bad it was without having lived through it yourself. I would rather die than go through anything like that again. I don't know how I can afford to take the chance on you. I still don't know *you,* not the way you know me. You're so secretive that I can't tell who you really are. How can I trust you when I don't know you?"

"And if you did?" he asked in a harsh tone. "If you knew all there is to know about me?"

"I don't know," she said; then they looked at each other and broke into snickering laughter. "There's a lot of knowing and not knowing in a few short sentences."

"At least we know what we mean," he said, and she groaned; then they started laughing again. When he sobered, he reached out and slid his hand underneath her heavy curtain of hair, clasping the back of her neck. "Let me give something a try," he urged. "Let me have another shot at changing your mind."

"Does this mean that if it doesn't work, you'll stop trying?" she asked wryly, and had to laugh at the expression on his face. "Oh, Tom, you don't even have a clue about how to give up, do you?"

He shrugged. "I've never wanted anyone the way I want you," he said, smiling back just as wryly. "But at least I've made some progress. You've started calling me Tom again."

He dressed and roughly kissed her as he started out the door. "I'll be back as soon as I can. It may not be today. But there's something I want to show you before you make a final decision."

Elizabeth leaned against the door after she had closed it behind him. Final decision? She didn't know whether to laugh or cry. To her, the decision had been final for the past six months. So why did she feel that, unless she gave him the answer he wanted, she would still be explaining her reasons to him five years from now?

Chapter Nine

The doorbell rang just before five on Sunday morning. Elizabeth stumbled groggily out of bed, staring at the clock in bewilderment. She had finally set the thing, but surely she had gotten it wrong. Who would be leaning on her doorbell at 4:54 in the morning?

"Quinlan," she muttered, moving unsteadily down the hall.

She looked through the peephole to make certain, though she really hadn't doubted it. Yawning, she released the chain and locks and opened the door. "Couldn't it have waited another few hours?" she asked grouchily, heading toward the kitchen to put on a pot of coffee. If she had to deal with him at this hour, she needed to be more alert than she was right now.

"No," he said. "I haven't slept, and I want to get this over with."

She hadn't slept all that much herself; after he'd left the morning before, she had wandered around the apartment, feeling restless and unable to settle on anything to do. It had taken her a while to identify it, but at last she had realized that she was lonely. He had been with her for thirty-six hours straight, holding her while they slept, making love, talking, arguing, laughing. The blackout had forced them into a hothouse intimacy, leading her to explore old nightmares and maybe even come to terms with them.

The bed had seemed too big, too cold, too empty. For the first time she began to question whether or not she had been right in breaking off with him. Quinlan definitely was *not* Eric Landers. Physically, she felt infinitely safe and cherished with him; on that level, at least, she didn't think he would ever hurt her.

It was the other facet of his personality that worried her the most, his secrecy and insistence on being in control. She had some sympathy with the control thing; after all, she was a bit fanatic on the subject herself. The problem was that she had had to fight so hard to get herself back, how could she risk her identity again? Quinlan was as relentless as the tides; lesser personalities crumbled before him. She didn't know anything about huge chunks of his life, what had made him the man he was. What if he were hiding something from her that she absolutely couldn't live with? What if there was a darkness to his soul that he could keep under control until it was too late for her to protect herself?

She was under no illusions about marriage. Even in this day and age, it gave a man a certain autonomy over his wife. People weren't inclined to get involved in domestic "disputes," even when the dispute involved a man beating the hell out of his smaller, weaker wife. Some police departments were starting to view it more seriously, but they were so inundated with street crime, drug and highway carnage that, objectively, she could see how a woman's swollen face or broken arm didn't seem as critical when weighed in that balance.

And marriage was what Quinlan wanted. If she resumed a relationship with him, he might not mention it for a while—she gave him a week, at the outside—but he would be as relentless in his pursuit of that goal as he was in everything else. She loved him so much that she knew he would eventually wear her down, which was why she had to make a final decision now. And she *could* do it now—if the answer was no. She still had enough strength to walk away from him, in her own best interests. If she waited, every day would weaken that resolve a little more.

He had been silent while she moved around the kitchen,

preparing the coffeemaker and turning it on. Hisses and gurgles filled the air as the water heated; then came the soft tinkle of water into the pot and the delicious aroma of fresh coffee filled the room.

"Let's sit down," he said, and placed his briefcase on the table. It was the first time she had noticed it.

She shook her head. "If this requires thinking, at least wait until I've had a cup of coffee."

His mouth quirked. "I don't know. Somehow I think I'd stand a better chance if your brain stayed in neutral and you just went with your instincts."

"Hormones, you mean."

"I have nothing against those, either." He rubbed his beard and sighed wearily. "But I guess I could use a cup of coffee, too."

He had taken the time to change clothes, she saw; he was wearing jeans that looked to be at least ten years old, and a soft, white, cotton shirt. But his eyes were circled with dark rings and were bloodshot from lack of sleep, and he obviously hadn't shaved since the morning before the blackout. The blackness of his heavy beard made him look like a ruffian; actually, he looked exactly like the type of people he hired.

When the coffee stopped dripping, she filled two mugs and slid one in front of him as she took a seat at the table. Cautiously sipping the hot brew, she wondered how long it would take to hit the bloodstream.

He opened the briefcase and took out two files, one very thin and the other over an inch thick. He slid the thin one toward her. "Okay, read this one first."

She opened it and lifted her eyebrows when she saw that it was basically the same type of file that he'd had on her, though this one was on himself. Only it seemed to be rather sketchy. *Bare bones* was more like it, and even then, part of the skeleton was missing. It gave his name, birthdate, birthplace, social security number, physical description, education and present employment, as well as the sketchy facts of his brief marriage, so many years ago. Other than that, he seemed not to have existed between the years of his divorce and when he had started his security business.

"Were you in cold storage for about fifteen years?" she finally asked, shoving the file back toward him. "I appreciate the gesture, but if this was supposed to tell me about you, it lacks a little something."

He eyed her warily, then grinned. "Not many people can manage to be sarcastic at five o'clock in the morning."

"At five o'clock, that's about all I *can* manage."

"I'll remember that," he murmured, and slid the second file, the thick one, toward her. "This is the information you wouldn't have gotten if you investigated me."

Her interest level immediately soared, and she flipped the manila folder open. The documents before her weren't originals, but were a mixture of photostats and faxes. She looked at the top of one and then gave him a startled look. "Government, huh?"

"I had to get a buddy to pull up my file and send it to me. Nothing in there is going to reveal state secrets, but the information is protected, for my sake. I could have hacked into the computer, but I'd just as soon not face a jail term, so it took some time to get it all put together."

"Just exactly what did you do?" she asked, not at all certain that she wanted to know. After being so frustrated by his lack of openness, now that his life lay open before her, she wasn't all that eager to know the details. If he had been shot at, if he had been in danger in any way…that could give her a different set of nightmares.

"No Hollywood stuff," he assured her, grinning.

"I'm disappointed. You mean you weren't a secret agent?" Relieved was more like it.

"That's a Hollywood term. In the business, it's called a

field operative. And no, that isn't what I did. I gathered information, set up surveillance and security systems, worked with antiterrorist squads. It wasn't the kind of job that you talk over with your buddies in the bar after work.''

"I can understand that. You got in the habit of not talking about yourself or what you did.''

"It was more than just a habit, it could have meant people's lives. I still don't talk about it, because I still know people in the business. Information is the greatest asset a government can have, and the most dangerous.''

She tapped the file. "So why are you showing me this?''

"Because I trust you," he said simply; then another grin spread across his face. "And because I didn't think you'd believe me if I just said, 'I can't talk about myself, government stuff, very hush-hush.' You would have laughed in my face. It's the kind of crap you hear in singles bars, hot-shot studs trying to impress the airheads. You aren't an airhead.''

After flipping a few pages and scanning them, she said, "You're right. I wouldn't have believed this. Most people don't do this type of work.''

He shrugged. "Like I said, I went to Cal Tech, and I was very good at what I did.''

"Did?" she asked incredulously. "It's what you still do. It's just that now you do it for yourself instead of the government.'' An idea struck her. "The people you hire. Are they—?''

"Some of them," he admitted.

"Like the biker?''

He laughed. "Like the biker. Hell, do you think I'd hire anyone who looked like that if I didn't personally know him? He really was an operative, one mean son of a bitch.''

"They come to you for jobs when they retire?''

"No, nothing like that. I'm not a halfway house for burned-out government employees. I keep track of people, contact them to see if they're interested in working for me.

Most of them are very normal, and it's just a matter of moving from one computer job to another.''

She closed the file and pushed it away from her. Quinlan eyed her with alarm. ''Aren't you going to read it?''

''No. I don't need to know every detail of everything you've done. A brief overview is enough.''

He drew a deep breath and sat back. ''Okay. That's it, then. I've done all I can. I can't convince you, prove it to you in any way, that I'll never treat you the way Landers did. *I* know I won't, but you're the one who has to believe it. Elizabeth, sweetheart, will you marry me?''

She couldn't help it. She knew it wasn't the way a woman was supposed to respond to a marriage proposal, but the relentlessness of it was so typical of Tom Quinlan that she couldn't stop the sharp crack of laughter from exploding into sound. She would probably hear that question every day until she either gave him the answer he wanted or went mad under the pressure. Instead of making her feel pressured, as it would have before, there was a certain amount of comfort in knowing she could depend on him to that extent. Seeing that file had meant more to her than he could know. It wasn't just that it filled in the gaps of his life, but that he trusted her to know about him.

She managed to regain her composure and stared seriously at him. Somehow, what had happened during the blackout had lessened the grip that Eric Landers had still had on her, even after so many years. During the long hours of that hot night she had been forced to truly look at what had happened, to deal with it, and for the first time she'd realized that Eric had still held her captive. Because of him, she had been afraid to truly let herself live. She was still afraid, but all of a sudden she was more afraid of losing what she had. If it were possible to lose Quinlan, she thought, looking at him with wry fondness. But, yes, she could lose him, if she didn't start appreciating the value of what he was offering her. It was sink or swim time.

He had begun to fidget under her silent regard. She inhaled deeply. "Marriage, huh? No living together, seeing how it works?"

"Nope. Marriage. The love and honor vows. Until death."

She scowled a little at him. He was as yielding as rock when he made up his mind about something. "Yours could come sooner than you think," she muttered.

"That's okay, if you're the one who does me in. I have an idea of the method you'd use," he replied, and a look of startlingly intense carnal hunger crossed his face. He shivered a little, then gathered himself and raised his right hand. "I swear I'll be an absolute pussycat of a husband. A woman like you needs room."

She had taken a sip of coffee, and at his words she swallowed wrong, choking on the liquid. She coughed and wheezed, then stared at him incredulously. "Then why haven't you been giving me any?" she yelled.

"Because I was afraid to give you enough room to push me away," he said. He gave her a little half smile that acknowledged his own vulnerability and held out his hand to her. "You scare me, too, babe. I'm scared to death you'll decide you can get along without me."

She crossed her arms and glared at him, refusing to take his outstretched hand. "If you think you'll get a little slave, you'll be disappointed. I won't pick up after you, I don't like cooking and I won't tolerate dirty clothes strewn all over the place."

A grin began to spread across his face as she talked, a look of almost blinding elation, but he only said mildly, "I'm fairly neat, for a man."

"Not good enough. I heard that qualification."

He sighed. "All right. We'll write it into our wedding

vows. I'll keep my clothes picked up, wash the whiskers out of the sink and put the lid back down on the toilet. I'll get up with the kids—''

"Kids?'' she asked delicately.

He lifted his brows at her. She stifled a smile. God, dealing with him was exhilarating! "Okay,'' she said, relenting. "Kids. But not more than two.''

"Two sounds about right. Deal?''

She pretended to consider, then said, "Deal,'' and they solemnly shook hands.

Quinlan sighed with satisfaction, then hauled her into his arms, literally dragging her across the table and knocking her mug of coffee to the floor. Oblivious to the spreading brown puddle, he held her on his lap and kissed her until her knees were weak. When he lifted his head, a big grin creased his face and he said, "By the way, I always know how to bypass my own systems.''

She put her hand on his rough jaw and kissed him again. "I know,'' she said smugly.

Over an hour later, he lifted his head from the pillow and scowled at her. "There's no way you could have known.''

"Not for certain, but I suspected.'' She stretched, feeling lazy and replete. Her entire body throbbed with a pleasant, lingering heat.

He gathered her close and pressed a kiss to the top of her head. "Six months,'' he grumbled. "And it took a damn blackout to get you to talk to me.''

"I feel rather fond of the blackout,'' she murmured. "Without it, I wouldn't have been forced to spend so much time with you.''

"Are you saying we never would have worked it out if it hadn't been for that?''

"I wouldn't have given you the chance to get that close to me,'' she said, her voice quiet with sincerity. "I wasn't playing games, Tom. I was scared to death of you, and of losing myself again. You never would have had the chance to convince me, if it hadn't been for the blackout."

"Then God bless overloaded power grids," he muttered. "But I'd have gotten to you, one way or another."

"Other than kidnapping, I can't think how," she replied caustically.

He went very still, and the silence made her lift her head to give him a suspicious glare. He tried to look innocent, then gave it up when he saw she wasn't buying it.

"That was what I had planned for the weekend, if you refused to have dinner with me Thursday night," he admitted a bit sheepishly.

"Ah-ha. I *thought* you waylaid me that afternoon."

"A man has to do something when his woman won't give him the time of day," he muttered. "I was desperate."

She said, "It's six-thirty."

A brief flicker of confusion crossed his face; then he glanced at the clock and grinned. "So it is," he said with satisfaction. She had just given him the time of day—and a lot more. With a lithe twist of his powerful body he tumbled her back into the twisted sheets and came down on top of her.

"I love you," he rumbled. "And I still haven't heard the 'yes' I've been waiting for."

"I agreed. We made a deal."

"I know, but I'm a little more traditional than that. Elizabeth Major, will you marry me?"

She hesitated for a second. Eric Landers had lost the power to keep her a victim. "Yes, Tom Quinlan, I certainly will."

He lowered his head to kiss her. When he surfaced, they were both breathing hard and knew it would be a while yet before they got out of bed. He gave the clock another glance. "Around nine," he murmured, "remind me to make a couple of phone calls. I need to cancel the kidnapping plans.''

She laughed, and kept laughing until his strong thrust into her body changed the laughter into a soft cry of pleasure, as he turned that relentless focus to the task of bringing them both to the intense ecstasy they found only with each other. She had been so afraid of that part of him, but now she knew it was what made him a man she could depend on for the rest of her life. As she clung to his shoulders, a dim echo of thought floated through her brain: ''God bless overloads!''

IF A MAN ANSWERS
Merline Lovelace

Dear Friends,

Readers sometimes wonder how writers come up with the plots for their stories. The idea for this book popped into my head one night at dinner, when my niece mentioned a call she'd received earlier. Turned out it was a wrong number, but that was enough to start the ole wheels turning.

What if you accidentally dialed a mobster's number? What if you heard something you weren't supposed to hear? What if…

Well, now you can see how nasty, diabolical writers can spin even the most innocuous dinner conversations into murder and sizzling romantic suspense.

I had a ball plunging Molly and Sam into danger *and* into love. I hope you enjoy reading their story as much as I enjoyed writing it.

All the best,

Merline Lovelace

Chapter 1

"Dammit! Doesn't the blasted man *ever* sleep?"

Yanking her pillow out from under her neck, Molly Duncan mashed it down over her head. Even with both ears covered, she still couldn't shut out the nasal lament that drifted across the desert night from the house next door.

She despised country music. She despised dragging herself out of bed after groggy, sleepless nights. She was fast coming to despise her new neighbor.

Until Sam Henderson had moved into the house next to hers, Molly had thoroughly enjoyed her life in Las Vegas. She'd moved to Nevada only six months ago, after dumping a fiancé more into control than her independent spirit could tolerate. Eagerly, she'd traded cold, wet Boston winters for the year-round desert sunshine and a position as a translator and tour consultant for the Las Vegas Trade and Convention Center. From the moment she'd crested the hills and driven down into the sparkling jewel that was Vegas, she'd reveled in its gaudy glitz. Buying her very first home had been the icing on the cake of her new life.

Then, just a few weeks ago, the Major had moved in next door.

She'd received several letters addressed to him in her mailbox by mistake, so Molly knew he was a retired Air Force major...a major pain in the bohunkus, in her considered opinion. She couldn't believe how swiftly their initial skirmish over a dented garbage can had escalated into an undeclared war.

And she'd never even spoken a word to the man!

Okay, so maybe the note she taped to his trash can the morning she ran over it, requesting that he keep the darned thing on his side of their parallel driveways, was a bit, well, unneighborly. But she was late for work, and picking up someone else's smelly garbage wasn't exactly her idea of a fun way to start the day.

Still, that was no reason for Henderson to fire a broadside in return. Even now, the memory of the note she'd found shoved under her front door that same night steamed her. The terse missive had assured Ms. Duncan that he'd keep his trash can in a safe, no-fire zone. In return, she might consider taking a few driving lessons. Judging by the ruts she dug in the lava rock between their driveways when she squealed out of the garage each morning, she could use them. Or maybe she was just feeling the aftereffects of the several cases of empty beer cans he'd observed in *her* recycling bin?

Molly didn't dignify the obnoxious note with a reply. The fact that she slathered a beer-based facial across her nose and cheeks every night to keep her splatter of freckles under control was no one's business but hers. She did, however, respond to the notice she received from Henderson a few days later, informing her that the oleander hedge she'd planted for privacy when she first moved in was actually three feet beyond her property line. According to the contractor hired by Major Sam Henderson, the hedge would have to come down to accommodate the pool he wanted to put in his backyard. The hedge's fate, Molly had replied in a scathing letter to the contractor, would be decided by the county surveyor's office.

She humped the pillow over her ears, furious all over again at the thought of anyone wanting to tear up the row of beautiful hot pink oleanders she'd put in with her own hands. The nerve of the man!

It was just her luck that her new neighbor's personality didn't live up to his admittedly gorgeous physique. In the past few weeks, Molly had caught a few glimpses of the reclusive Major, stripped to the waist and poking around under the hood of a classic, flame-colored Mustang convertible. She had to admit that he possessed a set of world-class buns. And, yes, his glistening, sweaty pecs had pretty well closed down her respiratory system. Based on those gorgeous muscles alone, she might have called a truce in their war and learned to peacefully coexist if Sam Henderson's damned nocturnal habits hadn't destroyed all hope of a cease-fire.

A morning person, Molly always faded fast when the sun went down. Her neighbor, she'd decided soon after he moved in, was part vampire. If he ever slept, she didn't know when. The soul-searing country music he listened to hour after hour seemed to drone on all night. Every night. She'd put up with it as long as she could, but finally had to protest.

The first time she'd called to complain, a sultry-voiced female promised to give Sam the message...when he got out of the shower.

The second time, she'd let the phone ring and ring with no answer.

This time, she vowed, dragging her head out from under the pillow, she meant business!

She glanced at the clock radio sitting atop the overturned

cardboard box she used as a nightstand and groaned. Ten after one, for heaven's sake, and she was scheduled to meet a delegation of Japanese businessmen for breakfast at seven.

Shoving her flyaway blond hair out of her eyes, she sat up and rummaged around in the scatter of papers on the box for the envelope she'd written her neighbor's number on. The scribbled digits blurred a bit, probably from the wet glass she'd left on top of the envelope. Tilting it to a different angle, she reached for the receiver. Seven quick punches and the phone started to ring.

Tapping her bare toes on the smooth oak floorboards, Molly marshaled her thoughts. She refused, absolutely refused, to allow another husky-voiced female to fob her off. This time she'd insist on speaking to the Major himself...even if she had to march next door and confront him in person.

She didn't have to march anywhere. A man answered on the third ring.

"Yeah?"

Molly blinked, surprised by the distinctive twang in the single syllable. Her trained ear placed the accent immediately. New Jersey. Possibly lower New York, but most likely upper Jersey.

Based on his choice in music and worn, low-heeled cowboy boots, Molly had assumed Henderson hailed from somewhere west of the Hudson River. Not that she cared *where* the man came from as long as he lowered the volume on his blasted CD player.

"This is Molly Duncan, next door. Would you *please* turn down that..."

A doorbell shrilled in the background. Unceremoniously, her neighbor cut her off.

"Hang on. There's someone at the door."

"Wait a minute! I just want you to...."

"Hold the phone, doll."

The receiver dropped onto a hard surface. Molly winced at the loud clatter, then scowled at the framed poster of Las Vegas by night on her whitewashed walls. Crossing one knee over the other, she swung her leg impatiently. Another sad lament drifted through her window, telling the story of a trucker who lost his wife to a city boy.

She wished she could lose her neighbor. In fact, she wished she could lose him, his music, his confounded garbage cans, his....

"Don't shoot! God, don't shoot!"

The hoarse cry ripped like a jagged knife through her rambling thoughts. She jerked upright, her jaw dropping. What the heck?

"I have to," a soft, cultured voice replied. "Surely you understand why."

Upper Midwestern, Molly catalogued without conscious thought. Wisconsin, most likely.

"No! No! I won't say nuthin', I swear!"

She'd just decided that the dramatic dialogue had to be emanating from some B-grade movie on her neighbor's TV when she heard a queer little pop. An agonized, gurgling shriek. Another pop. A thud.

Then only silence.

Frozen with disbelief, Molly gripped the phone.

It had to be the TV! Surely that desperate plea hadn't come from her neighbor! Surely those weren't real shots she'd just heard!

She strained, listening for something more. Anything. A bit of dialogue. A dramatic surge of background music to indicate the TV show had just reached a climax.

After what seemed like an eternity, someone picked up the receiver. Quietly. Deliberately.

"Hello?"

Molly's throat closed.

Good grief! This was no movie. The same soft, cultured

voice she'd heard a moment ago was now speaking directly to her. She couldn't reply. Couldn't force so much as a squeak through her frozen vocal chords.

Silence descended once more. The person at the other end of the line listened. Just listened.

Like an animal suddenly sensing danger, Molly slammed the receiver down. Her heart hammered. Her whole body shook in a delayed reaction. Trembling violently, she stabbed at the phone buttons once again.

"Hello, 911," a Hispanic female replied with practiced calm. "What is your emergency?"

"A shooting! There's been a shooting!"

The woman's voice took on a sharper edge. "Have you been shot?"

"No! No, I…uh…my neighbor…."

"You shot your neighbor?"

This wasn't the time for Molly to admit that she'd thought about it. More than once.

"No, I heard someone shoot him. Over the phone. The doorbell rang. My neighbor shouted a protest, and then I heard shots. You have to send someone right away. Whoever fired them is still in his house!"

"I have your name and address on my screen. Are you Ms. Duncan?"

"Yes!"

"Please confirm your neighbor's address?"

"Uh…sixty-seven-nineteen…No, sixty-seven-twenty-one South Valley. I think."

She threw a frantic glance at the curtained windows, trying to get her bearings. The mountains were behind her house. The interstate just a couple of miles away ran north and south.

"His house is to the north of mine. At the end of the cul-de-sac."

"Please hold on the line while I dispatch the police, Ms. Duncan."

The operator came back a moment later, her voice once more calm and steady.

"There's a squad car only a few blocks away. They're on their way. Are you by yourself?"

"Yes."

"Are you safe? Do you feel threatened?"

"Nooo...."

Just scared to death, she thought with a shiver.

"Please stay away from the windows and remain on the line. Can you give me any more information that might aid the police when they arrive?"

While Molly added what little she could to the details she'd already provided, she couldn't help picturing the scene next door. Her neighbor might be lying in a pool of blood. His life might be seeping away second by second. Oh, God! He might already be dead. Waves of guilt for all the awful things she'd wished on Sam Henderson came crashing down on her.

"Ms. Duncan?"

"Maybe I should do something. Try to help him."

"No!"

"He could be dying. Bleeding to death."

"Ms. Duncan, listen to me. The last thing we need is for you to go next door and put yourself in danger. Please, just remain on the line until the police arrive at the scene."

"Yes, but..."

She searched her bedroom for a weapon. The most lethal object she could spot was a tennis racket she'd been intending to take in for restringing. Maybe she could sneak through the oleander hedge and lob the racket through her neighbor's window. Set off his alarm. Scare the shooter away.

The realization that she might also scare herself right into the line of fire of a cold-blooded killer added another kink to the knot in Molly's stomach. Suddenly, a siren wailed in the distance. She heaved a ragged sigh of relief.

"Thank God! I hear the police."

"Stay put until they contact you."

The tennis racket forgotten, Molly mumbled an assent and hung up. Her bare feet slapped the oak floor as she hurried down the hall to the upstairs front bedroom. Lifting the shade aside a few inches, she watched two black-and-white patrol cars pull into her neighbor's drive. Weapons drawn and angled at the night sky, they approached the red-roofed, stucco house. After peering in the darkened front windows, one officer skirted the garage and headed for the back. The other disappeared into the shadows on the far side of the house.

Molly had no idea how long she crouched there in the front bedroom, her nerves crawling. It felt like hours. To her mingled relief and consternation, nothing happened. No gunfire shattered the night. No shouts sounded from the house or yard. No ambulances pulled into the driveway, sirens flashing.

Finally, the officers returned to the front. From where she crouched, Molly couldn't see whether they kicked in the door or found it unlocked. In any case, an oblong of yellow light slashed through the darkness.

Shivering, she let the shade fall. Whatever the police found next door, she'd better get dressed. The operator had said they'd want to talk to her.

Her doorbell sounded just as she was splashing away the remnants of her facial. Hastily, she swiped a towel over her face and pulled on a soft gray cotton top and leggings. The wide-necked tunic slipped off one shoulder as she hurried on down the stairs and into the hall that led to the tiled front entryway.

Scrunching one eye shut, she peered through the peephole with the other. At the glint of a silver metal shield prominently displayed on a dark-shirted chest, she yanked off the chain, twisted the dead bolt, and threw open the door.

"Ms. Duncan?"

"Yes!"

"I'm Officer Dennis Rodriguez. My backup, Officer Corrigan, is in his patrol car, notifying central dispatch."

"Thank God you got here so quickly. What did you find next door?"

"He found me, Ms. Duncan," a deep voice snarled. "Alive, unshot, and, at this point, thoroughly ticked off by your stupid stunt."

Molly jerked back, startled by the half-naked male who stepped forward to confront her. Unsnapped jeans rode low on his hips. A white towel dangled around his neck. Sweat glistened on his heavily muscled torso.

Her nerves snapping like live electrical wires, Molly dragged her stunned gaze from that acre or so of smooth, muscled chest to the face that went with it. Too rugged for handsomeness, too square-jawed for charm, it was the kind of face that would make any woman back up a step, even when it wasn't tight with anger...which at this point, it definitely was! Below a thick pelt of sweat-slicked hair so dark a brown it looked black in this light, his slanting brows slashed to a *V*. Slate gray eyes lasered into Molly.

"Is this your idea of a joke?" he demanded in a scorching drawl.

No trace of New Jersey there, she thought, torn between relief and confusion. Her neighbor definitely hailed from west of the Hudson. Somewhere in the Southwest, she thought. Arizona, or maybe he was one of that rare genus, a Nevada native.

Obviously, this wasn't the man who answered her call a while ago. Frowning, she responded to his irate demand.

"No, of course it isn't a joke."

His big fists gripped the ends of the towel, knuckles white. "If you insist on continuing this damned feud you started, you should at least have the guts to do it in person."

"The feud *I* started?" Molly practically sputtered with indignation. "Let's get something straight here. I wasn't the one who put my garbage cans smack in the middle of someone else's driveway. Nor was I pulling some stupid stunt when I called the police tonight. I heard shots and thought you'd been wounded or killed. Next time," she promised darkly, "I won't bother to report it."

"Next time," her neighbor fired back, "you might consider laying off the beer and maybe you won't hear strange noises in your head."

Hastily, the uniformed police officer intervened.

"Could we take this inside, folks? I need to ask Ms. Duncan a few questions."

Tight-lipped, she led the way down the tiled entry hall to the archway that opened onto the living area. A flick of a wall switch bathed the high-ceilinged, open-beamed room in soft, recessed light. It also illuminated the fact that the room's furnishings consisted of a single rattan chair cushioned in cool desert mauves, a gnarled cypress stump that did duty as an end table, and a scattering of oversized pillows.

When she'd walked away from her ex-fiancé, Molly had subleased her Boston co-op fully furnished. Eager for a new beginning in Vegas, she'd emptied her bank account to make the down payment on this house. She'd almost saved up enough to splurge on the leather sectional sofa and chair she had her eye on. After that, she intended to work on a table and chairs for the dining room. Right now, though, she made do with cardboard boxes, gnarled tree stumps and a tall stool pulled up to the kitchen counter.

With a wave of one hand, she gave the two men a choice

of chair or pillow. Both opted to stand. Officer Rodriguez pulled out a notebook and pen.

"Will you tell me exactly what you heard, Ms. Duncan?"

"I heard the most god-awful wailing coming from next door," she replied with a searing glance at her neighbor. "I've been hearing it for the past two or three hours."

The Major appeared taken aback for a moment, then his scowl deepened. "I take it you're referring to my Buck Randall CDs?"

"If that's who's putting out that tinny, wheezing noise night after night, yes."

Henderson shook his head in disgust. Even Rodriguez looked faintly disapproving. Obviously, this country crooner was a local favorite.

"If my music's been bothering you, why the hell didn't you call and let me know?"

"I did," Molly retorted, her Boston-Irish temper up. "Twice. The first time, some whipped cream and chocolate-voiced woman promised to pass you my message. The second time, no one answered the phone. Why don't you get an answering machine?" she muttered irritably.

"Right. So you can leave obnoxious messages on it about my garbage cans instead of taping them to my front door?"

Refusing to respond to that deliberate provocation, Molly continued. "After listening to this Boots Randolph..."

"Buck Randall," the two men chorused.

"...Buck Randall for two agonizing hours, I got up, turned on the light and dialed Major Henderson's number. A man answered." She jerked her head at her neighbor. "I thought it was him."

"And then what happened?"

She ran through the sequence of events, shivering a bit when she got to the part about the eerie silence after the shooting.

"Is it possible that you dialed the wrong number?" Rodriguez asked when she finished.

"Yes, it's possible," she admitted, having already come to that conclusion herself. "The numbers were a bit blurry."

"Why am I not surprised?" the Major said with a little snort. "You put out more empties in the morning than a waterfront dive. And that's not chicken soup I smell coming from the kitchen."

What he smelled was her grandmother's recipe for beer-bran mush. Molly had brewed up a fresh batch earlier this evening, but she was damned if she was going to explain that fact to Major Sam Henderson. Her jaw tight, she finished her report.

"Then I dialed 911 and reported what I thought was a shooting."

"Well, if there was a shooting, it didn't occur at Major Henderson's residence," Rodriguez concluded, stating the obvious.

"There was a shooting," Molly insisted. "I heard it."

The police officer flipped his notebook shut. "We'll get the phone company to verify the number you dialed and make a few calls of our own, just to see who or what turns up."

Molly started to point out that dead persons don't answer the phone, but kept her mouth shut. She was already beginning to feel more like the perpetrator of a hoax than the reporter of a possible crime.

Rodriguez headed for the entryway. "It could have been kids. Pulling a late-night prank."

She followed more slowly, shaking her head. "Those weren't kids I heard."

"Well, if we find out anything, we'll let you know."

"Please do. It was so real." As balmy as it was, the desert air raised a chill on her arms. "So frightening."

Nodding, the police officer headed for the black-and-white squad car. The Major followed him out, but turned halfway down the paved walk. He searched Molly's face, his own cast in shadows.

"Look, I'm sorry about the music."

The gruff apology surprised her. After the way he'd all but called her a drunk, however, Molly wasn't about to accept it with any degree of graciousness.

"You should be."

"I didn't realize the sound carried so clearly across our yards...and I didn't get your previous message."

His tone implied that he had doubts she'd ever left it. Molly bristled all over again.

"I'll keep the volume turned down in the future."

"Thank you."

Curling his hands around the towel ends, he studied her a moment longer. "You all right?"

The reluctance behind the question came through loud and clear. Obviously, he didn't want to get involved with someone he considered a drunk or a neurotic, at the very least.

"No," Molly replied acidly, "As a matter of fact, I'm not all right. I'm tired, I have an early appointment in the morning, and I just heard someone get shot...I think," she finished on a mutter.

By this time, she wasn't quite sure what she'd heard. All she wanted to do was to climb back into bed, pull the covers over her head and try to blank this whole, nightmarish incident from her mind.

With a curt good-night, she turned and slammed the door.

Sam walked barefooted across the concrete driveways that divided the front of his property from that of his prickly, pesky neighbor.

The headache he'd been trying to drive out of his mind with a punishing workout before the cops had pounded on his door had now doubled in intensity. Instead of lancing through the back of his head with knife-like precision, the damned thing roared around in his skull like a high performance jet in full thrust.

Damn! As if ejecting helmet-first through a malfunctioning aircraft canopy and being placed on a temporary disability retirement list weren't bad enough. Now, just when he needed time and space and quiet to figure out what the hell he was going to do if the medical evaluation board put him out to pasture permanently, he had to move in next door to a beer-guzzling wacko.

He still couldn't quite buy her story about hearing a shooting. It wouldn't surprise him if she'd called the cops just to harass him. She'd been on his case since the day he moved in, starting with her snippy note about the garbage can, then threatening to take him to court over her weedy bushes...which she'd planted on *his* property, for Pete's sake!

No doubt about it. Despite those mile-long legs and flashing green eyes, the woman was trouble.

Too bad. In another time, or with another woman, he might have found a way to satisfy this crazy urge to rake his fingers through that tumble of wheat-colored, shoulder-length hair. Or maybe tasted that sulky mouth, which might have been luscious if she hadn't kept it all tight and unsmiling. He certainly would have teased a smile into those green eyes that went from nervous to indignant to confused as the interview progressed. Of course, Sam thought with a snort, all those Coors she'd been tipping might have something to do with that haze of confusion.

She hadn't sounded drunk, though. Hadn't acted it, either.

Frowning, he slammed his front door and twisted the dead bolt. Maybe the woman *had* heard a shooting. Or what someone wanted her to think was a shooting. Maybe she'd really called the police to come to his rescue, instead of sending them to his door to harass him, as he'd first assumed.

He shook his head at the memory of his less than appreciative response, then winced as the abrupt movement sent fingers of white-hot fire from one side of his skull to the other.

Dammit, he'd sort it all out tomorrow. Maybe even apologize to his neighbor...and mean it this time. Someone had to call a truce in the ridiculous war that had sprung up between them. First, though, he had to get through the rest of the night.

Mindful of her acid comment about his choice in music, Sam crossed to the built-in bookshelves that took up one wall of his great room and turned down the volume on the CD player. Buck Randall's tribute to the night dropped to a ribbon of mournful sound.

He tossed his towel at the couch shoved up against the wall to make room for the universal gym he had installed shortly after he moved in. His feet sinking into the protective rubber pad under the steel structure, he stretched out on the narrow bench. He grasped the handlebar, grunted, and slowly worked his way back into the rhythm of the punishing routine the police had interrupted. It took a while, but eventually the intense strain on his body blanked both the pain and the tantalizing image of his neighbor from his head.

He finished his workout an hour later, then showered and prowled the house for a while before hitting the sack. He dozed off just before dawn, only to awaken to the sound of tires squealing down the driveway next door. Sam winced, thinking of the new ruts he'd find in the tiny strip of desert landscape that separated his drive from his neighbor's.

He'd better forget about trying to effect a truce, he told himself wryly. Forget about going next door with another apology. The less he had to do with the ditzy, tumble-haired

Ms. Molly Duncan, the better. He didn't need to complicate his life any further with the kind of baggage she carted around with her.

He finally drifted off to sleep, unaware that his ditzy, tumble-haired neighbor would come crashing through her damned oleanders that very night and throw herself and a whole bagful of complications right into Sam's arms.

Chapter 2

Molly's Tuesday morning started off bad and went downhill from there. After tossing and turning for what was left of the night, she hit the snooze button on the clock radio a few too many times. Full consciousness didn't occur until a newscaster came on and finally broke through her grogginess. She listened to his patter for a few drowsy seconds until he announced the time. Jerking her head out of the pillow, she stared at the clock in disbelief.

"Six-thirty! Oh, no!"

Throwing off the covers, Molly dashed to the bathroom and splashed cold water on her face. Thankfully, her honey blond, shoulder-length waves didn't require anything more than a quick run through with a brush and a hand-scrunch or two. She slapped on a matte foundation to cover her freckles and protect her skin from the fierce Nevada sun, dabbed a mascara wand at her lashes, swiped on some lipstick and spun out of the bathroom.

After a quick search of her closet, she pulled on strappy

black sandals and yanked a silky chiffon black-and-white polka-dot dress off the hanger. Tying the sash on the run, she snatched up a black scarf and her purse and raced out of the bedroom. Downstairs, she threw a look of intense longing at the coffeepot on her way to the garage. She had no time for coffee. No time for anything if she was going to make her seven o'clock meeting with the president of Sato Motors International.

Early September heat already shimmered above the concrete as Molly shoved her car key in the ignition. With a twist of the ignition key, she squealed out of the garage and peeled down the drive. In the process, she took the curve onto the cul-de-sac a bit too wide. The tires threw up a spray of lava rock from the landscaped area that separated her drive from the Major's.

Wincing, Molly flicked a quick glance at her neighbor's house. The shades were drawn, thank goodness, and the place showed no signs of life. After snide cracks Sam Henderson had made about her driving last night, she hated to hand him any more ammunition to use in their continuing battle.

Although…

For a moment there, Molly had sensed a slight lessening of hostilities. She had to admit that his apology had surprised her. Okay, everything about the man surprised her, from his nocturnal habits to his gruff personality. What a shame that a bod like his was wasted on someone with such a touchy disposition.

A mental image formed of the Major as she'd last seen him, bathed in streetlight, muscles gleaming, jeans riding low on his hips. At the memory of his raw maleness, an unexpected dart of heat arrowed right through Molly's stomach. Startled, she dug her nails into the leather-wrapped steering wheel. It took a conscious effort of will to relax them.

For heaven's sake, she didn't even like the man! If he continued in his pigheaded determination to dig up his whole backyard…and her bushes with it…they might well end up in court. She had no business imagining what his rugged face would look like without that tight scowl, or recalling the dark hair that swirled down his stomach to disappear inside his jeans. Shaking her head to dislodge the persistent image, Molly concentrated on zigzagging down the hill that led from her housing development.

The open stretch of road at the bottom of the hill tempted her to nudge the speed limit just a bit. The flat desert landscape wouldn't remain empty for long, Molly saw with a twinge of regret. Already huge round concrete culverts lined either side of the road, waiting to be buried. The steel girders of a new high school rose from the desert floor. With a fleeting regret for the loss of this stretch of wild, desolate beauty, she whizzed past saguaro cacti and silvery tumbleweeds.

Fourteen minutes later, her little white Trans Am convertible screeched to a halt at the pillared entrance to the Addagio, the Strip's newest and most expensive resort and casino. Re-created to look like a fourteenth-century Venetian palazzo, the complex covered several city blocks. Tossing the keys to the parking valet, Molly hurried through a lobby filled with replicas of gorgeous antiques and glittering neon. After confirming her appointment with the concierge, she stepped into a private elevator that accessed the penthouse suite. The elegant, paneled cage whirred her upward.

A quick peek at her watch had her sagging against the wall in relief. She'd made it, with two minutes to spare! A few quick jabs with her fingers restored her hair to a casual disorder. Several deep, calming breaths restored her poise.

Mr. Sato and his entourage were waiting for her in the magnificent suite. The sitting room alone contained more square footage than the entire downstairs of Molly's house. Even more spectacular was the 270-degree view of Las Vegas and the surrounding mountains in early morning sunlight.

The view at night, she knew from previous visits, had to be seen to be believed.

The men rose at her entrance. Smiling, she greeted Mr. Sato in fluent Japanese, then switched to English for the benefit of the hotel's vice president for sales.

"I see you're ready to begin your presentation, Mr. Hamilton."

"As soon as we finish breakfast, Ms. Duncan. Would you care to sample the buffet?"

Molly's stomach somersaulted in delight as she took a quick trip into the dining room. The Addagio had pulled out all stops in its effort to impress Mr. Sato and company. They certainly impressed her. The artfully presented array of hot and cold dishes constituted a major test of her willpower. With real regret, she limited herself to just two of the mouth-watering pastries, a plate of fruit and the most delicious sushi she'd ever eaten. She'd developed a taste for the cold rice cakes during her junior year in college, which she'd spent in an exchange program at the University of Tokyo.

As soon as the attentive wait staff had cleared the dishes and refilled everyone's cups, Mr. Hamilton began his presentation. Without seeming too eager, the sales director made it clear that the Addagio wanted to host Sato Motors International's annual convention for the year 2001. They were well aware of the millions that SMI's well-paid employees would drop in the casino before, during and after their convention.

Although most of the Sato executives spoke and read English, Molly was on hand to interpret, if necessary. She would also escort Mr. Sato and his staff to the various sites they wanted to scout in the area. Unfortunately, the visiting CEO had somehow formed the mistaken impression that her duties extended to more than escorting and interpreting. On the first morning of his visit, Mr. Sato had offered Molly a staggering sum in exchange for her exclusive companionship at night. She'd politely refused. Since then, she'd discovered that he had difficulty understanding "no" in either Japanese or English.

Twice during the Addagio's long presentation, she removed his pudgy fingers from her thigh. The second time, she pinned a bright smile on her face and let him know in a private aside that she'd send him home to his wife in two separate suitcases if he touched her again.

After grinding out a polite farewell, Molly finally left Mr. Sato and his group to a night of gambling and whatever debauchery they cared to seek out. She also left a sublimely happy vice president of sales hugging a signed contract to his Versace-clad chest. Worn out by her long day and even longer night, she drove to the Las Vegas Convention and Visitors Authority just off Paradise Road. Her boss had asked for a full report. As expected, Davinia Jacobbson whooped with joy at the news that Sato had signed with the Addagio.

"That means some ten thousand Sato employees will descend on the city, along with their families and assorted friends. Good goin', kiddo."

Her infectious delight pulled a grin from Molly. A former college student turned showgirl turned entertainment attorney, Davinia still flashed long legs and a ten-megawatt smile. Now director of convention management, she had recently shucked her third husband and was actively auditioning candidate number four.

"This calls for a celebration," she exclaimed. "The Center's got some tickets for the big fight at the arena tonight." She waggled eyebrows a shade or two darker than her gloriously platinum hair. "Want to go watch while two hunks of superb maleness pound each other into a bloody pulp?"

"No thanks," Molly replied, laughing. "I'm too pooped for pulp."

Davinia shook her head in despair. "Good golly, Miss Molly, we have to find something or someone who can keep you awake after the sun goes down. Vegas doesn't fizz to life until midnight."

"Vegas might fizz to life, but I fizzle out. Besides, I had a long night last night."

"Oh?" Davinia's face brightened with interest. "Don't tell me you actually lived it up for once."

"I wouldn't call spending half of the night listening to some honky-tonk cowboy with seriously overdeveloped adenoids named Boots Randall and the other half with the police living it up."

"If you mean Buck Randall," Davinia drawled, "he and his adenoids are headlining at Caesars next week. But what's this about the cops?"

"Well, you know the running war I've been having with my neighbor...."

"The phantom of the night?" She bristled on her employee's behalf. "Has that jerk been hassling you again?"

"Well...."

"I wish you'd let me turn ex-number-two loose on him. John's a total pig most of the time, I'll admit, but he aced property law and civil torts when we were in law school together. He'll tie your creep of a neighbor into so many legal knots, the man won't know his backyard from his backside."

Molly smiled at the tempting offer, but declined. "There's no need to loose number two just yet. The Major didn't exactly hassle me, except with his taste in music. And I did a bit of hassling in return."

Briefly, she recounted the previous night's events. Davinia's eyes rounded as Molly described her disturbing phone call, the police response, and her neighbor's half-naked and wholly irate appearance on her doorstep shortly afterward.

"The police officer who came out to the house promised to get a record of my outgoing calls from the phone company," Molly finished. "He said he'd let me know if he found anything."

"You'd better check your voice mail," Davinia advised, frowning. "Your calls have been piling up all day."

With her boss trailing behind her, Molly headed for her office.

The sleek glass cubicle contained less than half the square footage of her Boston office, but Molly didn't mind. She wasn't hung up on the trappings of power or the latest in modular office equipment. The wide-ranging scope of her new job and the excitement of living in Las Vegas more than made up for the smaller digs.

Skirting the walnut console, she punched the play button on her phone. Sure enough, one of the recorded messages was from Dennis Rodriguez. The phone company computers had experienced some kind of glitch, he reported. He hadn't been able to get the information he'd requested. He'd call back when he did.

Molly wavered between disappointment and relief. Part of her had hoped that the police could trace the call and verify what she'd heard last night. Another part was willing to be convinced that she'd imagined the whole thing.

"I'm going home," she announced, pushing her chair back. "After what I went through last night and with Mr. Sato today, all I want is a cool glass of wine, a hot bath and a night of blissful, uninterrupted sleep."

She managed only one out of the three.

As she drove home, the beauty of the desert landscape went a long way to soothing her frazzled nerves. With the approach of dusk, the hundred-degree-plus heat of the day had softened to a balmy eighty-five or so. The warm air rippled like silk against her skin. Even the dust thrown onto the road by the bulldozers digging trenches for the massive concrete culverts caused only a momentary annoyance as she sped by. She soon left the dust behind and took the winding road that led to the houses tucked in the rolling foothills.

When she swung the wheel to turn into her driveway, the city shimmered in the rearview mirror. Molly drank in the spectacular sight while the garage door rumbled up. Even at its gaudiest, Vegas had its own unique beauty.

Feeling relaxed for the first time all day, she sent the door rumbling down again and went inside. Her home welcomed her with a graciousness that still gave her a thrill after six months. Even the empty spaces seemed elegantly spare, not stark and uninviting.

Tossing her purse on the kitchen counter, she revised her planned agenda. She'd indulge in a long, hot shower first. Then pour herself a relaxing glass of wine. Then, if her neighbor stuck to his promise to keep Boots/Buck to a low wail, she'd sink into blissful oblivion.

She went upstairs, shedding her dress, shoes and underwear in careless abandon as she crossed her bedroom. She wasn't a messy person by nature, but there was something to be said for the freedom of picking up when and where the mood struck her. A quick twist of the faucet soon steamed the shower. With a sigh of contentment, Molly stepped inside.

When she finally flipped off the pulsing jets, she felt as limp as overcooked linguini. Pulling on a pair of purple satin boxer shorts and her favorite midriff-baring University of Syracuse T-shirt, she towel dried her hair. Under the glare of the bathroom lights, she slathered several generous dollops of fresh-brewed facial across her nose and upper cheeks.

The beer-bran mush tightened her pores with a satisfying tingle. As she knew from long experience, the home-brewed facial would also keep her splatter of freckles from multiplying like busy little rabbits while she slept. The downside, of course, was that the concoction dried to a tight mask and flaked all over her pillow during the night. That was a minor inconvenience, in Molly's considered opinion. Her grandmother still turned heads at seventy-eight, and a complexion like Rose Duncan's was worth a few flakes on the pillow.

Brady hadn't agreed, of course, but that was only one of Molly's personal quirks her former fiancé had begun to criticize. When he'd started in on her friends, her taste in clothes, and even her decision to splurge on the little white Trans Am instead of the yuppie four-wheel-drive Explorer he thought they should have, Molly had finally rebelled. The ensuing argument had *not* been pretty, but the angry, hurtful confrontation had led to her new life and her new house.

Wondering why in the world she'd put up with her overly controlling ex-fiancé as long as she had, Molly headed downstairs for her long-anticipated glass of wine. She'd just poured her favorite California blush into a stemmed glass and lifted it for a taste when she heard a thump in the living room.

Startled, she jerked around. In the process, she splashed most of the wine down her front. The soft cotton soaked up the chilled liquid like a sponge. Molly in turn soaked up the sound of quiet footsteps in the hallway leading to the kitchen.

She froze, eyes wide and staring at the dimly lit hall. When she spotted what looked like a shadow moving toward the kitchen, Molly did what any reasonably intelligent, semi-intrepid woman would do.

She turned tail and ran.

The wine glass crashed to the floor. The door leading to the back deck banged behind her. Molly tore across the wooden deck and into her yard. Instinctively, she headed for the closest signs of human habitation—the light spilling from her neighbor's back windows.

The oleander hedge proved only a minor obstacle. She crashed through it, not even wincing when the thin, leafy branches whipped at her bare legs and slashed her arms. She was so intent on who was behind her that she didn't see the still figure ahead of her. A moment later, she plowed right into him.

"What the…!"

Sam stumbled back, grabbing at the body plastered against his. Small, high breasts flattened against his chest. A hip bone crunched into his. Instant, electric awareness jolted through him, firing nerves from his knees to his neck.

Even before she'd cannonballed into him, he'd recognized his neighbor. Now, he recognized the fact that she packed more curves on her slender frame than the baggy, gray tunic she'd worn last night had suggested.

Hard on the heels of that stomach-clenching discovery came the realization that she'd added wine to her regular beer consumption. From the light, fruity fumes rising in waves to assault his senses, she'd already downed several glasses too many.

Only after he'd untangled his arms and legs from hers and stepped back a pace did Sam realize that she hadn't downed all her wine. If the wet splotch that had transferred from her chest to his shirt was any indication, she was wearing a good portion of the bottle…and little else, he noted with a sudden tightening of his throat.

"Someone's in my house!"

The panic in her voice snapped Sam's attention from her bare belly button. "What?"

"Someone's in my house," she repeated, digging her fingers into his arms. "I heard him moving."

The possibility flashed into Sam's mind that his tipsy neighbor got her kicks by reporting imaginary assaults and attacks. As quickly as the thought came, he dismissed it. He could see she wasn't drunk, despite the wine she was wearing, and he'd been around enough to recognize real fear when he saw it.

He'd flown F-15s in Desert Storm. Later, he'd commanded a detachment of test pilots. The men and women he served with knew how to mask their inner doubts and fears, but Sam had enough experience under his belt to recognize the tight lines at the corners of the eyes. The quick glance at the distant sky when no one was looking. The grin and the cocky thumbs-up that was as much a prayer as a promise. The swagger that disguised all doubts, all private fears.

Molly Duncan didn't try to disguise anything. Her frightened green eyes grabbed at his gut. Her full mouth trembled. Her fingers dug into Sam's forearms like talons. Something or someone had shaken her right down to her pink-painted toenails.

Through the silvery hedge, Sam gave her stucco house a quick, searching once-over. He didn't see anything or anyone moving in the brightly lit kitchen. Darkness shadowed the rest of the house.

"There's someone there," she insisted, twisting around to follow his narrowed gaze. "Or there was."

"Did you see him?"

"No. I was in the kitchen and I heard a thump and I ran."

"A thump? What kind of a thump?"

A flicker of impatience pushed some of the fright from her eyes. "How do I know what kind? A thump is a thump."

She was recovering, Sam thought. Fast.

"Then I heard a squeak," she added in a rush. "Like sneakers walking on the tile."

"Go inside and call 911."

He disengaged her clawlike grip and started for the hedge. With a small shriek, she grabbed his arm again.

"You can't go over there. Not alone. Wait for the police!"

"I'm just going to watch the exits, in case whoever or whatever you heard decides to depart the premises before the police arrive. Go on, make the call."

"But...."

"Lock the patio door behind you."

Sam went in low and slow and very, very quiet. He'd grown up hunting with his father and brothers on their northern Arizona spread. Air Force jungle and desert survival schools had refined those silent, predatory skills to the point that Sam had no doubt of his ability to observe without being observed.

It didn't take him long to made a quick circuit of Molly's house. The back door still yawned open from her hasty exit. The garage and front doors remained shut. Sam didn't see any signs of forced entry, but he did find a first-floor window that gave when he tested it. Frowning, he returned to the front of the house just as a squad car pulled up in his driveway.

Molly rushed out of Sam's front door to greet the officer. A backup car arrived in the drive at the same time Sam did. The patrolmen took a disjointed report from Molly and a considerably more coherent one from Sam.

"I didn't leave that window unlocked," she protested. "I'm sure I didn't."

"We'll check it out, ma'am. You'd better wait in the Major's house until we go through yours. You, too, sir."

A still nervous Molly retreated back inside the house. She stationed herself in the tiled foyer, bending a bit to stare through the narrow windows beside the front door. Sam tried *not* to stare at her purple satin boxer shorts. He really tried. The effort raised a small sweat on his temples.

His neighbor wasn't feeling the same heat, though. She curled one bare foot over the other and wrapped her arms around her waist, as if to ward off a chill. Belatedly, Sam realized that she was under the arctic blasts coming from the air-conditioning vents. He'd gotten in the habit of keeping the house cool during his workouts.

Tearing his appreciative gaze from those clinging purple shorts, he headed down the hall to turn up the thermostat. A quick detour to the laundry room retrieved a well-washed yellow T-shirt showing one of the 442d Test Squadron's F-15s in flight over the desert.

"Here. You'd better put this on before you catch cold."

She spun around, startled by his gruff offer. When he saw

her face in full light for the first time, Sam was more than a little startled himself. It took him a moment to identify the brown, peeling stripe laid across her nose and cheeks as some kind of a facial mask. He was still staring at the crusted layer when she reached for the T-shirt.

"Thanks." Her smile tried for grateful and came up shaky. "This wet top and the idea of someone prowling through my house is enough to raise goose bumps all over my skin."

That wet top was enough to raise a few goose bumps on Sam's skin, too. More than a few.

"I wouldn't want you to catch cold and sue me."

He'd meant the oblique reference to the scorching letter she'd sent his contractor, threatening legal action if he touched so much as a leaf of her oleanders, as a joke, as nothing more than an attempt to ease the tension that radiated from her in waves. She didn't take it as one.

"No, I'm sure you wouldn't," she zinged back, tugging the oversized shirt on over her head.

Sam waited until she'd settled the yellow cotton shirt over her hips. "I was kidding, you know."

"I wasn't," she replied coolly. "In my letter, I mean."

"A few scrawny bushes aren't worth going to court over. We'll work something out."

Her mouth settled into a pucker. "I spent most of my landscaping budget on those scrawny bushes. They're not coming down without a fight."

How the hell could the woman manage both scared and stubborn at the same time? Not to mention sexy as hell? A tiny tendril of pain started to curl around the base of Sam's skull.

"We'll work something out," he repeated firmly.

With a tight little nod, she turned her attention back to the windows. Sam tried to turn his attention from the long stretch of bare thigh below the hem of his yellow T-shirt. Despite his best efforts, his stomach tightened. At the same moment, the pain at the base of his skull sent out fresh shoots.

Dammit! Ever since he'd butted headfirst through that malfunctioning canopy, he'd lived with this pain. At best, it was a teeth-grinding annoyance. At worst, it felt like the entire Brazilian soccer team was taking free shots at the back of his skull.

The team had been on break until this moment. He hoped he'd make it through the rest of the night without having to pummel his body and his mind into numbed submission. Now...

Now his neighbor had barreled into his arms and set off all kinds of alarms in his head. Sam knew he should heed the warning signals. Even without the blossoming pain, his instincts told him to back off. The wisest course of action would be to let this aggravating, enticing female sort out her own problems...which is exactly what he might have done if the police hadn't come down Molly's front walk at that moment.

She threw open his door and hurried outside to meet them. Sam followed, a frown settling between his brows as they gave their report.

"We searched the house, ma'am. We didn't find anyone inside."

"Someone was there," she insisted.

"If he was, he's gone now. We need you to take a look through the house and see if anything's missing."

While the backup officer reclaimed his squad car and drove off, Molly led the way into her house. For the second time in as many nights, Sam found himself in her very spacious, very empty living room. He waited with the patrolman while she made a quick inventory of her possessions.

It didn't take long.

"I don't see anything missing," she said slowly.

The officer hitched up his belt. "Well, there's always the

possibility that something or someone other than an intruder caused the noise you heard. The house settling, maybe. A rock thrown against the wall by a passing car. I drove over some lava rock in the road in front of your house."

Nobly, Sam refrained from pointing out that a fresh scattering of rock ended up in the road every time his neighbor tore down her drive.

"What about the shadow I saw on the wall?" she demanded. "And the squeaking sound?"

"Lights from a passing car could have caused the shadow, too. I'm not saying that's what it was, you understand, but...."

"Ms. Duncan made another 911 call last night," Sam interjected.

"Yeah?"

His interest piqued, the police officer swung back to Molly. She stared at Sam, then the portion of her face not covered in brown went white.

"I heard a man shot. Or...or thought I did."

Briefly, she ran through last night's bizarre events. The officer made another annotation, then flipped his notebook closed once more.

"There's probably no connection between what you heard last night and tonight, but I'll let Rodriguez and the folks in Investigations know about your suspicion that someone entered your house...."

"Someone did."

"Yes, well, either Rodriguez or one of the detectives will get back to you. In the meantime, you might want to keep your windows and doors locked and think about a security system."

"I will."

The waver in her reply had Sam cursing under his breath. He hadn't intended to scare her by bringing up last night's incident. At this point, he didn't know if there was any link between the shooting she'd heard and her unknown intruder tonight. Hell, he didn't even know if she'd really *heard* a shooting. He just thought they should consider all possibilities.

When Molly turned to him, her face pale under its crusty stripe, he saw that she'd considered the possibilities, too, and didn't much like them. Her gaze darted nervously around the room before centering on Sam.

"Would you like a cup of coffee? Or some wine? I opened a bottle just before...." She managed a wobbly smile. "Just before I came charging through the oleanders."

Sam knew he should leave. The pain at the back of his skull hadn't reached the jaw-breaker stage yet. With luck and a few hours of hard, mind-numbing exercise, he could head it off at the pass. More to the point, he knew he should put some distance between himself and his neighbor. Even in his oversized T-shirt and cracked facial mask, she did serious damage to his self-control.

"Coffee would be good," he heard himself reply.

Chapter 3

Since the basic amenities inside Molly's home didn't run to more than the one easy chair, scattered pillows and a single stool pulled up to the cobalt blue kitchen counter, she and Sam took their coffee to the back deck. There the builder had incorporated two long, curved-backed benches into the railing that defined the rectangular deck.

Molly flipped on the spots and settled on one bench, tucking a bare foot under her. Her neighbor's oversized yellow T-shirt settled around her like a cloud, covering her from neck to knee.

Sam rested his hips against the rail beside her. In the bright wash of light coming from the spots mounted high on the wall, he looked solid and reassuring. He'd *felt* solid and reassuring, too, she remembered, when she'd flung herself into his arms and wrapped herself around him like a wet sponge.

Thinking about how she'd gone chest-to-chest with the Major, Molly squirmed on the cushionless bench. As Henderson had reminded her only a little while ago, they had yet to resolve their property differences. She'd surprised herself by offering him coffee. He'd surprised her even more by accepting it. She wasn't exactly sure why she'd extended that rash invitation, except that her empty, echoing house didn't seem quite as…welcoming…at this moment as it usually did.

"I'm sorry I barreled into you earlier," she said, breaking the stillness of the star-studded night.

"No problem." His mouth curved in a half smile. "I survived four older brothers and almost fifteen years in the military. I've taken worse hits over the years."

She could believe it. Sam Henderson didn't look like the kind of man who went out of his way to avoid trouble, with his brothers or anyone else. Under the bright patio lights, she couldn't miss the blunt angle to his chin or the slight flattening at the bridge of his nose.

Even his clothes seemed to reflect his rugged individualism. He wore his jeans like someone who felt completely at home in them. His soft blue cotton shirt sported a little designer logo on the pocket, but he'd rolled the sleeves up to reveal strong, tanned forearms. Tonight, his dark brown hair had been tamed with a neat side part, unlike last night when the short layers had sheened with sweat and stood up in spikes.

Thinking about last night, and tonight, and the possibility of a connection between the two, Molly suddenly shivered. The abrupt movement slopped coffee over the mug and into her lap.

"Oh, no!"

Just in time, she yanked up the T-shirt hem and thrust her legs to one side. The hot liquid missed her skin, but spread a soppy brown stain across the cotton. She stared at the splotch in dismay. First the wine. Now coffee. What else could she spill all over herself tonight? What else could happen tonight?

"I'm sorry," she said again. "I'll get the stain out, I promise."

To her horror, her voice wobbled. Even worse, the hand holding her half-full mug still shook.

Sam reached down and relieved her of the mug. "Don't worry about it."

But she did. For some reason, the stain spreading across the shirtfront assumed the proportions of a near tragedy. Helplessly, Molly grabbed the shirt hem and twisted it into a tight screw, over and over, as if she could wring out both the coffee and the fear that had suddenly invaded her life.

Sam's brows pushed down as he watched his neighbor's jerky movements. He understood her sudden attack of nerves. He'd seen these kinds of delayed reactions often enough after a dangerous mission. Concern slid into sympathy, then into a need to soothe her.

Careful, he told himself. Go real, real careful here. He didn't need to get tangled up with a woman wearing a pungent combination of beer, wine and chocolate hazelnut decaf, for God's sake, any more than he needed the pain streaking up the back of his skull. The way her full mouth trembled shouldn't hit him in the gut. The sheen of tears she furiously blinked back shouldn't curl his hands into fists, either.

Oh, hell. He couldn't take seeing her twist the shirt into knots like that, any more than he could take her sniffles. Hunkering down, he laid his hands over hers. She lifted her face with its cracked and peeling mask to his, and Sam knew he was in trouble.

Big trouble.

"It's okay," he said, gentling his voice. "It's okay, Molly."

She scowled, then glanced down at their joined hands. A

small piece of brownish crust flaked off her left cheek and landed on Sam's bent knee, which caused her to scowl even more.

His heart twisted. Resigning himself to the inevitable, he nudged her to one side of the bench and eased in beside her. His arm went around her shoulders, drawing her into his side.

"It's okay, sweetheart."

The endearment didn't mean anything. Sam knew it. Molly obviously knew it, too. She resisted a bit, keeping herself stiff in his loose hold.

"I can't believe I'm acting like such a twit," she muttered. "I don't usually come apart at the seams like this."

"You're not coming apart. You've had a traumatic night. Two traumatic nights. You're just experiencing a delayed reaction. Relax, Molly."

She sank slowly against his chest. To Sam's consternation, she felt as though she'd been carved specifically to fit him. He kept his arms loose and his hands above the swell of her hips, but he experienced a delayed reaction of his own when she shifted to find a more comfortable position.

Gritting his teeth, he willed himself to stay loose. The determined effort sent pain shooting up the side of his skull. For a moment the stars splashed across the sky overhead blurred.

"...you do so late at night, Sam?"

Slowly, the stars regained their luster. The pain became bearable. He picked up the question in Molly's voice, if not her actual words.

"What?"

"What do you do so late at night?"

"I work out. Sometimes I putter in the garage."

"I've seen you out there early in the mornings, when I leave for work. Do you stay up all night?"

"Sometimes."

"Why? Are you part vampire or allergic to sleep or something?"

"I don't need much sleep."

She wasn't letting him get away with that. Tilting her head back, she frowned up at him. "Why not?"

Sam wasn't ready to tell her about the pain. He hadn't told anyone, not even his brothers, how bad it got at times. He'd been sure he would conquer it in time. Now, he wasn't so sure. Nor were the docs.

Instead, he answered the question in her eyes with a small, careless shrug. "I guess I got used to irregular hours in the Air Force."

She was quiet for a while. Sam could feel the tension in her limbs slowly easing. Contrarily, the more she relaxed against him, the more he had to fight the urge to tighten his arms around her.

"What did you do?" she murmured. "When you were in the Air Force?"

"I flew test aircraft," he replied with considerable understatement.

Flying didn't begin to describe what he'd done as a test pilot. Sometimes, he'd throttled to full power and flung his experimental aircraft right at the sun. Sometimes, he'd hurtled it straight down. He'd stressed the wings, stressed the weapons load, stressed himself with every twisting spiral.

"And now you're retired?"

"Yes."

Sam still had trouble with the word. Retired. At thirty-six. The Medical Evaluation Board had assured him that they'd consider removing him from the Temporary Disability Retired List when and if he conquered the headaches. The possibility seemed as remote tonight as it had six months ago.

"Were you stationed at Nellis?" she asked, her voice drowsy and indistinct.

"Yes, I was."

He rested his chin on the top of her head. Her mix of scents tugged at his senses. Shampoos, coffee, that crazy, crackly stuff she wore on her face. The feel of her body slanted against his tugged at more than his senses.

"I was assigned to the Four-forty-second Test and Evaluation Squadron," he told her, as much to distract himself as to keep the conversational ball rolling. "We conducted operational tests for Air Combat Command on new hardware and equipment upgrades in simulated combat environments."

"Mmm?"

The mumble could have signaled interest or incipient unconsciousness. Sam suspected it was the latter. He hesitated, debating whether to continue.

He hadn't talked about the life that had ended the night he went headfirst through that damned canopy in a long time. Too long. Somehow, it was easier here with Molly. The calm night air and black velvet sky seemed to wrap them in a private world. More to the point, the casual, one-sided conversation seemed just what she needed after her earlier fright.

"The four-forty-second is a mixed unit," he said slowly. "We flew fighters and attack helicopters. Most of the equipment we tested is classified, but I can tell you that we did a lot of night flying, and that we developed new methods of employing the Low Altitude Navigation and Targeting Infrared for Night system."

He knew his listener was falling asleep even before she gave one of those reflexive little jerks that come with relaxation of the muscles. He smiled at her mumbled apology, and deliberately kept his voice to a low, steady monotone. Not so deliberately, he tightened his hold and brought her onto his lap.

The low bench back cut into his back. The wooden seat

numbed his butt. He shifted, angling his body into the wedge formed by the angle of the rails. When Molly shifted as well, draping herself across him from shoulder to hip, the singeing contact instantly upped Sam's discomfort factor by a multiple of ten. Her breath warmed his neck. Her legs tangled with his. Sam refused to let himself dwell on the way her breasts flattened against his chest, or the long length of thigh that stretched beneath the hem of his squadron T-shirt. Despite his best efforts, his lower body went hard.

Great! The pounding at the base of his skull was bad enough. He didn't need this tight, coiling ache in his belly to add to it. Briefly, he debated taking her inside before the still-warm desert night cooled.

From long, painful experience, Sam knew that cooling wouldn't occur until just before dawn. He'd spent enough nights watching the moon sink and listening to the distant coyotes. If he concentrated on something other than the soft tush in his lap and the warm wash of breath against his neck, he could take another hour or two. By then, his prickly neighbor should have regrouped, regained her equilibrium, maybe even revived enough to resume her battle over the blasted bushes.

Sam eyed the tall, silvery bushes. He supposed he'd have to get the contractor to redesign the pool. Maybe angle it a bit to give him the length he needed for straight laps. His doctor had recommended swimming instead of pumping iron to refocus his mind when the headaches threatened to get out of control.

Like now.

Dammit! This one was going to be a real winner. After six weeks in the hospital and almost as many months in physical therapy, Sam knew the signs. Cursing to himself, he started counting the stars.

Molly woke slowly. Her cheek felt numb where it pressed against something hard and unyielding. Her neck ached from bending at an odd angle. Overriding those minor annoyances, though, was the delicious sensation of curling into warmth and the steady, reassuring drum of a strong heartbeat in her ear.

For a confused moment, she thought she was back in Boston, snuggled up in Brady's arms. Mumbling, she slid a hand across the chest under her cheek. Her hips wiggled a deeper nest in his lap.

Strange. Brady's chest had never felt this hard or this muscled before. Nor, Molly thought with sleepy surprise, had she ever heard him mutter such a colorful curse under his breath.

The realization that the hard, contoured chest under her palm didn't belong to her former fiancé registered on Molly's consciousness at about the same instant she identified the southwestern drawl in that curse.

She pushed upright, dismayed to find Sam's tight-clenched jaw just inches from her own. Oh, great! Not only had she draped herself across her neighbor like an afghan, she'd dropped off into total oblivion in the midst of his telling her about his Air Force days. Mortified, she tried to scramble off his lap. His arms flexed for a brief instant, holding her in place, then dropped. In an undignified scramble, Molly got to her feet and tugged the yellow T-shirt down over her hips.

"I'm sorry," she mumbled for what seemed like the umpteenth time that night.

Her embarrassment doubled when she saw Sam's face. Distant and withdrawn, it held none of the understanding he'd shown when he'd taken her into his arms...when?...a few minutes ago? An hour ago?

"I didn't mean to fall asleep on you," she said in a strangled voice.

"No problem."

The response came out short and too clipped. He got to his feet, unfolding his body with a stiffness at odds with his earlier easy grace. Once upright, he held himself rigidly erect, as though the mere act of moving was an effort.

Good grief. Had her dead weight stiffened him up like that? How long had she sprawled on top of him and pinned him to that bench, anyway? He answered her silent question before she asked it.

"I was going to wake you up in a few minutes. It can get chilly out here just before dawn."

Dawn! Molly shot a disbelieving look at the eastern horizon. Sure enough, the sky showed a distant tint of golden red.

"I can't believe we spent almost the whole night on that bench."

"Believe it."

Something that might have been a smile started at the corners of his mouth. It twisted suddenly, and ended in a near grimace. "I have to go," he said abruptly. "Why don't we take another walk through the house before I leave? Just so you feel comfortable about going inside."

Molly had to admit that she felt decidedly *un*comfortable at that moment, not to mention embarrassed and confused. Her tumbling emotions had nothing to do with a reluctance to reenter her house. They did, however, have a whole lot to do with Sam Henderson's Jekyll-and-Hyde personality.

"Thanks, but you don't need to go through the house. I've already, uh, imposed on you enough."

Imposed hardly came close to describing the way she'd pinned the man to the bench, but she hoped her slight understatement might at least crack the rigid cast to his face. No such luck.

"I'll do a quick sweep," he bit out.

He disappeared into the house, leaving Molly now almost as irritated as she was confused. What was with this guy, anyway? Had she dreamed his friendliness earlier? Had he really drawn her onto his lap and cradled her? Maybe she'd just sort of landed there, and he'd been too polite to shove her away.

No, she decided, polite didn't figure among Sam Henderson's more significant character traits…as he demonstrated when he returned a few moments later.

''All clear. Good night.''

Her jaw sagging, Molly stared at his back as he marched stiff-legged across her yard. A moment later, the oleanders swallowed him up.

She snapped her mouth shut. She had no idea what the heck Sam's problem was, but she darned well wasn't going to spend the little that was left of the night trying to figure it out. With luck, she could grab two or three more hours of sleep before she had to get ready for work. Spinning around, Molly marched inside the house. The patio door banged shut behind her.

In a distant corner of his brain, Sam recorded the snapping sound, just as he'd recorded the surprise on Molly's face when he'd left her so abruptly. He couldn't think about either at this moment, though. He needed all his concentration just to put one foot in front of the other and make it to his own back door.

He couldn't believe he'd been such a fool! He'd known better than to just sit there, breathing in his neighbor's unique, intriguing combination of scents, while the demons in his head took possession of his body. He should have put her out of his arms hours ago. Gone back to his own house. Pounded the damned pain into submission with a grinding workout.

He knew his abrupt departure had bewildered her. Better bewilderment than pity, Sam thought savagely. He didn't need her pity. Any more than he needed commiserating slaps on the back from his former squadron mates or worried

calls from his brothers. He'd beat this thing. He'd prove the
doctors wrong and beat it, and he'd do it without doping
himself up with painkillers every night.

Until he did, though, he sure as hell wasn't much use to
anyone…particularly a green-eyed, long-legged blonde who
seemed to attract trouble like a magnet. Slamming his own
patio door shut with a force that added another bright color
to the kaleidoscope whirling through his head, Sam stripped
off his shirt. His mouth grim, he headed for the well-worn
leather bench.

Molly puzzled over her neighbor's strange behavior off
and on for most of the next morning…until the call from
the Las Vegas Police Department drove all other thoughts
right out of her head.

It came just after lunch, as she was walking out of her
office for a meeting with the director of the new fifty-four-
million-dollar Star Trek museum and entertainment center
at the Las Vegas Hilton. The spectacular fifty-four-million-
dollar center had just opened, and the director had promised
Molly and a number of the media a sneak preview. A long
time trekkie, she was looking forward to the tour. Impatiently, she leaned back over her desk to catch the phone.

"Molly Duncan."

"Hello, Ms. Duncan. This is Detective Kaplan, from the
LVPD Homicide Unit. I wanted to let you know that we
traced the call you made at one-twelve yesterday morning."

Her heart skipped a beat. "Yes?"

"The number you dialed belongs to a man named Joe
Bennett. His rap sheet lists a number of aliases, but we know
him as Joey the Horse."

"Rap sheet? You mean he's a criminal?"

"A small-time drug dealer with a weakness for the po-
nies. He also supplements his income by pimping for the

high rollers. Or he did. He won't be supplementing anything anymore."

"Is he…?" Molly gripped the phone. "Is he dead?"

"As the proverbial doornail," Kaplan confirmed with a notable lack of sympathy for the deceased. "The landlord let our guys into his apartment this afternoon. They found Joey with a nice, neat hole in the middle of his forehead and a not so neat one in his chest."

Molly sagged against the edge of her desk. Over and over, a desperate plea echoed in her mind.

"Oh, God."

"I'm in court this afternoon on another case," the detective continued, "but I'd like to talk to you about your phone call. Can you swing by the station in the morning? Hello? Ms. Duncan?"

"What?" She shook herself out of the shocked trance. "Oh. Yes, of course."

"Ten o'clock okay?"

"Ten o'clock," she repeated numbly, then Kaplan shifted gears with a disconcerting suddenness.

"I understand you also reported hearing some noises in your house last night?"

"Yes, I did."

"There's probably no connection between the two incidents, but until we clear up this business with Joey, I've asked the city desk to increase the patrols through your neighborhood. Call 911 if you see or hear anything that makes you nervous."

Anything that made her *more* nervous, Molly corrected silently as she dropped the receiver onto the cradle. She stared at the phone as if it were an instrument of evil.

She'd heard someone shoot another human being. Really and truly shoot him. The reality stunned her. And curled her stomach into a tight, frightened knot. She was still standing motionless beside her desk when her boss whirled in on a cloud of Arpege and brisk efficiency.

"Hey, girl! I thought you had a two o'clock at the Hilton."

"I did. Uh, I do."

The mumbled reply brought Davinia's perfectly arched brows snapping together. "What's the matter? You look like you've seen a ghost."

"I think the operative word is heard, not seen," Molly said weakly.

"Huh?"

"The police just called."

"Really?" Davinia hitched a hip on the corner of Molly's desk and swung a long, nyloned leg. "Did they trace the call you made?"

Molly nodded. "Evidently I called a Mr. Joey the Horse Bennett, a drug dealer and occasional pimp."

"You're kidding!"

"I wish!"

Gathering her scattered thoughts, she relayed her brief conversation with Detective Kaplan. When she finished, her boss swung her leg in a slow, thoughtful arc. Her three-inch clear acrylic heel caught the light and threw back a rainbow of color.

"A drug-dealing pimp with a New Jersey accent, a weakness for the horses and a hole in his forehead. This doesn't sound good, girl. Not good at all."

"As a matter of fact, it sounded awful," Molly replied with a little shudder. "You should have heard him, pleading with the killer for his life."

"Well, yes, but that wasn't what I meant."

Waving a hand tipped with long, silvered nails, Davinia dismissed the now-deceased drug dealer with the same casual callousness Detective Kaplan had.

"Las Vegas has pretty well cleaned up its act in the past

decade or so," she said, "but there are still a few of the old school around. Men with connections."

"Connections?"

"You know, the old families."

Molly stared at her boss in dismay. "Are you suggesting that I overheard a mob execution?"

"It's a possibility."

Groaning, she reached for her purse. "Thanks a lot! Now I won't get any sleep tonight, either."

Davinia took her lower lip between blindingly white teeth. "Why don't you come stay with me for a few days? Just until the police work this case?"

Molly almost took her up on the offer. Somehow, the thought of going back to her empty house didn't hold quite the same appeal it had before. Davinia had just moved the latest candidate for husband number four into her condo, however, and Molly didn't want to impede the matrimonial tryouts.

"You don't need any more company," she replied. "You've got Antonio."

"Nonsense. He'll love having two women to practice his techniques on. Not that he needs much practice," she added with a wicked grin.

Since the hunky Latino had recently graduated with top honors from massage school, Molly didn't doubt it. She did, however, doubt that he'd appreciate another woman's presence in the house. Particularly when her boss had hinted that she'd instituted a program of total seduction and surrender...her seduction and Antonio's surrender.

Gracefully, Molly refused Davinia's offer and headed home. It was only as she pulled into her driveway and spotted the lights in Sam's house that she realized a good part of her reason for refusing Davinia's offer was the knowledge that her confusing, intriguing neighbor was only a hedge away.

Chapter 4

Molly leaned down to snag the yellow T-shirt from the dryer. When she pulled it out, a fragrant cloud of fabric softener came with it. Holding the garment up to the light, she examined its front. After two washings, the brown coffee splotch had pretty well disappeared. The little that remained was so faint that it blended right in with the faded, streaky yellow.

Laying the shirt on top of the dryer, she smoothed the wrinkles with her palms. The faded blue patch on the front caught her gaze. The lettering below it read 442d TES, whatever that meant.

Vaguely Molly recalled Sam telling her about the unit he'd been assigned to at Nellis. She'd hovered somewhere between sleepy exhaustion and total unconsciousness at the time, so she had only hazy memories of his voice rumbling under her ear. The sensation of Sam's thighs shifting under hers hadn't exactly added to her powers of concentration, either. Nor had the steely strength of his arms folded around her.

Thinking back to those hours on the deck, Molly had to admit that Sam's solid strength had given her the oddest sense of comfort. Not that she really needed it, of course. She didn't want any man flexing his muscles in her life, even figuratively. She'd had enough of that with Brady. Still, for a few hours, she felt warm and comfortable and safe in Sam's arms.

She frowned, disturbed by the idea that she required anything or anyone to feel safe in her own home. This was her castle. Her sanctuary.

She glanced through the laundry room door at the brightly lit kitchen. On any other night, the sand-colored plaster walls with their border of blue and gold Aztec sun signs would give her a small thrill of pride, just as the long, clean sweep of cobalt blue counter fed her need for color and brightness.

Tonight she saw only the kitchen's empty corners. Slowly, she shifted her gaze to the windows. A silvery path of light spilled from her neighbor's high living room windows and traced across her yard. Molly contemplated the shimmering trail for several moments. Although she couldn't hear Sam's music, thank goodness, that trail of light lured her like a beacon.

Folding the T-shirt, she decided to follow that beacon. After a quick detour to the powder room just off the kitchen to twist her hair up in a clear plastic clip decorated with pink rhinestone flamingos, courtesy of the famous hotel's gift shop, she slipped into a pair of similarly decorated plastic mules. She smiled, thinking how the gaudy accessories that were so much a part of the Vegas scene would have brought a pained look to her former fiancé's face. Molly, on the other hand, loved them. Thank goodness she'd walked away from Brady before the man had smothered her or she'd strangled him.

On that cheerful thought, she marched out the kitchen

door and followed the silvery path through her backyard to Sam's. She wouldn't linger at his place. Not after his abrupt good-bye and hasty retreat this morning. She'd just return his T-shirt and give him an update on Detective Kaplan's call, keeping a nice, neighborly distance in the process.

Molly had pushed through the hedge before she realized that she should have approached his house from the front and rung the doorbell. It was a little tacky to stroll into his backyard and walk right up to his patio. It was even more tacky to gape at the sight that greeted her through the open windows.

Sam lay astride a narrow leather bench, wearing only a pair of blue nylon athletic shorts and a grimace. Above him towered the jungle of gleaming steel bars Molly had rushed past to get to a phone last night. She didn't rush anywhere tonight. Tonight, she stood rooted to the patio, her feet planted as firmly as her oleanders, and watched her neighbor in motion.

He moved to a rhythm that appeared as strenuous as it was beautiful. On a beat that only he could hear, his tendons corded. His glistening muscles gathered. A black column of weights lifted almost to the top of the steel structure. A moment later, he sucked in a breath and relaxed. The weights plunged.

Slowly, he gathered himself and flexed once more.

Molly stood in the shadows, transfixed. She wasn't into sweat herself. In fact, she generally tried to avoid any activity that raised even the faintest hint of moisture on her skin…with one or two notable exceptions, of course. She had to admit, though, that the sheer perfection of Sam's movements gave a new perspective to the whole question of exercise.

Molly hated to interrupt him, but she wasn't into voyeurism any more than sweat. Not usually, anyway. After watching Sam in motion, she could almost understand how masses of people got off on purely spectator sports. Clutching the folded T-shirt to her chest, she rapped on the glass patio door. He didn't hear her. She tried again, knuckling the glass with a little more force. Still no response. Finally, she gave the tempered sliding door a solid whack.

The weights froze, and Sam twisted on the bench. He pinned her with a narrow, piercing glance, his face wearing the same expression it had this morning. Hard. Tight. Unwelcoming.

Wishing now that she'd stuffed the T-shirt and a note in his mailbox, Molly pasted on a smile that strove for a balance between neighborly and distant. She didn't want the man to think that she'd come running to him in a fright again or that she was hounding him. Considering their brief and somewhat brittle acquaintance, though, she supposed he couldn't think anything else.

Thankfully, his grim expression eased when he took in her unfrantic face. Peeling himself off the bench, he reached for the gray sweatshirt draped over one of the crossbars. By the time he unlocked the patio doors and slid them open, he looked almost friendly. Only a woman who'd spent the night in his arms might notice that the creases at either side of his mouth went far too deep to constitute a smile.

"Hello, neighbor. Everything all right on the far side of the oleanders?"

"More or less."

He cocked his head. His dark brown hair glistened, shining almost black in the overhead light.

"Is my music bothering you again? Sorry. I thought I had the volume turned down low enough to keep it from carrying."

Molly hadn't even noticed the lament for a lost dog…or was it for an ex-wife?…threading through the air until Sam mentioned it.

"No, the volume's fine."

He invited her inside, and she declined with a little shake of her head.

"I just wanted to return your T-shirt. I got most of the coffee stain out."

"You shouldn't have bothered. The thing's seen better days. Much better days," he added, taking it from her outstretched hands. His eyes went to the patch on the front. He thumbed the lettering for a moment, then shook his head, as if to clear it of unwanted memories, and tossed the shirt aside.

"Sure you won't come in? I don't have any hazelnut decaf, but I think I can scare up some instant. Or some cold beer, if you prefer."

Molly decided it was time to correct that particular misconception. "I don't drink the stuff," she informed him loftily. "I just wear it."

His mouth kicked up to a half smile. "I hadn't noticed."

"Liar. I probably flaked all over your shirt last night."

"What are a few flakes between neighbors? Look, why don't you come in? I'll turn off the CD player, I promise. You won't have to suffer through Buck and company, if that's what's holding you back."

Molly knew darn well what was holding her back... Sam Henderson's on-again, off-again charm. In the early hours just before dawn, his icy stare had frozen her to her deck. Now, that half grin of his was causing a minor meltdown in her circulatory system. Much against her better judgment, she caved.

"Well, if you promise...."

He slid the patio door shut behind her and crossed to the washed-oak cabinets built into the wall beside the fireplace. The high-tech electronic equipment that filled the cabinets looked powerful and sophisticated enough to launch the space shuttle *Atlantis*. They'd certainly sent Bucky Boy soaring through the night on a number of previous occasions.

Sam punched a few buttons, and the low, lonesome wail segued into the haunting strains of a violin concerto. Molly blinked in surprise. Buck Randall and Mozart? On the same CD player? Her conflicting impressions of her neighbor took a turn into serious confusion.

"Come on into the kitchen while I zap some water," he invited.

She trailed him through the house, seeing it with an eye for the details she hadn't noticed last night. Aside from the soaring, two-storied great room which Sam had turned into his own personal gym, the rest of the place held a mix of comfortable, masculine furnishings and artwork from every corner of the world. Asian batiks and carved African masks hung in a dazzling display on one wall. A collection of delicate watercolors depicting European street scenes decorated the long central hall.

But it was the well-furnished and fully equipped kitchen that gave Molly a real pang. She sighed, lusting instantly for the rectangular, washed-oak table and six high-backed chairs. Behind the table, a glass-and-brass étagère drew her envious eye. The piece took up most of the far wall, and displayed to perfection a truly remarkable collection of beer steins.

While Sam rummaged in the cupboard for cups, Molly examined the collection. Colorful coats of arms decorated the front of each stein, and military figures exquisitely detailed in pewter and silver perched atop the lids. Some of the figures sat astride prancing steeds. Others stood at attention or lunged with weapons drawn. All wore tall shakos and what looked like fur cloaks thrown over one shoulder. Enchanted, Molly traced a finger along a raised silver sword.

"These are beautiful."

"They're Prussian regimentals. I picked them up when I

was stationed in Germany a few years ago. They have pictures glazed into the bottom that become visible when the owner drains his beer.''

"Really?'' Molly thumbed back a lid.

"Most of the scenes depict the unit's arms or insignia. A few are more, uh, artistic.''

"So I see,'' she drawled.

Letting the pewter lid drop on the over-endowed and underdressed fräulein who smirked up at her, she settled into one of the chairs. Another twinge of envy attacked her as she glanced around the comfortable kitchen.

Aside from the living room/gym, Sam had managed to make his house into a home in a remarkably short period of time. Or, she wondered suddenly, did he owe the comfortable arrangements to the sultry-voiced female who'd answered the phone the first time Molly had called to complain about his music?

Or had she even called Sam that first time? Maybe she'd misdialed then, too. The thought sent a shiver down Molly's spine and reminded her all too graphically of her second reason for pushing through the oleanders.

"The police contacted me today,'' she told her host. "They traced the number I dialed the other night.''

He shot her a quick look over the steaming mugs of hot water. "And?''

"And it belongs to a man named Joey the Horse Bennett...recently deceased.''

Sam swore. Quietly. Succinctly. Dumping spoonfuls of dark granules into each mug, he gave them a quick stir and joined Molly at the table.

"Tell me the details.''

She took a sip of coffee first, finding that the telling seemed to get harder, not easier. With each repetition, the victim became more that just a disembodied voice. She imagined a short, wiry dark-haired man. Heard his desperate pleas. Tried not to see a bullet hole blossom in his forehead.

"A Detective Kaplan in Homicide asked me to come downtown tomorrow at ten," she finished, swirling the dark liquid in her mug. "He wants to go over exactly what I heard."

"You okay with that?"

She looked up to find Sam studying her with a frown in his gray eyes.

"No," she admitted. "I get a little queasy every time I think about that phone call. My phantom visitor last night didn't exactly help matters, either."

"I did a walk-around of your house before you got home tonight," Sam said, surprising her. "All the doors and windows were secure. I'll make another check after you go back inside."

Molly didn't think he'd intended that as a hint for her to leave, but she decided to use it as an exit cue. Pushing her mug aside, she rose.

"Thanks. I'm enough of a coward to appreciate the offer."

"No need to rush off. You haven't finished your coffee."

She didn't tell him that she'd lingered too long as it was. For a belligerent ex-military type with vampire habits and a Jekyll-and-Hyde personality, Sam Henderson could certainly turn on the charm when he wanted to. She'd better get the heck out of Dodge, or in this case, out of his beautiful kitchen, before she did something stupid. Such as get too friendly with a man who turned his emotions on and off like a faucet.

"Coffee's the last thing I really need tonight," she confessed, detouring around the steel jungle of his living room. "My boss suggested that I overheard a mob execution. That cheerful thought is enough to keep me awake without the added stimulus of caffeine."

"A mob execution," Sam echoed, frowning. "I suppose that's one possibility. This Joey character could have welched on his bets or gotten crosswise of a major drug distributor."

"Hey! For a guy who's trying to reassure me by checking my doors and windows, you're going about it all wrong! Besides, the man I heard shoot Joey the Horse didn't sound like a mobster."

"Oh? Have you carried on conversations with a lot of mafioso before?"

She threw him a nasty look. "This guy came across as educated, sophisticated."

"You think today's hoods aren't?"

"Okay, okay. What if it was the mob who rubbed him out? Unless the police can put a face to the voice I heard, it won't make any difference."

She didn't know who she was trying to convince, herself or Sam. In any case, she got the answer to her question the very next morning.

Molly had only visited City Hall once before. Her boss had taken her down to meet the mayor and city council, who maintained a close working relationship with the Convention Center. At the time, the multistory elliptical glass structure on the corner of Fourth and Stewart hadn't particularly impressed Molly. Nor had the shallow, empty fountain in front of the building. Devoid of even a trickle of water, the dry fountain had struck her as incongruous in a city bursting with vibrant energy.

The interval between Molly's first and second trip to the municipal building hadn't improved its appeal. The grim purpose behind her visit only emphasized its stark, uninviting facade. After asking directions from the receptionist at the front desk, she made her way to the police department located in the rear annex and asked directions to Detective

Kaplan's office. A uniformed officer directed her up two flights of stairs and down a long hall.

She found the Homicide Division…and Sam Henderson ensconced in one of the uncomfortable-looking plastic chairs placed in front of a modular desk unit.

He rose at her approach, tall and calm and smiling a little at her surprise. For the first time in their brief acquaintance, he wore something other than jeans, sweats or thigh-skimming athletic shorts. Even in loafers, black slacks and crisp, blue cotton shirt, however, he looked like a man who knew his way around a gym.

Chiding herself for the strange little rush of pleasure his presence generated, Molly inquired what he was doing there.

"Kaplan called this morning and asked me to come in as well. I guess he was hoping that I could add some detail to your initial report. So far, I've come up blank. Here, have a seat."

She had just taken the other chair when a short, compact individual in wrinkled gray slacks and a tan sport coat approached.

"Miss Duncan?" He tossed a file on the desk and held out his hand. "I'm Al Kaplan. Thanks for coming down."

Molly's ear picked up a hint of an accent. German, she was sure. Judging by his dark jowls and sturdy build, the detective had no doubt descended from first-generation immigrants.

"Have you met Major Henderson?" Kaplan shook his head at his own question. "Oh, sure you have. He's your neighbor, the one you lodged the complaint against the night you heard the murder."

Avoiding Sam's sardonic gaze, Molly nodded. "Yes, he is."

"I've read the police reports filed as a result of your two calls to 911," the detective continued, seating himself opposite the two, "but I'd like go over them with you in detail."

"Both of them?" she asked with a little frown.

"Both of them."

"Why? Do you think there's a chance that the two incidents are related?"

"We can't discount the possibility. You said in your statement that the killer picked up the phone while you were still on the line."

"Yes, he did."

Even now, in the bright light of day, she could hear the echo of the victim's desperate pleading and the killer's cold, calm response.

"You probably shook him as much as he scared you," the detective theorized, shuffling through the files on his desk. "Could be, he decided to check you out. Wouldn't have been hard to track you down. Especially with your name and phone number on Joey's caller ID."

Molly felt the blood drain from her face. "He had caller ID?"

"Yeah. Everyone and his brother's got one of those gadgets these days."

She barely heard the offhand remark. The abstract possibility that the shooting she'd heard was somehow connected to her uninvited guest had been disturbing enough. The fact that the killer had instant access to her name and telephone number at the time of the murder lifted the matter out of the realm of possibility and put it down on just the other side of scary.

"…again exactly what you heard."

She stared at Kaplan, too shaken to reply.

"Ms. Duncan?"

In the seat next to her, Sam cursed under his breath. He hadn't missed the shock that darkened her green eyes or the pallor of her face. He reached for her hand, cradling it between both of his.

"Molly?"

Turning a white, frightened face to his, she gripped his fingers with bruising force. Protective instincts he had no business feeling for this woman leaped into his chest. The need to take her in his arms slammed into him. He restrained himself, but only because Molly released her death grip on his hand at that moment and turned her attention back to Kaplan.

"I'm sorry. The idea that the man I heard fire those shots knew exactly who he was speaking to when he picked up the phone got to me."

The detective picked up a pencil and leaned forward. "Let's talk about that. What, exactly, did he say to you?"

"'Hello.'"

Both Sam and Kaplan waited expectantly. When she didn't volunteer anything more, disappointment flattened the detective's face.

"That's it?" At Molly's nod, he tossed his pencil on top of the reports and scraped a hand across his cheeks. "'Hello' is not going to get us far."

She pulled in a breath. "No, it won't. But I also heard him talking to Joey before he shot him. He spoke with an accent, faint but definitely upper Midwest. From the way he rounded his vowels, I'd guess Wisconsin or Michigan. He also attended school or worked on the East Coast."

Kaplan gaped at her. "You got all that from just a few phrases?"

"Languages are my profession and my specialty," she answered with a shrug. "My grandparents on one side are first-generation Irish, and second-generation Polish on the other. I could swear fluently in Gaelic or in Polish by the time I was three."

"So how does Gaelic translate to upper Midwestern?"

"My dad worked for the Great Northern Railroad. We moved every few years, and I picked up the local slang wherever we happened to live. Since then, I've studied seven additional languages, including German, French, Japanese and Korean."

Sam was impressed. Kaplan even more so.

"I'd recognize the man's voice instantly if I heard it again," Molly finished.

"*If* you hear it again," the detective pointed out. "I'll run what you gave us through the PD's database to see if we turn up anyone with a Midwestern background and a record. We'll also work the local pawn shops to see if anyone with that particular accent purchased a .38 recently. It's a long shot, but worth a try."

He flipped the file folder shut, then hesitated. Sam sensed what was coming next. He felt the worry in his gut even before Kaplan voiced it.

"In the meantime, Ms. Duncan, you'd better stay alert. It also wouldn't hurt to have the locks on your doors changed and a security system installed. Whoever killed Joey the Horse knows who you are and may or may not have paid you a visit already."

"As if I needed that reminder!"

Molly pushed through the outer glass doors into the dry, searing heat. She stood on the broad steps for a moment, face lifted to the sun, willing the warmth to chase away the chill of Kaplan's remark.

Sam saw the pallor under her scattering of freckles and felt the knot cinching his gut tighten another notch. He knew he should walk away. Now, while he still could. He had enough problems of his own without adding Molly Duncan to the list.

But he couldn't just stroll off and leave her to deal with

the shock of knowing that a cold-blooded killer had taken her name and phone number off a caller ID unit.

"It may take a while to get that security system installed," he said slowly. "With all the building going on in Vegas these days, I had to wait two weeks for mine."

"Two weeks!"

Dismay darkened her eyes to a deep, shadowed green. Sam held out for five seconds. Ten. Almost a half minute.

"I've got three empty bedrooms at my place," he forced out. "You're welcome to use one until you get your house wired."

She glanced up, as surprised by the offer as he was by having made it. He saw the polite refusal forming in her eyes and bit back a sigh of relief. He'd offered. He'd done his neighborly duty.

To his consternation, she hesitated. He could almost see her mind working, clicking through her friends and acquaintances. Her brows drew together, carving a little groove down the middle of her forehead.

"Maybe...."

The tentative reply stopped his heart. He held his breath while she nibbled delicately on her lower lip and the heat rose in shimmering waves around them.

"Maybe I'll take you up on that. If you're sure?"

Sam glanced down into her freckle-dusted face. At that moment, he knew he was about to commit what the military termed "a serious mistake in judgment," a catch-all phrase for any irresponsible act leading to total and irrevocable havoc.

"I'm sure."

Chapter 5

"You're staying with the jerk?"

Davinia lifted a perfectly arched brow in disbelief.

"The creep?" she asked melodramatically, as if doubting her subordinate's nod. "The defiler of the airwaves and would-be slayer of oleanders?"

"Only for a night. Two at most."

Or so Molly hoped! Avoiding her boss's incredulous stare, she plopped the thick yellow pages down on her desk. A quick thumbing brought her to the section on burglar alarms.

"I must have missed something here," the older woman mused. "When did your surly neighbor go from obnoxious to so hospitable that you two are going to shack up for the weekend?"

"We're not shacking up," Molly sputtered. "We're just spending a night or two under the same roof."

"Suuuure you are."

Davinia, as her employee well knew, didn't ascribe to the

theory that platonic friendships between men and women were possible, or particularly desirable. Swinging a shapely foot encased in a lizard shoe sporting a three-inch, hourglass shaped heel, she gave her subordinate a speculative once-over.

"Come on, girl. Let's have it. Why are you sleeping with the enemy instead of staying at the condo with Antonio and me this weekend?"

Smiling, Molly ticked off the reasons. "One, because you gave me a fairly detailed outline of what you were going to do to and with Antonio when you got him alone this weekend and I didn't want to get in the way."

"You wouldn't have been in the way…much."

"Two, I need to be at my place to give the security folks access. And, three…?"

"Yes?"

"All right," Molly admitted. "The Major and I have, well, declared a truce."

"Aha!" Her boss's turquoise eyes gleamed. "I knew it."

"A truce, Davinia. That's all." She shoved a hand through her hair. "If I'd been thinking rationally this morning, I would've made arrangements to stay at one of the hotels. I guess that business with the caller ID rattled me."

Her boss's smug expression disappeared. "That would have shaken me, too." She drummed a long nail on the desk. "Ex-number-three knows some folks in the construction business. Do you want me to see if he can recommend a reliable alarm company?"

"Yes, please!"

By shamelessly exploiting Davinia's ex-husband's connections, Molly arranged for Allied Security Systems to survey her house that very afternoon. She drove home to meet the company rep at four-fifteen.

Surveying the house was one thing, she soon learned. Installing the system was another. After alternately begging, brow-beating, and acting the frightened female...which didn't really take all that much acting...Molly finally wrung a promise from the harassed rep to send a work crew out tomorrow.

"No, wait. Tomorrow's Saturday." He shoved his ballcap back and swiped the sweat off his bald crown. "I've got all three of my crews working overtime on that new housing development off Flamingo Road. Hafta be Sunday. Or Monday, if we run behind."

"But..."

"That's the best I can do, Ms. Duncan. Take it or leave it."

Molly blew out a slow breath. "I'll take it."

Twilight hung in a soft purple haze outside her bedroom windows when she dumped a sleep shirt and a few vital necessities into a plastic tote decorated with a glittery gold MGM lion.

This house-sharing arrangement with Sam would work, she told herself again. Molly would make it work. She'd get up early and get out of Sam's way. She had plenty to do at the office to keep her busy over the weekend. Allied promised to call when they were ready to come out. She'd meet them here, then move right back into her own home. That way, she'd inconvenience her host and herself as little as possible.

That was the plan, anyway, when Molly slipped on a pair of low-heeled thong sandals in the same cherry red as the short-sleeved top she wore with her jeans, then made her way downstairs.

Sam unfolded himself from the rattan chair in her living room and eyed the little plastic tote. "Do you have everything you need?"

"Everything I need for tonight. Hopefully, I won't have to impose on you longer than that."

"You travel light," he replied with a smile that creased his tanned cheeks. "And as for imposing on me, we've already covered that ground. Several times. I wouldn't have invited you if I didn't want the company."

Given his on-again, off-again personality, Molly wasn't so sure. Tonight, though, she had to admit he was on. Definitely, devastatingly, one-hundred-percent on. His easy smile could charm the bark off a tree. It certainly peeled away a few of Molly's outer layers.

He'd traded the black slacks he'd worn earlier this morning for his customary jeans, but still wore the blue cotton shirt. He'd shoved up the sleeves to his elbows and acquired a small grease stain on one cuff, probably from the Mustang he'd been working on when Molly had pulled into her driveway.

She didn't think he'd been waiting for her specifically since he spent a good number of his evenings bent over the fender of the little red classic, but his solid presence had given her a surprising spurt of pleasure and…okay, she could admit it…relief. When he strolled across their parallel driveways and accompanied her inside her empty house, she'd been more than happy to let him do a quick search of the premises.

As Molly walked beside him now through the deepening twilight, her sandals crunching on the lava rock, she grappled with the disturbing fact that the narrow strip between their properties now seemed more like a safe passage than a hostile fire zone. She didn't like the fact that she'd been frightened out of her own home, but she liked the possibility that a killer might be watching her and her house even less. Sam shouldered open the door to his home, stepping back for her to enter. "Take your pick of the rooms upstairs. Come on down when you're settled and I'll throw some steaks on the grill."

Molly paused with one foot on the stairs. It was well past

eight o'clock. She'd made it a point to work late and grab a taco on her way home so she wouldn't impinge on Sam's hospitality any more than she had to. Turning down his offer seemed a bit rude, though.

"I got a fresh shipment of prime cut this morning," he added casually. "Compliments of the Double Bar."

"Okay, I'll bite. What's the Double Bar?"

"A small spread in northern Arizona. The brand is sort of a sideways 'H.'"

"The 'H' standing for Henderson, I assume?"

He nodded, and Molly gave herself a mental pat on the back for correctly placing his faint drawl the first time she'd heard it.

"Is this spread yours?"

"Just a small corner of it. My mother sold off most of the land when my father died. My brothers and I run a few thousand head with the Double Bar brand on what's left. My oldest brother, Jake, manages the place for her, in addition to his own."

Molly's store of knowledge about ranching would fit on the tip of the proverbial pin, but a few thousand head sounded like a pretty good-sized operation to her. Curious, she tilted her head to study Sam Henderson, onetime rancher, ex-Air Force Major, and currently unemployed as far as she could tell. "So why did you settle here in Vegas if you own land in Arizona?"

He hesitated a mere fraction of a moment, then lifted his shoulders in a shrug. "It's more convenient here."

Molly wondered at that brief pause, and at the deliberate casualness of his reply. Obviously, Sam Henderson didn't like talking about his past. Or was it his present that put that touch of cool reserve into his voice? More curious than ever about her mysterious neighbor, she decided to bend her self-imposed no-meals, no-mingling rule. Just for tonight.

"A steak sounds wonderful…if you're sure it's no trouble?"

"I'll fire up the grill while you get settled."

It didn't take Molly long to choose between the three upstairs bedrooms. The one at the top of the stairs obviously doubled as a study. A sophisticated computer system sat atop a desk, while the rest of the room was taken up with bookshelves and a striking hunter green leather sofa. An antique sleigh bed and a massive Korean chest in teak and brass dominated the second room. Suppressing a pang of serious envy over the beautiful chest, Molly peeked in the third room.

It had to be the master suite, since it ate up the whole back half of the second floor, but the huge room hardly looked lived in. Granted, the giant-sized bed attached to a wall unit filled with books was truly awesome. And, yes, Molly would have committed serious mayhem for the comfortable, high-backed leather chair and ottoman in one corner. Yet she didn't get a sense of sanctuary, of welcoming retreat, as she did in her own, far more sparsely furnished bedroom. Nor did she spot a single item of clothing draped over the back of the chair or tossed on the floor. Either Sam's military training had turned him into one of those disgustingly neat obsessive-compulsives, or he didn't spend a lot of time in his bedroom.

Considering the nights she'd laid awake listening to Buck Whatsisname, Molly supposed it was the latter. More curious than ever about her neighbor's nocturnal habits, she deposited her tote on the sleigh bed in the guest room and headed back downstairs. The aroma of hot, sizzling charcoal drew her to the patio.

"How do you like your steak?"

"Burned black on the outside, no trace of pink on the inside."

Molly braced herself for the usual argument. Everyone

from waiters to friends to ex-fiancés…particularly ex-fiancés…gave her grief about her preference for meat cooked to the consistency of blackened shoe leather. To his credit, Sam merely winced.

"This could take a while." He forked a slab of beef a good three inches thick onto the grill. "Would you like a cold beer while you wait?"

"I don't drink beer," she reminded him with just a hint of priggishness. She hadn't completely forgotten the nasty cracks he'd made about her empty beer cans during their initial skirmishes.

"That's right." His eyes glinted above the glow of the coals. "You only wear it. How about a glass of wine, or do you only wear that, too?"

"Just on special occasions." She replied, grinning. Her gaze drifted past Sam to the dark outline of her house. Slowly, her smile evaporated. "Like when I hear things go bump in the night."

Who had made that noise? she wondered for the gazillionth time since her meeting with Detective Kaplan this morning. Whose shadow had she seen moving along the wall? Had Joey Bennett's killer come after her, too? Was he lurking somewhere close by right now? Watching her? Waiting to get her alone? She shivered and edged a step closer to Sam.

He caught the small movement. As she had, he shot a quick look at the darkened house beyond the hedges. His chin took on a determined tilt, but his voice held only calm assurance.

"You're safe here, Molly. My security system came with a whole battery of motion-activated floodlights. I turned them on this morning. No one can get anywhere near this place without lighting it up like a Christmas tree…and answering to me."

That went a good way toward soothing Molly's jittery

nerves. Settling in a springy, striped patio chair, she hooked a heel on its crossbar and wrapped her arms around her knee.

"I can't believe I got myself involved in such a bizarre situation. Brady would, though. He was always telling me that I was too impulsive, that I needed to slow down and think things through."

"Brady?"

"My onetime fiancé. I left him and most of my furniture back in Boston when I sublet my apartment and moved to Vegas six months ago."

That explained her empty house, Sam thought. It didn't explain the sudden, inexplicable kick of satisfaction he got from knowing that his quirky neighbor was currently unattached.

Or was she?

"Six months, huh?" He probed her steak with the long-handled fork, raising a chorus of spits and sizzles. "Do you still miss him?"

Her full mouth curved in a slow, impish smile that did strange things to Sam's lungs.

"I miss my couch more."

He was still trying to recover from his momentary lack of oxygen when Molly turned the tables on him.

"What about you? The first time I called here, a woman answered the phone. Is she someone special? Someone who might wonder what your neighbor is doing camped out in your guest room?"

Sam thought briefly of the sexy, red-haired intelligence officer he'd been seeing off and on before his accident. Smart, talented and ambitious, Janet Green had wanted to take their relationship to the next level. They were a perfect match, in her view. Both dedicated to their jobs, both on the fast track to the top, they understood the pushes and pulls of a military marriage.

All during Sam's long rehab, Janet had remained convinced the Air Force wouldn't put him out to pasture. He was too valuable a resource, too experienced a test pilot. She'd been shocked when he accepted without a fight the Medical Evaluation Board's ruling of a temporary retirement. She'd come by several times after he'd hung up his uniform and moved into this house, trying to understand, even offering to put her own fast-moving career and upcoming transfer to Washington, D.C., on hold while he contested the MEB's decision.

Sam knew when and how to pick his battles. This wasn't one he intended to fight. Until he conquered the blinding pain that attacked him all too frequently, he couldn't fly, couldn't give his usual two hundred percent to any job. Hell, at times he could hardly see.

There was no way he was pulling any strings to get back on active duty. He wouldn't do that to the Air Force, or to himself. After their last argument over his decision, Janet had left, disappointed and hurt, although Sam suspected that her disappointment stemmed primarily from learning that their "perfect match" wasn't so perfect after all. She hadn't been back since.

"No," he told Molly, adding his steak to the grill beside hers. "There's no one special. Do you want to eat out here? I nuked a couple of potatoes in the microwave. I'll bring them out while these finish cooking."

"I'll get them."

She pushed out of the patio chair and went inside. Sam kept one eye on the sizzling meat and one on the swing to Molly's backside. She filled out a pair of jeans nicely, he had to admit. Very nicely.

Without warning, the memory of how she'd snuggled against him last night came rushing back. It had taken a concerted effort, but Sam had managed to keep that particular memory at bay most of the day. He'd darn well better keep it tucked away for the short time Molly would spend under his roof. He couldn't let himself think about the way her breasts had pressed against his chest. Or the neat fit of her bottom in his lap. Not if he was going to make it through the next few days without doing something stupid…like forgetting that his prickly neighbor could put out more sharp spikes than a desert cactus when she wanted to. Or that he wasn't in any condition to take up where he and Janet had left off.

No, he'd play it easy and friendly for the next few days. That approach seemed to be working well tonight. His neighbor hadn't snuck in any digs about his music or her bushes, and Sam didn't feel any aggravating curl of pain around the base of his skull. With luck, that surprisingly pleasant state of affairs would hold until Molly moved back into her own quarters.

Easy and friendly lasted all through dinner, eaten by the light of the stars and a couple of candles Molly had found in one of his cupboards.

It took them through an hour of idle, after-dinner conversation, where the topics drifted from Boston to Arizona to Vegas. From her newfound passion for the spangles and spandex so popular here, and his for the '67 Mustang he was restoring. From her current job, which Sam found fascinating, to his former one. He even opened up a bit himself, admitting that a flameout over the desert and a head-to-head with a stubborn canopy had forced him into a temporary medical retirement. When pressed, he said only that his nightly workouts were slowly getting him into better physical condition than anyone would have predicted six months ago.

Easy and friendly even got them through an awkward moment Friday morning, when Sam came downstairs to find Molly about to return to her own house. She hadn't wanted to wake him, she explained, but she had to shower and change for work.

Sam didn't bother to remind her that he'd gotten used to operating with little or no sleep…or that he'd spent half the night trying not to picture her sprawled across the bed just down the hall, and the other half wishing he could go downstairs and work off the tension that gripped his lower body when he did. He simply walked her home, checking the entire house before returning to his own.

There was nothing even remotely easy or friendly about Sam's condition late Friday night, however. His head pounded like the jackhammers heard constantly all around Las Vegas. An entire construction crew could have been riveting steel beams in there.

He prowled the darkened downstairs, desperately needing exercise but reluctant to wake Molly by pumping the clacking, clattering weights. He needed the distraction of one of Buck Randall's lonesome laments. He needed….

"Sam?"

He spun around, and the pain slam-dunked through his brain. The sight of Molly wearing a wide brown stripe across her nose and cheeks and a baggy T-shirt that dropped down to her knees didn't help his condition, either. How the hell could the woman manage to look sexy in a cotton sack?

"What do you want?"

He didn't realize he'd barked at her until she took a quick step back, blinking. She recovered before he did, her surprise morphing into concern.

"Are you okay?"

"I'm fine. Go back to bed."

Ignoring his growl, she padded into the darkened room. "What's the matter? Why can't you sleep? Why don't you ever sleep?"

"I sleep when I want to," he ground out, adding a silent "sometimes."

"Uh-huh. That's why I see lights on at your place all hours of the night."

Sam was in no mood to argue. He couldn't.

"All right. I get headaches once in a while. That's what happens when you butt headfirst through a supposedly shatterproof canopy."

"Have you got one now?"

"Yeah," he admitted, trying not to grind his teeth. "Go back to bed, Molly. It'll go away. They always do."

Eventually.

"Can't you take something?"

She floated toward him in the darkness, all pale, sleep-tossed hair and flaky brown facial. Above the peeling stripe laid across her upper cheeks and nose, her eyes were wide with a concern that teetered so close to pity that Sam's jaw tightened another notch.

"Didn't the doctors give you some pain pills?"

He would have snorted if he didn't know the effort would blow off the top of his head. "I've got a whole pharmacy full of pills upstairs. Every color and variety you can name."

"Tell me what you need. I'll go get it."

"No."

"But...."

"No!" His lips pulled back in a snarl. "I'll be damned if I'm going to spend the rest of my life doped up and out."

To Sam's surprise, she didn't back down. She didn't even flinch. She stood toe to toe with him, her face scrunched up under her half mask.

"So you're going to spend the rest of your life living like a vampire? Pacing through the night? Listening to that..."

She caught her breath.

"Listening to Buck Randall and pumping iron," she finished slowly. "That helps you? That...that punishment in the form of exercise? And the music?"

"Sometimes."

She frowned, dislodging a small shower of flakes. "Well, why aren't you doing either?" With a swift, indrawn breath, she answered her own question. "You didn't want to keep me awake. That's it, isn't it, Sam?"

"No."

"I've interrupted your routine, haven't I?" She searched his face, her own troubled, then spun around. "I'm going back to my own place. I shouldn't have imposed on you like this."

"Molly, wait."

He caught her arm, bringing her back around. As little as Sam wanted to spend the rest of the long hours until dawn with this splintering pain, even less did he want his neighbor alone and unprotected in her house with a killer on the loose. The stubborn tilt to her jaw told him that she wouldn't give in without a fight. Sam couldn't manage even a minor battle tonight.

"You won't help matters by going home," he said brusquely. "I'll still be awake and worrying about you."

"I'm not going to stay here and interfere with your regimen."

"Okay, okay. We'll compromise. I'll work out for a little while..."

"For as long as it takes," she insisted.

"And you stay put. Agreed?"

"Well..."

"I'll forgo Buck," he offered by way of inducement. "You pick the music."

"I have a better idea. Instead of music, why don't I just sit here and keep you company? I'll talk to you while you work out. Unless you think it would be too distracting?"

At the moment, Sam couldn't decide which was more

distracting...the jackhammering in his head or Molly Duncan curled up on his couch, her long, slender legs tucked under that sexy bottom. All he knew was that he wanted to get rid of one, badly, and not the other, almost as badly. He conceded with something less than graciousness.

"Sit here then."

Stripping off his shirt, he stalked to the Universal gym and set the pin on the weights.

"Okay," he instructed, fitting his back to the bench. "Start talking."

Carrying on an easy flow of conversation in any one of several languages had never been a problem for Molly. Tucking her legs under her, she sank onto the sofa that had been pushed against the far wall to accommodate the gym.

"Have you been to the Addagio yet?" she asked. "It's gorgeous. All marble floors and tall, round columns. It's supposed to replicate the interior of a famous Venetian palace. I've never been to Venice, but if the buildings look anything like the Addagio, I have to add it to my growing list of places to visit before I die."

Sam gritted his teeth and pulled the cold steel bar down to his chest. "Where...else...is...on...your...list?"

"Don't talk," she ordered. "Just do your thing and listen. Where else do I want to go? Well, I spent a year in Tokyo on an exchange program while I was in college. I'd love to go back there again. Especially in the spring. Everyone should visit the Imperial gardens when the cherry trees blossom and a breeze catches the petals. It's like walking through a pink, perfumed snowstorm."

Slowly, Sam worked into his routine. The clanking weights took on a familiar beat. A light sweat filmed his chest and arms as they bunched, released, bunched. Even Molly's monologue seemed to pick up the rhythm, taking on a curious lilt. From her Irish grandmother, Sam guessed, his breath gusting with effort. The one with the secret recipes.

"And I want to see the pyramids," she said dreamily. "I've never been to Egypt, although I did take a side trip to Morocco once."

He could listen to her all night, he decided.

Yeah, right, an inner voice scoffed. Like listening was what he really wanted to do all night with Molly. Even with the top of his skull about to blow off, all he had to do was sneak a glimpse at his neighbor curled up on the sofa, those gorgeous legs curled under her, and he got as hard as the damned steel frame caging him in.

Grunting, Sam yanked the bar to his chest.

Molly struggled to maintain her monologue as long as she could. The clank of metal on metal had kept her wide-awake at first. Gradually, she picked up the cadence buried in the jarring sounds. Before she knew it, she was pitching her voice to match it.

Maybe she could have kept her lids up if she'd been able to see Sam's face. Or watch him as he strained and flexed his superb muscles. But they hadn't turned on a light, and he was a pale blur in the darkness.

She had no idea when she lost the battle with her up-at-dawn, down-at-dusk internal body clock. She barely stirred when Sam slipped his arms under her and carried her up the stairs. Burying her face in the towel draped around his neck, she clung to him sleepily. The plush terry smelled of laundry detergent, she noted through a haze of weariness, and raw, elemental male. Groggy and disoriented, she nuzzled deeper into the towel. She had almost sunk back into sleep when Sam deposited her in the sleigh bed. Hovering in that hazy state of semiconsciousness, she didn't immediately react to the light kiss he brushed across her mouth.

"Good night, Molly. Thanks for the company."

The husky whisper finally penetrated. Her eyes drifted open. Sam's face hovered just inches from hers. All she had to do was lift her hand. Draw him back down an inch or two. Bring her lips to his once again.

"You're welcome," she muttered, confused and just a little stunned by the need that coursed through her.

"Sleep well."

Sure she would! Awake now and fully aroused, Molly watched him cross the darkened room to the door. It took a hard bite on the inside of her lower lip to keep from calling him back.

She wasn't ready for this, she thought in dismay. She shouldn't be fighting this sudden, urgent need to follow Sam down the hall to his own room. This greedy urge to peel off her T-shirt and take up where his kiss had left off. She shouldn't ache to slide her hands down those awesome abs. To let his powerful body crush her into the covers and...

Heat flooded her face. Her neck. Her belly.

She groaned and pulled the sheet up over her head. She had to get a grip here! She barely knew the man.

Okay, he wasn't the bloodsucking vampire or the foul-tempered martinet she once thought him. And she could have wept for the pain she'd glimpsed in his eyes when she went downstairs tonight. But Molly had learned her lesson with Brady. She'd gotten engaged to a man she thought she knew and didn't really know at all. She wouldn't jump recklessly into a relationship again.

Not that Sam showed any signs of *wanting* a relationship right now, with her or with anyone else. Obviously, he had problems of his own to work through. So did she...in the form of a nameless, faceless killer who may or may not be stalking her.

That sobering reminder was enough to push Molly into full, frightened wakefulness. She huddled under the sheet for a long while, then spent the next hour restlessly thumping the pillow and alternating between the disturbing memory of the voice she'd heard over the phone and the equally disturbing memory of Sam's lips brushing hers.

Chapter 6

As the weekend progressed, Molly tried to remember all the reasons why she should maintain some distance between her and Sam. The remembering grew more difficult with each passing daylight hour.

It got even harder at night. Sam didn't press for her company after that first evening, and Molly made sure she stayed out of his way so as not to interfere with his exercise regimen. She stuck to her plan of leaving his house early in the morning and returning late. Still, just knowing he was down the hall…or prowling the darkened downstairs, unable to sleep…kept her awake long past her normal zonk-out time.

Thankfully, the alarm company finally showed up on Monday afternoon. Sam came over to check out the system after it was installed, testing the infrared sensors and the pressure points on the stairs. Molly winced every time he set off the Klaxon. The raucous noise was loud enough to wake the entire cul-de-sac.

She moved herself and her few belongings back to her own house that night, happy to be home in a nesting kind of way. She didn't miss Sam…much. Only enough to keep her standing at the bedroom window for long moments that evening. Frowning, she stared at the light spilling through the great room windows next door. Was he hurting? Putting himself through another grueling routine? She ached for him and his lonely vigils.

On Tuesday morning, Detective Kaplan called to report that his search of the police department's database and the local pawn shops had turned up no leads to anyone with a Midwestern accent.

"So what happens now?" she asked, chewing on her ballpoint pen.

"We're going to have another chat with some of the women Joey pimped for. Talk to the bookies he owed money to. With luck, maybe one of them will give us a lead, although I'm not holding out a lot of hope. Everything okay at your end?"

"So far. No more misdirected phone calls or uninvited visitors, anyway."

"For what it's worth, I think the killer must have realized that you can't ID him. If you could, we would have tagged him by now. My guess is that he's feeling pretty secure. Assuming that was our boy you heard in the house the other night, I don't think he'll be paying you any more late night visits."

"I hope not!"

Molly hung up a few minutes later, fighting a spurt of guilty relief. She certainly didn't want anyone to get away with murder. Far from it. She'd done her part to bring Joey's killer to justice. If that wasn't good enough, well, too bad. At this point, all she wanted to do was put the whole incident behind her.

Maybe not the *whole* incident, she amended. Certainly not the spin-off truce between her and Sam.

She propped her chin in her hands, thinking about her neighbor. She still hadn't thanked him for his hospitality, and didn't have a clue how to. As she'd discovered in the past few days, Sam Henderson had narrowed his world and his focus while he battled his private demon. He seemed to have cut himself off from his past and sidestepped any talk about the future. His needs these days, he'd told Molly with a casual shrug, were simple. So what could she give this self-contained, self-sufficient man to thank him for coming to his pesky neighbor's aid?

The question had stumped her all weekend. It continued to nag at her until her idle gaze snagged on the Convention Center circular containing the printed show schedule for the week. She stared at the two-inch letters announcing a gala opening night show at Caesars Palace, then jumped up and headed for the offices downstairs.

Molly drove home that evening with the Trans Am's top down and the wind streaking through her hair. Anticipation bubbled like sparkling water in her veins. She couldn't wait to see Sam's face when she handed him the tickets nestled in her purse.

Why not just admit it? a smug little voice mocked. She couldn't wait to see Sam's face, period. So much for tiptoeing around his house and making herself scarce all weekend! The hot air rushing past her cheeks seemed to blow away all those lectures she'd given herself, all those stern reminders that she'd just escaped one uncomfortable entanglement and didn't need to fall into another. Or maybe it was Kaplan's seductive suggestion that the killer recognized he was safe, that he had no reason to come after Molly.

Whatever the reason, she felt more lighthearted than she had in days. Her resurgent spirits took a slight hit when she drove up the cul-de-sac and spotted a truck parked in the driveway next door. The red lettering on the rear panels identified the vehicle as belonging to Aqua Aruzzo Spa & Pools.

Uh, oh! Sam's pool contractor.

The Trans Am screeched to a halt halfway up her drive. Fingers drumming on the wheel, Molly stared at the truck. Had her truce with Sam ended so soon? Were they going to resume their battle over their contested property line?

The thought gave her a sinking feeling. She didn't want to redraw the battle lines. She'd gotten too close to her neighbor to paint him as the bad guy any longer. If it came to a choice between her oleanders and extending their cease-fire, she concluded with a tug of regret, her beautiful bushes would have to go.

Crunching across the lava rock between their houses, she pressed the doorbell at the same moment the front door opened. A lanky, gray-haired stranger blinked in surprise. Just beyond him, Sam smiled a greeting.

"Hello, Molly. You're home early."

"A little. I saw the truck in the driveway. I came to talk to you about the hedge."

"It's not an issue any longer. I've asked Mr. Aruzzo to redesign the pool to leave the hedge intact."

She flashed Sam a look of surprise. "Thank you! That was very generous and..."

"Neighborly?" he suggested, his smile cranking into one of those heart-stopping grins.

"Neighborly," she echoed, trying to catch her breath. How in the world could a few crinkles at the corners of a pair of gray eyes and a crooked grin do such a number on her respiratory system?

"The new design might take some time," Aruzzo warned, climbing into his truck. "I'll have to see when our architect can get to it. With all the building in Vegas these days, we've got almost more business than we can handle.''

"Tell me about it," Molly muttered.

He keyed the ignition, then added a final caveat. "With the new design, you'll have to double your laps if you're going to get the distance the docs recommend.''

"I understand."

The contractor's truck backed down the drive and roared off as Molly swung to face Sam. Dismay rushed through her in guilty waves.

"Oh, no! Why didn't you tell me the pool was part of your therapy?''

"It's not a problem."

"It certainly is! Call this guy back. Tell him to go ahead with the original design.''

The dismay in Molly's eyes pierced Sam's pleasure at her unexpected appearance on his doorstep. That wasn't pity darkening them to a deep emerald, but it came too damn close for his pride to swallow in one bite. After spending a weekend in close quarters with this woman, the last thing he wanted or needed from her was pity.

Correction. He didn't *need* anything from her. But he wanted. Oh, yes, he wanted. He'd gone through six kinds of hell these past few nights knowing that she slept just a few yards down the hall from him, her face slathered with beer mush and those long legs bared to the balmy desert night. When she packed up her little plastic tote and returned to her own place yesterday morning, he'd felt relieved…and lonely for the first time in a long, long time.

He didn't like the feeling, any more than he liked the idea she felt sorry for him.

"Don't worry about the pool, Molly."

"But…."

"Let's drop it, okay? We can declare the war of the hedges officially over and done with.''

She tilted her head, her frown etching deeper. The afternoon sun haloed her windblown hair. Just enough breeze swirled by to ruffle the waves even more. Deliberately, Sam blanked out the memory of how soft that tangle of silk had felt against his chin when he'd carried his sleepy guest upstairs.

"Do you want me to go with you while you check out your house?"

"No, thanks. I just saw the truck and came over to, uh...."

He forced himself to relax. "Defend your property."

"Actually," she said with a little toss of her head, "I came over to concede defeat. And I wanted to thank you again for taking me in."

"You've already thanked me. Several times."

"I know. Bear with me one more time."

Rummaging in her purse, she pulled out a small envelope and handed it to him. Sam slid his thumbnail under the flap and drew out a pair of tickets. His eyes widened at the embossed printing.

"Buck Randall's opening performance at Caesars. How the heck did you wrangle these?"

"The Center reserves a block of tickets for visiting VIPs. I strong-armed them into letting me purchase two. I know it's short notice, but I hope you can make the performance tonight."

"I can make it." He glanced down at his watch. "The show starts at nine. We've got time for dinner first."

"We?" A wave of color rushed into her face. "I didn't get you these tickets with the idea that you'd take me to the show."

Obviously not, Sam thought. He followed the becoming wash of pink from her neck to her cheeks. Well, he'd already put one foot in it. Might as well drop the other.

"I think you should go. What better way to learn to appreciate Randall's artistry than to see him in person?"

"Artistry?"

Her little hoot of derision lifted his brow. Realizing that she'd just looked her own gift horse in the mouth, Molly hastily backpedaled.

"I'm sure he has talent."

"He does."

"I just don't have the, ah, educated ear to appreciate it."

"So it's time your ear got educated. I'll pick you up at seven."

She hesitated, then capitulated with a smile. "Seven it is. Let's get one thing clear, though. Dinner's on me. I still owe you for that steak."

Molly turned off the expensive new alarm system—which had set her acquisition of living room furniture back another three months—and tossed her purse on the hall bench. All right. She might as well admit it. She couldn't think of anything she'd enjoy less than sitting through a Buck Randall concert. Or anything she'd enjoy more than spending another evening with Sam.

She didn't even try to convince herself that she'd accepted his invitation out of common courtesy or as a result of his generous concession about the oleanders. Common courtesy didn't explain this pulse of excitement beating just below the surface of her skin. Sam's gracious concession hadn't generated this shivery sense of anticipation. Just the thought of being with the man for a few more hours had her quivering.

She'd been bitten by the vampire next door, she conceded, kicking her shoes in the general direction of the closet. Only time would tell how badly.

After a long, decadent bath, she dragged herself out of the tub, then debated about the proper attire for a Buck

Randall concert. She considered jeans, a dressy little two-piece suit, and silky palazzo pants with a silver tank top. Finally, she settled on her favorite cocktail dress. The concert was being held at Caesars, after all.

The short, sparkly dress blazed in a sinful red. Its swishy skirt swirled just above her knees. The halter-necked bodice plunged in front and dropped even lower in back. She might not have the lush curves of a Las Vegas showgirl, Molly mused, twirling in front of the bathroom mirror, but her legs weren't bad. Not bad at all.

Piling her hair on top of her head, she secured it with a rhinestone clasp that matched the clip on her little red bag. A dab of perfume, a fresh application of makeup, and she was ready. She went downstairs to wait for Sam, hoping she hadn't overdressed for the occasion.

He rang the bell a few minutes later. Her first sight of him resolved her doubts instantly. It also caused a minor cardiac infraction.

In casual clothes, he'd snag the attention of any female over ten or under a hundred. In more formal attire, he'd have even the post-centenarians craning around for a second or third look. He'd slicked back his dark hair. His tanned face was freshly shaven. An elegantly tailored charcoal gray suit was paired with a pale yellow shirt with a tie that splashed reds and blues and oranges in a paisley pattern. He was, Molly decided, when she gathered her stunned senses enough for coherent thought, every woman's fantasy come to life. Assuming, of course, that those fantasies ran to broad-shouldered, square-jawed, knock-you-down gorgeous males.

He flashed her a quick grin, and Molly knew she was done for.

"You look terrific."

"So do you."

"Ready to do some serious damage to your diet and your taste in music?"

Groaning, she punched in the alarm code. "As ready as I'll ever be."

She locked the door behind them, then Sam crooked an arm and led her down the walk. His gleaming, cherry red Mustang convertible waited in the driveway.

"We're going in style, I see."

"I've been working on this baby for over two years," he admitted. "Tonight's the first night I've taken her out in public. I hope she behaves herself."

"I hope so, too."

After duly admiring the restored chrome and original hood ornament, Molly slid into a leather seat that breathed saddle soap and loving hand-polishing. Her sparkly red dress swirled about her thighs before settling demurely.

Fighting to control the sudden surge of heat generated by a brief flash of leg, Sam thunked the door shut with far more force than his pride and joy deserved. And he'd thought just sleeping down the hall from his neighbor for a couple of nights was torture!

He'd needed only one look at her flushed, smiling face and throat-closing flame dress to know his torture was just beginning. Now that slither of silk stockings would thunder in his ears for the rest of the night. He didn't want to think what her light, fragrant scent would do to him.

Sam shoved the key in the ignition, realizing that he couldn't deny it any longer. He wanted her. More than he could remember wanting any woman, including the bright, ambitious redhead he'd once thought of combining careers and lives with. He might not be able to offer Molly any kind of a future, he thought with a slow twist in his chest, but he could sure give her one hell of a tonight.

Las Vegas by day could enchant the most blasé visitor. By night, it wove a gossamer, magic spell. Even after six months, Molly wasn't immune to its sorcery.

The coming dusk puffed dark clouds across the horizon as the Mustang purred its way down the cul-de-sac, behaving so well that both she and Sam were free to admire the glittering network of lights laid out below. The wind tugged her hair free of the rhinestone clip, but she vetoed Sam's offer to stop and put up the top. She didn't think she'd ever get enough of these balmy, star-studded desert nights.

Molly soon realized that Sam knew the city far better than she did. While her job had taken her to all the major hotels and tourist attractions, she hadn't yet sampled many of the small, out-of-the way places that the locals frequented. The Continental Grill was tucked away in the corner of a small strip mall and combined the best of both worlds. Its decor inside and out lacked the neon and flash of the big casino restaurants, but its menu did credit to a gourmand.

On any other occasion, Molly would have savored her chilled cucumber bisque and delicately peppered Pacific salmon and dawdled shamelessly over the cappuccino that followed. Tonight, the exquisitely flavored food and drink did little to satisfy her appetite. Sam's thigh accidentally brushing hers under the thick linen tablecloth had generated a different, far fiercer hunger. The gentle abrasion of his fingertips in the small of her back when they left the restaurant only added to it.

If she'd been a betting person, Molly would have wagered her next paycheck that three hours of Buck Randall would have killed those growing hunger pangs. Good thing she didn't. Her losses would have set the acquisition of a living room sofa back once again.

As tall and angular as he was rail-fence thin, the ex-con-turned-rodeo-stuntman-turned-recording-superstar electrified his audience with his energy. Molly still couldn't quite get past his nasal twang. Nor did she find a great deal of poetry in his lyrics, which encompassed every disaster from the death of his first love to the loss of all his worldly possessions at the hands of a devil woman named Angel. But she had to admit he threw himself into his performance and pulled everyone in the cavernous showroom in with him. His fans cheered each song. Piercing whistles accompanied each verse. Half the house belted out the choruses with him.

Even Sam got caught up in the act. Wedged next to Molly in the circular booth only a few yards from the stage, he tapped out a steady beat on her bare shoulder. At one point, his rich, deep baritone joined in the general sorrow over the theft of a piebald mare. The vibrations rumbling in his chest made Molly's nerves dance in response. She slanted a quick look sideways, her heart thumping when she observed the pleasure on Sam's strong, chiseled face. After seeing how pain had drawn it into a tight mask, she decided that Buck might just have some talent hidden somewhere under that twang after all.

She didn't really appreciate the full scope of that talent, however, until his final encore, when he pleaded with his listeners not to go to their graves without tastin' mescal or lovin' a green-eyed woman.

Sam's hand slid up Molly's neck to tangle in her hair. She turned her head to find his eyes on her. Silvery gray. Shielded by dark lashes. And hungry. So hungry her heart contracted, then exploded painfully against her ribs.

"Ever tasted mescal, Molly?"

Even with Buck amplified to forty zillion decibels and two thousand of his fans stomping feet and clapping hands, she couldn't miss the husky edge in Sam's voice.

"No."

"You've got something to look forward to then."

"If mescal is that stuff made from cactus, I don't think so."

His thumb made a slow circle on her nape. "You'll have to try it sometime. You might like it."

The applause faded to mere background noise. Buck's final refrain dimmed in her ears. Molly felt Sam's touch on her neck like a brand. Every square inch of skin that came in contact with his burned.

She didn't stop to think. Didn't try to analyze her body's response to his touch, let alone try to curb it. She leaned into him, until her breath touched his.

"Ever made love to a green-eyed woman, Sam?"

His gaze skittered, then locked with hers. For a moment, his face took on the hard edges she'd come to dread. For that same moment, Molly thought she must have misread him, misjudged the heat that rose in almost palpable waves around them.

She was searching for some bright, witty way to pass her comment off as a joke, when his face softened. A need that matched her own flared in his eyes, and he pulled her closer, nuzzling her temple.

"No, sweetheart, I haven't."

Molly melted into a puddle of bright, liquid need.

"You'll have to try it sometime," she murmured. "You might like it."

"I intend to."

Chapter 7

Consumed by the need racing through her, Molly didn't pay any attention to the whistles and shouts that erupted all around her at the end of the concert. Sam's husky promise sang in her head, drowning out every other sound.

In a shimmer of anticipation, she sat through two encores and a long, irreverent dialogue between Buck and his fans. Finally, Sam slid out of the curving booth and reached out to help her. His hand closed on hers, hard and warm, then burned a brand at the small of her back as he guided her out of the showroom and through the casino's streaming throngs.

Although it was close to midnight when they walked into the star-strewn night, Molly's inner clock hadn't sent its usual signals to shut down all systems at the first sign of darkness. Her whole body tingled with life and with an awareness of the man at her side.

She didn't want the night to end.

While Sam fished in his pocket for the valet parking

ticket, Molly glanced at the brightly lit Strip. The glittering neon signs beckoned like signposts to sin. She pulsed with the urge to follow their exotic, sensual lure…but it was the display of classic roadsters parked in the semicircle in front of the casino that snagged Sam's attention.

"Would you look at that?'' he breathed, riveted by a gleaming green monster loaded with chrome.

The awe in his voice made her smile. "I'm looking, but you'll have to tell me at what.''

"It's a '47 Studebaker.''

"I thought Studebakers went the way of the dinosaurs.''

"They did.'' While the valet loped away to locate the Mustang in the reserved parking lot, Sam steered Molly across the circular drive for a closer look. "Before they became extinct, though, models like this one set the auto-motive industry on its ear. See that rear window? The all-glass notch-back caused a design revolution just after World War II.''

She gave the wraparound back window respectful consid-eration.

"There were some protests to the radical new look, of course,'' Sam added with a quick, slashing grin. "The be-boppers and hepcats who enticed their dates into the back seat didn't particularly appreciate the cinemascope view it gave of their activities.''

The gleam in his gray eyes caught Molly right where it caused the most damage. Her head tried to tell her that her neighbor's on-again, off-again personality had switched to full power once more. That it could just as easily switch off. Her heart wasn't buying any of it. That rebellious organ thumped erratically against her ribs, until all Molly could think of was a line from one of Buck Randall's songs. Something about slidin' down the slippery slope and not bein' able to do a damned thing to break the skid.

"In fact,'' Sam continued, the gleam a definite glint now,

"it's my theory that every advance in automotive design pitted man's basic instincts against his baser instincts."

"This I have to hear," she murmured as the Mustang squealed out of the underground lot and screeched to a halt before them.

Passing the attendant a hefty tip, Sam got behind the wheel. Larger-than-life statues of Greek gods and goddesses gazed serenely down on them as the Mustang flowed into the stream of traffic leaving the casino.

"Take this gearshift, for example," he said, warming to his subject. "Over time, the old, original levers evolved into a single stick shift, which in turn gave way to an automatic drive on the steering column. Far more convenient, but not as much fun as slipping the clutch and sliding this baby into gear."

As if to illustrate his point, he maneuvered the convertible into second with an effortless partnership of hand and foot.

"Now we've come full circle. Today, every adolescent, young and old, wants a macho four-on-the-floor instead of a dull, boring automatic...and ends up cursing when the gearshift gets in his way on Saturday night."

Laughing, Molly shook her head. "Poor babies."

"You think I'm kidding?" His hand curled around the wood-grained knob. "This little gadget has been known to unman the overeager and unwary."

Somehow, she couldn't imagine Sam ever letting a little gadget like that get in his way. Grinning, she listened with mounting skepticism to his drawling recitation of the problems presented by various automotive designs on the male of the species. By the time he pulled into her driveway, his X-rated version of the evolution of bucket seats had her giggling helplessly.

"Come on! Do you really expect me to believe narrow seats are the automotive industry's counter to the sexual revolution?"

"Sure they are."

He cut the engine and slewed around with his back to the door. She shifted to give him more room, acutely aware of the way their knees knocked. Her heart was doing some knocking of its own, as well.

"Just think about it," Sam urged. "Bucket seats appeared on the scene about the same time as the Pill. Someone had to throw a few obstacles in the path of progress."

"Some obstacles! We're practically sitting in each other's lap."

The glint in his eyes gave Molly her only warning that she'd walked right into that one.

"Not quite. But where there's a will…"

In one easy motion, he scooped an arm under her knees and lifted her over the offending gearshift. She landed awkwardly, her legs tangling with his and one elbow digging into the back of the seat.

"…there's a way," he finished smugly.

"So I see."

Suddenly breathless, Molly attempted to extricate herself. Her elbow slipped, and she found herself wrapped tightly in Sam's arms.

For a moment neither of them spoke. Molly held her breath, wanting, aching for his kiss. He wasn't long in giving it.

This one didn't even remotely resemble the first kiss he'd given her. This wasn't any light brush of lips on lips. No casual, friendly touch of his mouth to hers. This one came down hard, and got harder.

Molly gasped, molding her mouth to his. Instant heat flared in her belly. White fire licked at her veins. She arched into him as much as her awkward position would allow, giving kiss for kiss and press for press.

She knew she was about to go up in flames when Sam buried one hand in her hair to anchor her head. His other slid up her calf, taking the swirly red skirt with it. When his palm encountered a patch of bare flesh guarded by a lace trimmed strip of elastic, his head jerked up.

"We have to throttle back," he said raggedly. "Or take this inside."

Her stomach did a little flip. He was offering her the choice. She didn't have to think for more than a second or two.

"Let's take it inside."

He stared down at her, his face grooving with stark lines that made her stomach take another flip. Oh, no! He wasn't going to switch personalities on her now, not when she was about to melt all over his damned bucket seat.

"If you want to," she tacked on hastily.

"I want, Molly. I want so bad I hurt with it. I have since the night you came careening through the oleanders and into my arms."

"Me, too," she said simply.

Sam shouldered open the door and untangled his long legs from Molly's. Effortlessly, he reached down and gathered her into his arms. He was halfway to her front door before he thought to ask if her somewhat sparse collection of household furnishings included a bed.

"A bed I have."

By this point, Molly craved Sam's touch so badly she would have made love to him on the kitchen counter. Thank heavens for her queen-sized mattress.

She lost her dress and frilly garter belt somewhere between the front door and the upstairs hall. Still carrying her tight in his arms, Sam didn't shuck his clothes until they gained the bedroom. He dropped her on the bed with more urgency than finesse and peeled out of his suit. Molly lay sideways across the bed, her stomach hollowing when he walked toward her.

Lord, he was magnificent. Pumping all that iron had

torched every ounce of fat from his body. He was rock hard, a solid mass of lean, corded muscle from his pecs to his glutes...and everywhere in between. Molly had never considered herself a connoisseur of the male physique before. A sense of humor and a keen mind rated far higher on her list of must-have qualities than a handsome face or a trim body. Now, she discovered, Sam's combination of all of the above shattered every one of her preconceived notions of raw male beauty.

On fire to touch him, she rose up on her knees. Her hands skimmed skin that felt like warm, supple leather. Entranced, she traced the expanse of his chest. The ridges and rounded slopes came alive under her fingertips, rippling at her touch.

"You almost make me want to take up exercise."

She pressed her lips to his shoulder, marveling at its smooth shape. He tangled his hands in her hair and tipped her head back. A smile sketched across his face.

"From the first day I moved in next door, you've made me want to do a lot of things, Molly. With no 'almost' about them."

She decided not to pursue that particular line of conversation. She didn't want to spoil the magic of the moment by careless references to run-over garbage pails or neighborly feuds. Instead, she slid her hands up and around his neck.

"What do you want to do now, Sam?"

His voice dropped to rawhide softness. "In the words of the immortal bard, I want to make love to a green-eyed woman."

With a silent, heartfelt *thank you!* to Buck Randall, Molly dragged Sam down. Or maybe he took her with him. However it happened, he proceeded to do exactly what he wanted. He made love to her. Slowly at first. Deliberately. Exploring every slope and valley of her body with his hands and his mouth.

No passive participant, Molly tried to match him kiss for
kiss, stroke for stroke. Before either of them was ready for
it, slow and deliberate couldn't satisfy the urgency that
speared through them. Her panties slid down to catch on
her ankle. A hair-roughened thigh slid in to press against
her core. Gasping, Molly arched at the pressure. Sam used
the small movement to rid her of her demi-bra. Her nipples
peaked at his touch. Her breasts quivered at the scrape of
his tongue and his teeth.

His mouth devoured her. Hers touched and tasted him.
She was panting with need, her breasts and belly slick and
aching, when Sam suddenly pulled away. The mattress
rolled under his weight as he pushed himself off. Molly
closed her eyes, fighting for breath, then levered herself up
on her elbows. Her heart broke at the tight cast to his face.

"Oh, Sam! Are you hurting?"

His mouth twisted in a wry grin as he scooped his pants
off the floor.

"I'm hurting, sweetheart. As bad as I've ever hurt in my
life. Just give me a moment and we'll fix it."

The little blue package of condoms he produced banished
Molly's wrenching concern. She fell back on the bed, laughing with relief. Relief gave way to singing, searing joy the
moment Sam took her in his arms. When he matched his
hips to hers and slid into her, she thrust up to meet him.
They found a rhythm that matched their need, slow and sure
at first, then harder, faster, more urgent. Pleasure centered,
swirled, spread.

Sam braced himself on both elbows, determined to see
Molly's face when she convulsed under him. He couldn't
count the hours lately he'd envisioned her like this…head
thrown back, eyes closed, face flushed with passion. Since
the moment she charged through the oleanders in those
skimpy purple boxers and half a T-shirt, he'd wanted her.
He'd fought it. Hell, he'd pumped more iron this past week

than he had at any time since the accident, and not just because of the ache in his skull.

Molly made him hurt in a way he hadn't hurt in a long time. Just the sound of her breathless little moans pushed the ache in his groin right past pain into a pleasure so intense he couldn't hold it. He thrust again, felt her slick, satiny heat grip him.

"Sam!"

She arched under him. He sank into her. The night fireballed around them.

Molly dropped into sleep with the abruptness of someone falling off a cliff. Sam wasn't surprised. He'd watched her sink into unconsciousness twice before. Tonight, she had the extra incentive of total physical exhaustion.

Smiling, he hitched her a little higher up on his shoulder. She mumbled a protest and threw an arm across his chest. One of her knees gouged into his thigh. A soft wash of breath bathed his neck.

Unlike Molly, Sam couldn't sleep. Not because his head ached, thank God. More from habit, he supposed. He'd gone so long with so little sleep, his body had accustomed itself to a lesser need.

He felt good, though. Great, in fact. The prospect of greeting the dawn without pain was joy enough. Greeting it with Molly in his arms would rank right up there among his greatest private pleasures. Better than riding out with his brothers on a cold, misty winter day to bring the cattle down from the high pastures. Even better, he thought with a grin, than the exhilaration of his first jet solo.

The grin slipped for a fraction of a second, then fixed firmly in place. For the first time, Sam didn't break out in a sweat of regret when he thought about the flying he suspected he'd never do again. He curled his arm, bringing Molly closer into his side. Slowly, deliberately, he let himself envision a future without the constant adrenaline high of the test business. Without the speed and the thrill and the edge that came with throwing high-performance aircraft across the sky.

He'd take it one day at a time, he told himself. One day at a time.

His fingers caught in the silk of her hair. He closed his eyes, breathing in her musky, womanly scent. No beer flavor this time. Not even wine or coffee. Just Molly.

The grin came sneaking back.

Maybe he'd take it one *night* at a time.

A sharp thrust to his thigh brought him jerking upright some hours later. He blinked, trying to orient himself in the dim, grayish light.

"Sorry," Molly murmured sheepishly, easing her knee away from his thigh and her bottom off the bed. "I didn't mean to wake you."

"Wake me?" Sam shook his head, still groggy. "Was I sleeping?"

"That's what it sounded like to me," she replied, her mouth curving.

"What time is it?"

"It's… Oh, no! It's after eight! I'm supposed to meet my boss at the new Visitors' Expo at nine."

She scooted off the bed and grabbed the nearest discarded garment, which happened to be Sam's shirt. As disoriented as he was, he still had time to appreciate the sight of her rounded bottom before it disappeared beneath the pale yellow cotton. He wasn't surprised when he felt his body tighten.

She turned to face him, her lower lip caught between her teeth. From the uncertainty in her eyes, Sam guessed that she was just beginning to feel the inevitable awkwardness of a morning-after.

"I have to get ready for work. Do you want to wait while I shower or, uh, do you need to get home?"

Definitely morning-after syndrome. Sam knew the cure for that. Unfortunately, he couldn't prescribe it right now. Molly had to get to work. Throwing aside the sheet, he reached for his slacks.

"You shower. I'll make coffee."

Nodding, she headed for the bathroom.

"Molly?"

She spun around, setting the shirttails to swirling and Sam's stomach to performing a full-engine stop.

"Yes?"

"I'd go to my grave happy this morning."

She stared at him blankly. Chuckling, Sam sang a few bars of Buck Randall's ode to cactus liquor and green-eyed women.

When he ad-libbed a few lines of his own that made reference to bucket seats and long-legged blondes, Molly blushed furiously and headed for the shower. She certainly wasn't ready to go to her grave this morning, happy or otherwise. Not when she felt so...so alive.

Alive and sated and the craziest bit shy. In the bright light of morning, she couldn't quite believe that she'd slept all night naked and plastered against Sam's side like wet newspaper. And that she'd taken him into her body not once, but twice. Or was it three times? She wasn't really sure, since she'd been pretty well out when he'd rolled her over and murmured certain lewd suggestions into her ear.

If those hazy memories hadn't been enough to fluster her, the sight of Sam jerking straight up in bed, the sheet barely covering his flanks, would have done it. Asleep, he'd set her pulse hammering. Awake and aroused, he'd short-circuited her entire system. And that scared her. Just a bit. Not enough to incite panic, but enough for some serious second thoughts.

Frowning, she stepped into the shower. The lukewarm water needled into her skin, sluicing away the last of her languor. Her hands impatient, she soaped her body. What the heck was her problem? Why had the sight of Sam taking up more than his fair share of her bed sent her stomach on a bumpy ride to....

To where?

Sam hadn't made any promises last night, Molly reminded herself sternly. He hadn't whispered any words of love in her ear.

And she didn't want any! Not yet. Not this soon. She still hadn't fully recovered from the break with Brady. If she needed any reminders of how the wrong kind of relationship could complicate her life, all she had to do was look around her empty house. In her determination to make a fresh start, she'd left Brady *and* her Boston co-op filled of furniture.

Which didn't explain why she lingered far too long in the shower, trying to conquer the traitorous urge to call Davinia, beg out of the meeting and drag Sam back down on the rumpled sheets.

Frazzled and more than a little exasperated with her uncharacteristic doubts, Molly towel dried her hair and swiped on some blush and lip gloss. A quick search of her closet had her shimmying into a melon pink silk jersey tank dress. Tugging on its matching short-sleeved jacket and a pair of heeled sandals, she followed the mouth-watering scent of coffee down the stairs.

Sam had turned on the small TV set atop the counter, but Molly paid no attention to the too-handsome newscaster rambling on with the morning traffic report. Her every sense was tuned to the man perched on her solitary kitchen bar stool, a mug in his hands and a smile creasing his unshaven cheeks.

He'd slipped on his gray suit, minus his shirt, which now lay in a yellow pool on her bathroom floor. His colorful tie hung out of one side pocket. The combination of bare chest and tailored charcoal gabardine made a fashion statement that sent Molly's breath right back down her throat.

"Got time for coffee?"

She didn't, but Davinia would understand if she was a few minutes late. Especially when Molly confessed that she and her neighbor had finally and irrevocably ended their feud.

"A quick one," she told him, wanting to kick herself for the fluttery confusion his smile generated in the pit of her stomach. She had to get a grip here.

"Traffic's clear all the way across town," he commented as she sipped gratefully at the steaming brew. "You won't even have to navigate around any orange barrels once you get past the bulldozers and culverts at the bottom of the hill." His eyes glinted with laughter. "You can take it easy coming out of the garage."

Letting that good-natured dig pass, Molly took another swig, then set the mug aside.

"I'd better go. Davinia will be waiting for me."

He pushed himself off the stool just as the newscaster's face gave way to a platform draped with bunting. A smiling politician started to extol the values of family, work and country.

"I'll walk out with you," He reached for the off switch on the little TV. "I have to..."

"Wait!" Molly shrieked. "Leave it on!"

Sam froze, his eyes slicing from her face to the flickering screen. The handsome, prematurely gray politician smiled and waved at a cheering crowd. His voice floated out over the speakers, smooth and erudite despite the tinny amplification.

"...won't guarantee a job for every person, but the welfare reform bill I introduced last year does guarantee every person's right to a job."

The scene faded to an American flag dancing against a robin's-egg sky. An announcer urged all listeners to vote for experience and results in November. A trailer appeared, showing dates and locations of a series of public forums at which the speaker would appear.

"Th...that's him!" Molly choked out as the newscaster reclaimed the screen. "That man. That voice. That's the one I heard on the phone!"

Chapter 8

Strung as tight as wire, Sam faced Molly across the shining blue countertop. She stared at the TV, her face paper white, her eyes huge with shock. For long moments, the only sound in the kitchen came from a very competent, very pregnant weather forecaster who informed her listeners that the mercury should hit a nice, comfortable eighty-nine by mid-afternoon.

Molly's stunned gaze jumped from the TV screen to Sam. "Did you hear him? Did you see him?"

"I saw him."

"That was him!" Her voice quavered, shot up an octave. "The man who shot Joey the Horse."

"Are you sure?"

"Yes! I've heard that voice in my dreams. I recognized it instantly."

She thrust a hand through her hair and raked the still damp waves. Her eyes locked on the TV once more. She stared at the flickering screen with a sort of fascinated dread, as if she expected the ad to repeat and the speaker to leap right out of the set.

"Do you know who that man is?" Sam asked, fighting to control his own shock.

"The banner said Congressman Somebody Walters. I've got to call Kaplan!"

Snatching up her purse, she upended it and shook furiously. A clutter of car keys, a wallet, a cellular phone in a red leather case, lipsticks, tissues, loose coins, laundry stubs and several white business cards dumped out onto the counter. Her hands frantic, she pawed through the jumble.

"Dammit, I know I have Kaplan's number here somewhere. I've got to tell him…"

"Molly, that was Congressman Joshua Walters."

Sam's flat remark pierced her absorption in her task. Her head shot up.

"So?"

He pulled in a deep breath. "So Josh Walters has represented this district in Congress for more than ten years."

"So?"

"He's well known in this area, Mol. He pushed through tough anti-crime legislation that helped clean up the Strip. He also secured tight defense department construction dollars for a new test facility at Nellis. Word has it that he was the architect for the family values platform in the last Presidential campaign."

"And that means he couldn't also pull a trigger and blow someone away? Come on, Sam, get real."

She shuffled through the jumble once more, then pounced on a card. She was reaching for the phone when Sam caught her wrist.

"I know him, Molly. I took him up for an orientation ride in an F-16 a few years ago. I shared a table with him and his wife in D.C. during the Air Force's fiftieth anniversary celebrations. I can't believe Josh Walters would have any dealings with a sleaze like Joey Bennett, let alone murder him.''

Storm clouds gathered in her green eyes. She yanked her hand away with an angry twist. ''Believe it or not, I know what I heard.''

Sam saw that he had to tread warily here. The woman who'd flamed in his arms just a few hours ago was now shooting angry sparks at him.

''You just caught a few words of the ad,'' he pointed out, struggling to sound calm and reasonable. ''Maybe you should listen to it again before you make any allegations against a man as powerful as Walters.''

''Maybe I should,'' she conceded grudgingly. ''So what do you suggest? That I sit around here all day waiting for the ad to air again?''

''Call Kaplan. Tell him to meet us at the TV station. We can review the clip there.''

''We?'' Her chin lifted. ''Are you sure you want to get mixed up in accusations against your buddy?''

''He's not my buddy, but I do like and respect the man. Give me a few minutes to clean up, okay? Then we'll drive down to the Channel Five studios. If Kaplan can meet us there, fine. If not, we'll get a videotape of the clip and take it to him.''

''All right.''

He brushed a kiss across her rebellious mouth and headed for the patio door.

Molly watched him disappear through the oleanders. Her nerves still jumped and spit like cold grease in a hot skillet from the shock of hearing the voice that had haunted her for the past week.

She sagged a hip against the counter, willing her heart to stop skittering all over her chest. How ironic that she'd hear the killer again just when she'd decided to put him and his damned voice out of her mind. When she'd started to feel safe again, secure in her own home. Her hand trembling, she reached for the phone. To her relief, Kaplan was in the office and more than willing to meet her at Channel Five in a half hour.

Sam reappeared a few moments later, neat and composed in khaki slacks, a teal knit shirt that hugged his muscled frame, and aviator sunglasses.

"Ready?"

Nodding, she extracted her keys from the jumble, then swooped her arm across the counter to dump the rest back into her purse.

"Want me to drive?" he asked.

"No, I will."

She needed to occupy her hands or she'd start gnawing on her nails. As it was, she barely missed scraping the side of the car on the garage when she backed out. Pointedly, she refused to meet Sam's sardonic glance. The white Trans Am was down the hill and skimming past the row of concrete culverts awaiting burial beside the road at the bottom of the foothills when she suddenly remembered her meeting with Davinia.

"Damn! I forgot to call my boss."

Dragging her purse onto her lap, she dug through the jumble for her cell phone. The steering wheel, the phone, and a bulldozer rumbling across the road all vied for attention. Sam reached over and tugged the little Motorola out of her hand.

"What's her number?"

"She'll have left her place by now. Her mobile is number three on the recall."

He punched the speed dial button and held the instrument to his ear.

"Try information," Molly instructed when he got no answer. She flung a look over her shoulder and ignored the reflex stomp of Sam's foot when she swung the Trans Am off the road and up the ramp to the interstate. "Get the number for the Visitors' Expo, would you? She might already be there. Her name's Davinia Jacobbson."

When he couldn't raise an answer at the Expo offices, Sam snapped the phone shut and calmly suggested they go by and leave a message for her. The Expo Center was on the way to the Channel Five studios...and Molly was certainly making good time.

Taking his advice and ignoring his gibe, she exited the interstate onto Paradise Road. The Trans Am pulled into the Expo Center's paved lot a few moments later, right behind Davinia's coal black Jag. Her boss slid out of her car, all long, curvy legs and bright orange heels.

"Hey, girl."

"Hi, Davinia." Slamming the convertible's door, Molly hurried across the few yards of asphalt. "I tried to reach you on your car phone."

"Antonio's got it," the blonde replied.

"I can't make the meeting this morning. Something's come up."

Davinia's turquoise eyes slid past her to the man unfolding his long frame from the Trans Am.

"So I see," she purred.

Molly swallowed a groan. She wasn't ready to explain Sam. Or last night. Or her confused second thoughts this morning. When he appeared at her elbow, however, she knew there was no way of avoiding the inevitable.

"Davinia, this is my neighbor, Sam Henderson. Sam, my boss, Davinia Jacobbson."

Sam peeled off his sunglasses and held out his hand. Davinia laid her palm on his, her full mouth tipping upward in unabashed, unrepentant female appreciation.

"Welllll, welllll. Now I understand why Molly opted for sleeping with the enemy instead of camping out in my guest room."

Sam shot the red-faced Molly an amused glance but thankfully didn't let Davinia know just how accurate her comment was.

"We've called a truce," was all he said.

"So she told me." A feline smile curved Davinia's lips. "Now I see why."

Her gaze lingered on Sam's face, but Molly knew darn well she hadn't missed an inch of the rest of his tall, muscled frame. How could she? That soft knit shirt showed off every square centimeter of it. Sure enough, Davinia's smile went up another few watts.

"You'll have to meet Antonio sometime. He's into bodybuilding, too. He's also got great hands, if you're ever in need of them."

Sam looked a bit startled at that revelation, but merely acknowledged the unknown Antonio's talents with a sort of half nod.

"We just stopped by because I couldn't catch you on the phone," Molly interjected hurriedly. "I heard the killer on TV this morning, Davinia. The man who shot Joey the Horse."

"No kidding!"

"We're on our way to the TV station to listen to the news clip again. The detective in charge of the case is meeting us there."

Instant concern darkened her boss's eyes to a deep aqua. "Make sure you watch yourself until this guy is in custody, okay? Or is that why you're along for the ride?" she challenged Sam.

"That's one of the reasons."

She looked as though she wanted to explore that flat, uncompromising comment. Molly didn't give her the opportunity.

"We've got to go. I'll see you later."

"Why don't you both see me later?" Davinia suggested

as they turned away. "Antonio will want to hear this, too. How about my place for dinner? Around seven, if you can make it."

"I'll let you know," Molly called over her shoulder.

Once back in the Trans Am, she threw Sam a quick apology. "Sorry 'bout that. My boss can be a bit overwhelming at times. Please don't feel obligated to take her up on her invitation."

"I don't." He slanted Molly a wry look. "Before I decide one way or another, though, you'd better clue me in. Just what does this Antonio do with his hands?"

A quick smile pushed its way through her tension. "He's a masseur. A good one, according to Davinia, and she should know. They've recently moved in together."

"In that case, I'm game if you are."

"I guess so."

The noticeable lack of enthusiasm in her reply lifted Sam's brows. Obviously, she still hadn't worked her way through those morning-after, what-have-I-started-here doubts. He could sympathize with her. He wasn't sure what he'd gotten into, either. He only knew that he'd come out of the first decent night's sleep that he'd had in months with Molly's scent on his skin and the driving urge to take her flushed face in both hands and kiss her until her toes curled.

Still, he might have pulled back and let their explosive attraction take its own, natural course if that damned campaign ad hadn't put such shock in her eyes again.

Sam still couldn't believe that the sound of Josh Walters's voice had painted that stark fear on her face. Christ! Josh Walters, of all people! Half of him was absolutely convinced that Molly had mistaken the man's voice. The other half...

The other half broke out in a cold sweat at the idea that she might find herself crosswise of the congressman. *If* he had killed someone, and *if* he believed for one minute Molly could finger him, Josh would make a formidable, dangerous adversary.

She had to be wrong.

His hope that a second hearing would shake Molly's conviction died ten minutes after they arrived at Channel Five.

Al Kaplan was waiting for them in the lobby. At his request, the receptionist summoned the station manager. A tall, desiccated chain-smoker, the manager's eyes glowed with the possibility of an exclusive as he led them back to a sound booth. It took him only a few moments to cue the tape to the paid political advertisement that punctuated the morning news show.

"That's him," Molly said fiercely. "That's the man I heard on the phone. I'm sure of it."

She listened to the tape once more, her arms wrapped tight around her waist. Encased from neck to knees in a long, clinging tube of melon-colored fabric, she formed a brilliant splash of color against the racks of equipment. She also, Sam noted with a notch to his breath, looked and sounded utterly convinced. Sam saw a shiver wrack her slender frame when the congressman's voice filled the booth once again.

"Listen to the way he rounds his vowels," she instructed. "He came from the upper Midwest, I'm sure. Wisconsin. Maybe Michigan. And there! Did you catch the way he pronounces 'i-dee-ah.' That's pure New England. The congressman traveled some before he took up residence in Nevada."

"She nailed him!" the station manager exclaimed. "We've got Walters's bio somewhere here on file, but if my memory serves me, he was born in Eau Claire, Wisconsin, and graduated with top honors from Harvard. He settled in Nevada after he married Jessica MacGiver, great-granddaughter of old Jessie MacGiver."

At his listeners' uncomprehending expressions, the manager flapped a hand tipped with brown, nicotine-stained fingers.

"MacGiver was one of the early prospectors in these parts. He discovered the Blue Diamond, which turned out to be the richest silver mines in this state. One of the richest in the country, as a matter of fact. The old man's son diversified into other minerals…copper, tungsten, lithium… and made another killing. Jessica MacGiver inherited a financial empire that would make Bill Gates's pile look like play money."

Kaplan eyed the man thoughtfully. "You know a lot about the family."

"I should." His smoke-wrinkled lips twisted. "MacGiver, Inc., owns this station, plus a half dozen newspapers around the state."

"I bet the congressman doesn't pay much for his political ads," Molly muttered.

The manager re-cued the tape, his pallid eyes zinging from the politician's handsome face to her taut one. "What's Walters done, anyway?"

"We don't know that he's done anything," Kaplan responded evenly.

"Come on," the newsman huffed. "What gives? Are you investigating him for illegal campaign contributions? Misuse of government aircraft?"

"Not at this time, and if I were you," Kaplan added laconically, "I'd be real careful about mentioning our visit here. To anyone. I doubt if Mrs. Walters would appreciate it if one of her employees started unfounded rumors flying about her husband."

With that unsubtle hint, the detective lifted the tape off the mixer. "I'll take this, if you don't mind."

"No, no, of course not."

* * *

After the controlled dimness of the TV station, the blazing morning heat hit Molly like a hammer. She stepped into the searing sunlight, half blinded and wholly shaken by the idea that she might have just identified a member of one of the most powerful families in her adopted state as a murderer.

"What do we do now?" she asked Kaplan, sliding on a pair of oversized sunglasses to shield her eyes from the shimmering white light.

He rubbed his hand across his jowls, his black eyes thoughtful. Obviously Molly's disclosures had had more of an impact on him than he'd let on inside the production booth.

"I'll check out Walters's whereabouts on the night of the murder," he said slowly. "I'll also see if there's any record that he owns a .38 special. I'll get back to you with whatever I find out."

Molly nodded, both disappointed and secretly a little relieved. While she wanted Walters brought to justice, she wasn't looking forward to what came next. She wouldn't mind taking a few days or weeks or even months to get over her jitters before she had to face the politician across a courtroom.

Kaplan started to turn away, then swung back. "Look, Ms. Duncan, you've convinced me that it could have been Walters you heard on the phone that day."

She anticipated the "but" before it came.

"The thing is, the D.A. won't press the case against him without some hard, corroborating evidence."

"And you don't think you'll find that corroborating evidence, do you?"

"No. Number one, a man like Walters is too smart to leave any. Number two..."

"Yes?"

"I've spent some twenty-three years on the Las Vegas

police force. During those years, I've seen supposedly up-standing citizens commit crimes that turned even my stom-ach. Yet I've never heard any snitch or undercover cop even whisper the congressman's name in conjunction with any-thing off-color. No gambling debts, no under-the-table do-nations to his campaign, nothing.''

"So what are you suggesting? That I forget what I heard? Or lie about it?''

"No, of course not. I'm just suggesting you keep quiet until I have a chance to check Walters's whereabouts the night of the murder, that's all. This case has the potential to get real nasty, real fast.''

"Thanks for the warning...I think.''

The detective shrugged and left with another promise to call when and if he turned up any information.

"Why the heck am I starting to feel like the guilty one here?'' she muttered to his back.

She slumped a hip against the Trans Am's fender. In-stantly, hot metal seared through her dress. With a short, pithy oath, she leaped away from the fender and smacked into Sam. He steadied her, his face tight behind the aviator glasses.

"Don't you start, too,'' she warned, pulling free.

She slid into the white convertible, wincing when the baked seats came in contact with the backs of her thighs. A quick twist of the key overcranked the engine, which in turn caused Sam to wince. Feeling even more disgruntled than she had when she slipped out of his arms and headed for the shower earlier this morning, Molly threw him an accus-ing look.

"I know this Walters is a friend of yours.''

"An acquaintance.''

"Whatever.'' Shoving the convertible into reverse, she wheeled it out of the parking slot. "I don't need you to remind me again that I only heard him for a few seconds. Or how powerful he is.''

''I hadn't planned to.''

''And I don't need anyone telling me that whole thing is going to detonate like a nuclear device when the media gets hold of it.''

''No, you don't.'' He slid his sunglasses down his nose and returned her glare. ''Would it do any good to remind you that I'm not the responsible party here, either?''

''You're just as responsible as I am,'' she shot back.

''Come again?''

Molly knew she was being unreasonable. She recognized that her emotions were riding a towering crest from last night and this morning. Still she couldn't hold back a snide little reminder.

''If you hadn't been inflicting Buck Randall on me night after night, I wouldn't have called to complain, I wouldn't have heard a shooting, and I wouldn't be about to finger a U.S. congressman for murder.''

Yeah, Sam thought. And I wouldn't be having dinner tonight with the divine Davinia and her masseur, instead of locking Molly's front door, dragging her down onto the nearest horizontal surface, and kissing her until her bones rattled, which was the only way he could think of at the moment to shake her out of her present snit.

Shoving his glasses back up the bridge of his nose, he tucked his arms across his chest. This was going to be a long day. And an even longer night.

Chapter 9

By the time Molly dropped Sam off at his place and got back to her office at the visitors' bureau, she'd recovered some measure of her equanimity. Thankfully, Davinia hadn't yet returned to the office. Molly's timely meeting with a German trade delegation at the Excalibur Hotel and Casino won her a further reprieve from the third-degree she knew her boss would subject her to.

After the lengthy meeting at the Excalibur, she dialed her voice mail to check her messages. Her stomach knotted when she heard Detective Kaplan's voice asking her to call him as soon as possible. When she reached him at his office, he cut right to the point.

"Walters has an airtight alibi for the night of the murder. He and his wife were the guests of honor at a fund-raiser at the Mirage. According to my sources, the governor, some two thousand assorted well-heeled contributors and an entire galaxy of Vegas's resident entertainers attended the bash."

Caught between relief and an instinctive need to refute

the evidence, Molly stared through the plastic shield of the phone booth at Excalibur's version of the haunted forest outside Camelot. Moss draped from shadowy overhead limbs, and a gray-bearded Merlin wandered the black-and-red carpeted floor, hawking puppets to a group of shy, smiling Japanese tourists.

"What time did the fund-raiser end?" she asked, frowning at Merlin.

"According to my sources, the entertainment ran longer than anticipated. The party started to break up just past one, but Walters and his wife lingered until most of the guests departed the scene. I've verified that he was at the Mirage until 2:00 a.m."

"The shooting occurred just after one," Molly murmured.

"We're still checking the gun records, but it doesn't look like the congressman is our killer."

"No," she conceded slowly, "it doesn't."

Molly hung up a moment later. Doubt swarmed inside her head like annoying little gnats. She would have staked everything she owned on the certainty that she'd heard Joshua Walters at Joey the Horse's apartment. Unless the congressman had a twin or he'd taken a few lessons from Sigfried and Roy in magic and illusions, she must have heard wrong.

She was still puzzling over the question of how Walters could have been in two places at the same time when she drove home a little past five that evening. The sight of the garage next door yawning open and Sam bent over the fender of the Mustang pushed the congressman to the periphery of her mind. Instant, deliciously carnal thoughts leaped to center stage.

Okay, she told herself as Sam unbent. All right. The dizzy loop her stomach just performed was perfectly natural, a normal, healthy woman's response to those thigh-hugging jeans and that stretch of white T-shirt across his broad chest. She didn't have to panic. She wasn't in love with him or anything. Only in lust.

Very much in lust, she admitted as he wiped his hands on a rag. She braked the Trans Am to a halt, waiting while he crossed the driveway. His dark brown hair gleamed with sweat at the temples, and the damp patches on his T-shirt had Molly's hands clenching on the steering wheel. But it was his face that twisted her heart.

His cheekbones jutted in stark relief, stretching his tanned skin into a thin membrane. His mouth formed a narrow slash. And his eyes... Molly could have cried at the tight, white lines fanning from their corners.

"Bad day?" she asked softly.

"I've had worse."

The clipped response warned her that he didn't want any sympathy. That and the hard line to his jaw.

"I talked to Kaplan a while ago," she said, burying her ache for Sam in the casual information. "Your friend Walters was the guest of honor at a fund-raiser the night of the murder. He didn't leave the gala until an hour or so after the shooting."

His expression didn't soften. If anything, it torqued up another degree. He was hurting, Molly knew. Badly. Her heart twisted for him.

"I won't say that I'm not relieved," he told her. "Josh Walters has done a helluva lot for this state and for the country. I like the man. I didn't like the idea that he's a murderer."

"I don't particularly like it, either. Look, Sam, do you mind if we take a rain check on dinner with Davinia and Antonio? We, uh, didn't get much sleep last night and I'm whipped."

He skimmed her face with tight, shuttered eyes. Heat rose in her cheeks. She didn't know which was worse. Remembering the strenuous activities that had precluded sleep last night or letting Sam believe that she didn't want to repeat them.

She did, she acknowledged. With every hormone in her body. But not until she'd worked through her own confused reaction to this man. And certainly not until he could look at her without pain gouging deep grooves on either side of his mouth.

"I'll call Davinia and beg off. She'll understand."

That was the understatement of the week. Her boss would not only understand, she'd put her own spin on things. No doubt she'd chuckle evilly and remind Molly that she and Sam needed to come up for air sometime.

Sam cocked his head slowly, as if wary of moving too fast. "Backing off, Molly?"

"A little," she admitted, sliding her hands back and forth on the steering wheel. "I think we might need to slow things down."

"Why?"

The simple question demanded the truth.

"I rushed into one relationship and ended up couchless." Her smile invited him to understand. "I don't want to rush into another one with a man I was about to declare all-out war on a week ago. Let's take this slow, Sam, and see what develops."

Sam told himself that she was right. Between the sharp spikes shooting into the back of his skull, he acknowledged that it wouldn't hurt to slow things down just a little. The problem was, he was afraid he'd gone beyond slow. He'd passed that point at Caesars Palace, when he'd glanced across the booth and watched Molly pretend to enjoy an art form she despised. Or maybe when she giggled helplessly and collapsed against him in the driver's seat of the Mustang. For sure when she shimmied and shivered and welcomed him into her body.

Sam had spent most of the day thinking about what he wanted from and with Molly Duncan, and it wasn't slow. All morning he'd tried to figure out how to shield her from the ugliness of this damned murder, which could have gotten even uglier real quick. A good chunk of the afternoon went to wondering just how she'd take to being shielded, from murder or from anything else.

Then the first distress signals had started. Low in his skull. Blunt at first. Gradually sharper and sharper. He'd worked out on the gym until his muscles screamed. Finally, he'd buried himself in the dim sanctuary under the Mustang's hood. Now, he fought to keep a rusty edge from his voice as he forced himself to agree with Molly.

"You're right. Maybe we'd better back off for a while." His mouth twisted in what he hoped was a smile. "For tonight, anyway. See you."

Molly couldn't let him walk away like this. Shoving the Trans Am into park, she pushed the door open and slid out.

"Sam! Wait."

He swung back to her, so stiff and taut he might have been carved from stone. Lava rock crunched under her soles as she closed the short distance between them. Her heart aching, she laid a hand on his arm.

"Would it help if I came over for a while? I could talk to you while you work out."

The muscles under her fingertips flinched. His eyes turned to slate.

"No, thanks."

"Sam, I can see you're hurting. Let me help. As a friend…or a pesky, interfering neighbor, if nothing else."

He hesitated, then lifted a hand to cup her cheek. His thumb brushed her lower lip.

"Thanks for the offer, neighbor, but you look as whipped as I feel. Get some sleep, then we'll take this discussion up where we left off."

The way his thumb teased her lip suggested that they'd take up more than the discussion. The kiss he dropped on her mouth confirmed it.

Molly watched him bury himself under the hood of his toy again. Feeling more confused than ever, she reclaimed her car and hit the garage opener. The door rumbled up, then down, closing out the slanting desert sunlight, the heat and Sam Henderson.

Five hours later, she blew out a long, irritated puff of air and let the bedroom shade drop.

Dammit! Sleep pulled at her like a high-powered magnet. The nest she'd made in the bedcovers sang out her name. She needed sleep. She craved total oblivion.

Even more, she craved the man next door. Her head could enumerate every reason why she should stick to her determination to put some space between them. Her body refused to listen to them. Her heart... Well, her heart bled every time she climbed out of bed and padded to the window to check the light spilling out of Sam's great room window.

She sank down into the nest again. Drawing up her legs, she plopped her chin on her knees. The facial slathered across her nose and cheeks cracked a bit. A flake or two drifted down to settle on the pale green duvet.

Sam didn't want her hovering over him. He'd made that clear enough. He didn't even want her talking to him. As grim as he'd looked earlier, he probably didn't even want to...

The shrill ring of the phone had her jumping half out of her Syracuse University sleep shirt. She waited until her breath returned, then reached across the covers to snatch up the receiver.

"Hello?"

"I saw your light. Are you all right?"

Sam's deep drawl sent a slide of relief through Molly. He sounded less strung out, almost relaxed.

"I'm fine," she murmured, hugging her knees. "I just couldn't sleep. How about you? Are you okay?"

"Not quite okay, but better than before."

"I'm glad," she said simply.

A small silence spun out between them, easy and companionable. The sexual tension was still there. It simmered just below the surface, like a rich, bubbling broth just removed from the burner. A layer of the friendship Sam had rejected earlier lay atop it right now. Molly had to admit the sex was better, much better, but this would do nicely.

He broke the stillness first. "Josh Walters's campaign ad came on again earlier this evening. I taped it, and watched it while I worked out."

"And?"

He hesitated. "And I remembered a small incident, nothing significant, but it got me thinking."

Molly sat up, her pulse quickening. "What kind of an incident?"

"Remember I told you I took the congressman up for a flight a few years ago?"

"I remember." A dry note crept into her voice. "As I recall, that came up right after you all but accused me of hitting the Coors again for suggesting Walters could be a murderer."

"Yeah, well, that might have been when it was."

Molly settled for that almost-apology. "So what was this incident you remembered?"

"I didn't see it," he cautioned. "I only heard about it second or third hand."

"Okay, okay, I got the picture." She scrunched up her nose impatiently, dislodging a small storm of brown flakes. "What happened?"

"Walters hit on one of the lieutenants at the base."

Molly shoved her knees under her and surged upright. "No kidding?"

"I shrugged the story off at the time because…"

She jumped in, excited and indignant. "Because you couldn't believe your paragon of virtue, your defender of truth, justice and the American way could step off the narrow path of righteousness."

"Because the lieutenant in question is well known around the squadron for her ability to lay a first-class lip lock on the unsuspecting and unwary," he finished dryly.

"Oh!" Chagrin and curiosity fought a short, fierce battle. Curiosity won. "Did she lay one on you, Sam?"

Molly could have sworn she heard him grinning.

"We're talking about Josh Walters here," he reminded her. "I thought I'd go out to the base tomorrow and, uh, feel this lieutenant out a little more."

She refused to rise to that obvious bait. "Let me know what you find out."

"I will." His voice dropped to a slow, rough caress. "'Night, Mol."

"'Night, Sam."

With the sun beating down mercilessly from a cloudless sky and the dust from a fitful breeze stirring lazy swirls across the desert, Sam drove out to Nellis Air Force Base the following afternoon.

Located eight miles northeast of Las Vegas, the sprawling military reservation covered more than eleven thousand acres. In addition to the base proper, restricted test air space ate up another three million acres of desert, with five million more set aside for shared use with civilian aircraft. One of the busiest air facilities in the world, Nellis was home to the Air Warfare Center, the USAF Thunderbirds, and a host of composite strike forces containing Army, Navy, Marine and Air Force elements. Sam felt its pulsing vitality the moment he drove through the front gate and returned the guard's snappy salute.

The forest green Blazer he drove every day in lieu of his cherished Mustang slowed to a crawl, its powerful engine growling a protest to the base's twenty-five mile per hour speed limit. Behind the row of tan-and-brown hangars, twin-tailed jets thundered down the runway and streaked into the air. The gut-wrenchingly familiar scent of jet engine exhaust drifted across the shimmering afternoon heat. Sam drew it into his lungs like another man might the scent of a woman.

He swung off the main boulevard and headed for the maintenance complex in an isolated sector of the base, where First Lieutenant Patricia Donovitch supervised a crew of highly skilled munitions handlers. After a long drive along the perimeter road, Sam pulled up at the gate to the restricted area and waited while the guard put in a call to the lieutenant.

The young security guard returned a moment later to inform him that she'd be with him as soon as her crew finished loading a batch of missiles. Sam climbed back in the Blazer and stretched out his legs. He squinted through his gold-framed sunglasses at the F-15 soaring into the sky at the far end of the runway. From this distance, the fully armed fighter seemed to move at a slower speed than the six hundred miles an hour Sam knew she was capable of.

He waited, mentally bracing himself for the kick to the gut he knew was coming. It slammed into him just as the sleek, twin-tailed jet spiraled into a sky so vast and so blue that a poet might describe it as a playground for the gods.

Christ, he missed it. All of it. Strapping himself into a cockpit and hearing the first whine of the engines revving. Wing tips tilting into the face of the sun. The soaring climb and dizzying drop. The brotherhood of arms, stripped to its barest essentials. Even the endless flight safety briefings and boring staff meetings. Would he ever get back to it?

The F-15 disappeared into a puffy white cloud, and Sam admitted the truth.

He wouldn't be climbing back into a cockpit in the foreseeable future. It was time he accepted that fact and got on with the rest of his life.

He was still sprawled in the Blazer, staring through the open window at the puff of cloud, when a dusty maintenance vehicle passed through the gate and pulled up nose-to-nose with the Blazer. Pat Donovitch spilled out, cheerful, bubbly, and packing her own load of lethal armament under her baggy battle fatigue shirt, Even with her thick curls stuffed under a navy ball cap and her feet encased in dusty web boots, she exuded an earthy sensuality that had made her so popular at the Officers' Club on Friday and Saturday nights.

"Hey, Major Henderson. How's the head?"

Sam shouldered open the Blazer's door. "Still there, Donovitch. How're you doing?"

Her lively face twisted into a wry grimace. "As well as can be expected with Red Flag kicking off in two days. You remember how that is."

"Yeah, I do."

Sam shoved aside vivid memories of those grueling training exercises when the "red" forces assigned to Nellis attacked and tried to prevent "blue" forces—U.S. and NATO units from all over the world—from penetrating their target. The simulated air battles in the skies over southern Nevada honed the Air Force's fighting edge and wrung every last ounce of emotion and energy from all participants, air crews and support personnel alike.

"I know you're busy, Pat. I won't keep you. I just wanted to ask you about Josh Walters."

"Congressman Walters?"

Sam caught the surprise that flickered in her blue eyes, followed instantly by a shadow of wariness. Her bright, cheerful smile dimmed. He hooked a thumb in his jeans, trying to think of any way to wrap the next question up in clean linen. There wasn't any.

"I remember hearing your name linked to the congressman's a year or so ago. I know it's none of my business and you can tell me to go to hell if you want to, but I need to know if there was anything more to that rumor than squadron scuttlebutt."

The lieutenant's face lost all trace of its former open friendliness. "You're right, Major. It's none of your business. Look, I have to go. We've got another load of SAMS to arm and…"

"I wouldn't ask if it wasn't important."

His quiet comment cut through her tumbled excuses. Even more wary, she threw him a nervous glance. "Important how?"

"A friend of mine thinks she heard Walters's voice in connection with a crime."

"What kind of a crime?"

It was Sam's turn to hesitate. He was reaching here, really reaching. He didn't want to start rumors flying around the base, or slander a man he'd always respected. Yet he couldn't discount Molly's on-target identification of Walters, any more than he could dismiss this sudden reluctance to talk on the part of a young woman not particularly known for her reticence.

"A man was murdered a week ago, a small-time drug dealer and occasional pimp."

"Murdered!"

Donovitch sucked in a quick breath. Under the bill of her ball cap, her face went stark white.

"There's no proof that Walters was involved," Sam said quickly. "I just came out to talk to you on a hunch. What can you tell me about the man?"

The lieutenant rubbed her palms down the sides of her fatigue pants. She looked everywhere but at Sam.

"Not much. He came through on a tour of our facilities and sort of, well, singled me out. He asked me what I thought about women in combat, and I got in a few good shots before his handlers hustled him off."

Sam kept his voice even. "Rumor has it he did more than just single you out during his tour."

"Yeah, well, he called me."

"At work?"

"At home."

Obviously on edge, she drew a line in the sand with the toe of her boot. Sam waited, his own edginess growing by the second.

"He said he wanted to hear more on my views about women warriors," she continued slowly, reluctantly. "He suggested that we have dinner. He also suggested that I keep it quiet, as the Air Force wasn't exactly pro-women-in-combat at the time, but, well, I was flattered. I guess I mentioned the call to a friend or two."

That's all it would take, Sam knew. The jungle beat would pick up that juicy morsel instantly and broadcast it all across the base. Donovitch confirmed his supposition with a disgusted shake of her head.

"Somehow word of the call got back to the General. From there, the tale shot straight up the chain to the Legislative Liaison office at the Pentagon."

"Ouch!"

"Ouch doesn't begin to describe it. The air staff went bananas. Some poor captain was even tasked to prepare issues papers for me to use in discussions with the congressman. My commander passed them to me with instructions to make sure that I understood the official Air Force position. God, what a mess!"

There was more. Sam heard it in her voice. Saw it in the

way her gaze slid sideways and fixed on the scrub beside the road.

"What did Walters have to say about the whole thing?"

Still she wouldn't look at him. "Publicly, he dropped it right in my lap. In that easy, cultured way of his, he implied that the little lieutenant had her own agenda about women in the military and was certainly going to extreme lengths to press it."

"And privately?"

She hesitated so long Sam didn't think she'd answer. Finally, she lifted her face. Defiance and an unmistakable note of fear threaded her voice.

"Privately, he called me at home again and warned me to keep my mouth shut. If I didn't..." She swallowed. "If I didn't, he had friends who would make me sorry...even sorrier than the last whore who tried to embarrass him."

The Blazer churned up a trail of dust. Sticking to the speed limit more by instinct than by conscious effort, Sam tooled the vehicle along the perimeter road. He barely noticed the two-ship flight of fighters lifting off at the end of the runway. The past no longer pulled at him. His whole being was focused on Molly Duncan and the immediate future.

His eyes slitted behind his sunglasses, Sam put Lieutenant Donovitch's short, bitter tale through a dozen different spins. With every twist and tumble, his lingering doubts that Molly had pegged the right man as the killer lessened and his uneasiness grew.

Damn! Josh Walters! Sam's knuckles whitened on the leather-wrapped steering wheel. Most of Nevada believed the congressman would breeze into the governorship after his next term in the House of Representatives. Even now, he was being touted as a possible presidential candidate after a stint as governor. Street-smart and highly educated, Wal-

ters possessed the necessary charm to propel him right to
the top. The fact that he'd married into big money certainly
hadn't diminished his prospects, either. He was a shoo-in
for re-election and a luminous political future…unless a
stubborn, green-eyed blonde with an ear for accents and a
splatter of freckles across her nose fingered him for murder.

The skin at the back of Sam's neck tightened. The thought
of Molly standing in Josh Walters's way to the governorship
and perhaps the presidency made his pulse skitter and stop,
then restart with a kick.

He took a quick look at the functional, stainless steel
watch strapped to his wrist. He'd head downtown and talk
to Kaplan, he decided. Then he'd wing by the Las Vegas
Convention Center and see what time Molly got off work.
Maybe he'd wait and follow her home. They might even,
he thought with a sudden, swift stab of need, pick up where
they'd left off yesterday, before Molly's morning-after
doubts and Josh Walters's campaign ad had complicated
matters considerably.

It was only after he'd left a thoughtful Detective Kaplan
that Sam realized his protective instincts had kicked into
overdrive. Keeping his pesky, irritating, seductive neighbor
in his bed for the foreseeable future now ranked a distant
but compelling second to keeping her safe. He was still
thinking about his priorities when he pulled into the parking
lot that skirted the visitors' bureau. He spotted Molly's
sporty white Trans Am a few moments later…at almost the
same time he spotted a hulking figure in a black collarless
shirt and gray sharkskin suit jimmying the lock on her car
door.

Chapter 10

"**W**hat the hell?"

With a squeal of brakes, Sam whipped the Blazer into park. He lunged out of the vehicle and across the asphalt at the same moment the individual bent over the Trans Am spun around.

If Sam had harbored any doubts about the man's intentions, the way he dropped into a fighter's crouch resolved them instantly. He was big, a real bruiser, and a street fighter. Sam didn't know whether he carried a weapon, but if he moved one of his hands a half inch toward his ankle or the inside of his suit coat, Sam would push his face into the asphalt. He approached slowly, keeping those huge, balled fists in his line of sight while he held the gorilla's gaze with his own.

"You want to tell me why you're trying to get in this car?"

Under a cap of glistening black curls, the intruder's narrowed eyes took his opponent's measure.

"Perhaps I shall tell you…if you tell me of what business it is to you?"

Sam didn't have Molly's ear for accents, but even he could tell the bruiser didn't hail from around these parts. What's more, someone had hand-tailored his double-breasted jacket to make it lie so smoothly over those bulging biceps. The suit must have set its wearer back a thousand bucks or more.

The realization that he wasn't dealing with a local punk raised the hairs on the back of Sam's neck. A dozen possibilities rifled through his mind, not the least of which was that Josh Walters had hired some big-time muscle to take care of Molly. The lieutenant's disclosures had planted more than a seed of doubt, he realized grimly. Adrenaline shooting undiluted through his veins, he curled his hands into fists.

"It's my business," he growled, "because I say it is."

"I think, perhaps, I do not like this way you talk with me."

"Tough."

"Tough?"

The curly-haired behemoth chewed on that for a moment. When he'd finished ruminating, delight sprang into his calf brown eyes.

"You wish to have the fight with me? *Bueno!*"

It didn't look too *bueno* from where Sam stood. The intruder outweighed him by some twenty or thirty pounds and had arms like giant sequoias. Sam had survived four older brothers, though, and every self-defense and escape and evasion course the Air Force had to offer. He knew how to fight dirty.

"We are of a size, you and me!" the brawny man exclaimed. "Only wait while I take off this so wonderful coat which Davinia has bought for me. Then we shall have the sport, yes?"

While his eager opponent attacked the two buttons on his sharkskin jacket, Sam eased out of his own half crouch.

"Davinia bought you that suit? Davinia Jacobbson?"

"Yes, she is most generous." Still smiling, he flexed an Olympic-sized set of muscles under the collarless black silk shirt. "I have not had the sport since I come to this country. Do we follow the rules, or do we most simply see who goes down first?"

Blood still rushed through Sam's veins at the speed of sound. The worry that had built during the drive in from Nellis and spiked right off the charts when he'd spotted this hulk fiddling with the door to Molly's car still knotted his gut. He craved an outlet for his tension, had pumped himself for knuckle-splitting violence, but a free-for-all with Davinia's lover in the Convention Center's parking lot wasn't the release he was looking for. He was about to tell the man so when a scolding feminine contralto floated across the parking lot.

"Hey, sweetcakes, you promised to get the car opened and the air-conditioning going before Molly and I..."

The svelte blonde halted, her turquoise eyes widening in undisguised pleasure.

"Hel-lo, Major. How convenient! Molly just called your place to see if you wanted to cash in that rain check you took last night. I see you've met Antonio."

"Not officially," Sam drawled.

"You are friends? You and Davinia?"

"He's Molly's neighbor," the blonde put in. "Major Sam Henderson."

"The one she fights with, then does not fight with?"

"Something like that."

He put out a hand, which the curly-haired Hercules regarded with undisguised disappointment.

"So, we do not have the sport?"

"Maybe next time," Sam replied, trying not to wince as his almost-opponent ground his bones together.

Molly's boss wrapped both her hands around her lover's arm and rubbed up against it like a cat.

"Can you join us, Major? We just finished the teleconference from hell and decided to let 'Tonio treat us to margaritas at the Hard Rock Cafe. Molly's on her way down. She'll want to hear about your trip out to Nellis. So do I, incidentally."

Sam fought to keep a frown from sketching across his brow. "She told you about that?"

"About Josh Walters, you mean?" Davinia waved a perfectly manicured set of nails. "She was pretty closemouthed about his identity at first, but I spent a few years as an attorney in a former life. I broke her down during cross-examination."

Before Sam could react to that, she organized matters with cool efficiency.

"Oh, good. Here comes Molly now. 'Tonio, you drive her car. I'll take mine, and she can go with the Major."

"I could not open the door of Molly's car," Antonio confessed with a shamefaced look. He uncurled his beefy paw to display a key ring. "I had not the right key."

"It's this one, sweetie. This one."

With a kiss that left her lover grinning foolishly, Davinia informed her surprised employee that they'd see her and Sam at the Hard Rock and climbed into her own two-seater Jaguar.

Molly looked from the Jag to the departing Trans Am to the Blazer planted sideways across three parking slots, its engine humming. Her brows lifting, she turned to Sam.

"Did I miss something here?"

"Almost."

Still pumped from his near brawl, Sam shoved a hand through his hair. He couldn't remember the last time he'd felt this kind of twisting, mounting tension. He had to get himself under control.

The sunlight painting Molly's hair to a nimbus of gold waves didn't help matters, either. Nor did the long, silky legs displayed to perfection under the thigh-skimming, hip-hugging tube of bronze knit that passed for a dress. How the hell did she bend over in that thing without getting arrested?

The puzzle presented all kinds of interesting solutions. With a wrench, Sam pulled his thoughts from acrobatics to actualities.

"It seems we're going to the Hard Rock Cafe."

"So I gathered." She accompanied him to the Blazer. "What are you doing at the Convention Center, Sam?"

"I was out at the base and came by to..."

To what? To report on his conversation with Lieutenant Donovitch? To counter the uneasiness that was knifing into him a little deeper with each passing hour? To satisfy a pressing need to keep this woman safe?

"To talk to you," he finished with a shrug. "And to Davinia, apparently."

He'd forgotten Molly's keen ear. Picking up on the underlying criticism in his offhand comment, she shot him a quick look.

"Do you have a problem with talking to Davinia?"

He had a big problem with it if the conversation resulted in the same kind of brushfire that Pat Donovitch's casual comment had sparked on base. Or the same threat to Molly.

"Kaplan's kept the station manager at Channel Five on a tight leash," Sam pointed out. "He doesn't want to spook the congressman or send the media into a feeding frenzy unless or until he's got something concrete to work with. I just hope Davinia can keep this between herself and sweet-cakes."

"She can," Molly retorted, flicking the man beside her an irritated glance.

She wasn't about to admit that she hadn't intended to spill every detail to Davinia. She'd tried, she'd really tried, to follow Kaplan's advice and keep the identity of the killer to herself for the time being. Dodging Lawyer Jacobbson's barrage of questions required far more stamina and skill than Molly possessed, however.

Of course, telling Davinia all also meant telling Antonio when he stopped by the office a while ago, but both parties had promised to keep the stunning revelation to themselves. Molly was sure she could trust them to hold to that promise. Sam, evidently, had his doubts.

She slanted him another quick glance. What was with him this afternoon, anyway? He didn't have that tight, white-lipped look that signaled one of his headaches, but his voice had a rough edge she hadn't heard since the night she sent the police to his house. He gripped the wheel with a curled fist, and his long, contoured body radiated a coiled tension. Molly had the sense of a sleek predator held rigidly in check. Quiet. Powerful. Deadly.

"What did you find out at Nellis?" she asked in an attempt to bridge the prickly silence.

His jaw notched. In an even voice that didn't quite match the sudden gridwork of lines at the corner of his mouth, he related his short conversation with Lieutenant Lip-Lock, as Molly had privately tagged her.

She was still trying to grasp the ramifications of the lieutenant's sobering story when Sam ushered her into the Hard Rock Cafe.

A symphony of sounds greeted them. Bruce Springsteen poured from speakers mounted on every wall. Early happy hour patrons shouted to be heard over the pounding beat.

Glasses clinked, waiters called in orders, and Davinia hailed them from a back booth.

Weaving her way through the noise and an assortment of rock-and-roll memorabilia that included platinum records, leather jackets and Bill Haley's motorcycle, Molly felt a momentary preference for Buck Randall's softer, if somewhat more nasal ballads. It faded, thank goodness, almost instantly. Over frosted margaritas and a gargantuan platter of green chili and chicken nachos, Sam related the gist of his conversation with the lieutenant. Davinia's eyes gleamed.

"So despite his squeaky-clean record and well-publicized family life, our boy has a history of hitting on nubile young women. This opens up all kinds of interesting possibilities."

Molly swirled the straw through her slushy margarita. She'd had time to think of a few possibilities, too, and she wouldn't describe them as interesting. Scary came a whole lot closer.

"Maybe Walters employed Joey's services as a procurer," Davinia mused. "Maybe Joey tried a little blackmail to supplement his income. Maybe the congressman decided he wasn't going to play that game."

Sam draped an arm across the back of the booth and stretched out his legs. Wedged in beside him as she was, Molly felt his hip and thigh connect with hers.

"We can 'maybe' this all night," he said slowly, "but that doesn't mitigate the fact that Walters has an alibi for the night of the murder."

"An alibi backed up by two-thousand-or-so assorted individuals," Molly muttered, stabbing at her drink.

"Hey, this is Vegas," her boss tossed out. "Two thousand people see Elvis reincarnated every night on stage at the Riviera. Thousands more watch white tigers disappear in a puff of smoke. Who's to say Walters didn't stage a theatrical appearance, then slip out when no one was looking?"

"*Quiera...*"

"Just a minute, sweetie." Patting Antonio absently on the thigh, Davinia focused her attention on the couple opposite her. "There's got to be a way to shake Walters's alibi."

"Assuming he's the killer."

"He is," Molly stated, sending Sam a glare.

Davinia tapped a nail on the table. Antonio started to speak once more, but she beat him to it.

"What we need to do is shake the man up, get him to..."

"What we need to do is let Kaplan handle this," Sam interrupted, making no effort to hide his scowl. "Josh Walters is too smart to let himself be shaken out of anything."

"*Quiera...*"

Shushing the hulking Spaniard with a wave of one hand, Davinia pounced on Sam's reply.

"Wrong! He made a big mistake when he called that lieutenant. What if she'd gotten him on tape? If he starts hearing rumors that he's under investigation and gets rattled, he may very well make another."

"I don't see it," Sam said stubbornly, shaking his head.

"He threatened this lieutenant, or so she claims. He might call Molly and try to intimidate her, too."

Or he may decide to pay her another visit, she thought with a shudder. She had no proof the same person she'd heard on the phone had slipped into her house the next night. Only her intuition, which, unfortunately, was working overtime at the moment.

"He doesn't have to call me," she said glumly. "He's got two-thousand-plus witnesses who can swear to his whereabouts at the time of the murder."

The patient Spaniard finally thrust himself into the conversation. "This *politico,* he is well known here, no? Like the movie star?"

"Very like the movie star," Davinia replied absently.

Antonio caught her chin and snared her attention by the simple expedient of tugging her face around to him.

"Listen to me, *quiera*. Someone who does Elvis, why could he not also do this Joshua Walters?"

"Huh?"

Grinning at her less than incisive reply, he dropped a kiss on her nose. "I have been to these shows on the Strip. I have seen the Elvis and the Julio Iglesias and the Marilyn Monroe. Why could someone who does the so-talented, so-handsome Julio not also impre...impro..."

"Impersonate Joshua Walters," Davinia finished for him in awe. "Ho-ly crappoli, you just might have something there!"

Her jaw sagging, Molly stared at her boss and the brawny masseur. She couldn't quite believe what she was hearing, or that Antonio's bizarre idea actually made sense. What had happened to the nice, serene world she'd created for herself here in Vegas? It was now populated by murdered pimps. Cold-blooded killers. Maybe even a professional impersonator who stood up for a U.S. congressman at a campaign fund-raising gala attended by half of Nevada!

That was insane.

But then...

Sanity had slipped away from her the night she made that blasted phone call. No, she corrected with an accusing glare at the man beside her, it had started slipping away the day Sam moved in next door.

If he caught her look, he ignored it. Like Davinia, he was staring at Antonio. Doubt, incredulity, and, finally, outright amusement chased across his face.

"I'd say that's as good a theory as any," he told the other man.

Antonio smugly crunched down on a nacho. Davinia grinned and flashed Molly a look of pure, feminine delight.

"Brains and brawn, girl, brains and brawn. How in the world did we get so lucky?"

By the time Molly and Sam parted from the others, her head whirled with the effects of two potent margaritas, the theories Davinia had tossed out with ruthless enthusiasm, and the press of Sam's hard, muscled thigh against hers in the narrow booth.

She walked into the night beside Sam, trying to decide which bothered her more…her body's clamoring insistence that she forget about slowing things down between them or his insistence that they stay out of the murder investigation and let Kaplan handle it.

Unlocking the Trans Am, she slid onto its leather seat. The trapped heat only added to her unsettled, disgruntled feeling. She missed the pull of the wind in her hair as she drove home through the gathering twilight, the Blazer's lights reflected in her rearview mirror. She'd put the top up this morning for the first time in ages. She'd even taken to locking her car doors.

As it had in the restaurant, a surge of resentment swept through Molly. Balling her fist, she pounded the steering wheel. Dammit, she'd come to Nevada to regain control of her life. She'd taken such joy in owning her first home, in wandering through the empty rooms and visualizing how she'd fill them. Now she'd barricaded herself behind a security system that could keep Fort Knox impregnable. She jumped at every shadow. She'd even gotten nervous about leaving the convertible's top down.

To heck with it! She was tired of sitting back and…and waiting. She wanted to *do* something.

Pulling into the garage, Molly grabbed her purse, slid out of the car, and hit the remote. A quick duck under the rumbling door brought her out into the cooling twilight. She waited while Sam tucked the Blazer into its berth next to his Mustang.

"Do you still have the tape you made last night?"

The Blazer's door thudded shut. "Yes."

"I'd like to take another look at it."

A frown settled in his gray eyes again as he ushered her inside. The house echoed only unbroken stillness. Tonight, the gleaming steel gym that took up most of his great room stood silent. No black weights rattled and clanged. No lonely lament wailed from the radio. Sam wasn't suffering tonight, thank goodness, even if he retrieved the cassette from the VCR and moved toward her with a slash between his dark brows. He tapped the videocassette against his palm.

"You sure you want to watch this again, Molly?"

"I'm sure."

"Why?"

She spun away, fighting a new surge of irritation. She didn't like having to explain herself, particularly when she knew Sam wouldn't agree with what she wanted to do. For an uncomfortable moment, she felt as though she were back in Boston again. Scowling at the jungle of smooth steel bars and beams that blocked her way, she took a deep breath and turned back to Sam.

"There was a trailer at the end of the ad. It listed dates and locations for a series of public forums Walters is attending to meet with his constituency."

"I saw it."

"I'm going to go to one of those sessions. Maybe if he sees me or hears my name, he'll know that I've recognized him and…"

"It's too risky," he said flatly. "I won't let you expose yourself to that kind of danger."

Her chin snapped up. "I don't recall asking for your permission."

Cursing his blunder, Sam knew he had to act fast if he wanted to recover. He tossed aside the cassette and moved to the gym. His hands folded around the well-worn grips of the crossbar.

"Bad word choice, Mol. Of course you don't need my permission, but I hope you'll take my advice. Let Kaplan handle this."

Let me protect you.

The words hammered in Sam's chest, worked their way to his throat. She wasn't ready to hear them, though. Anger stained her cheeks and sparked in her eyes. Struggling to keep his protective instincts on a short leash, he tried a different tact.

"You don't know Walters."

Sam could see at once that he'd pushed the wrong button.

"And you do?" Her eyes flashed green fire. "I know it's hard for you to believe that your sainted Josh Walters could kill someone in cold blood...."

"Dammit, you've convinced me, Molly. That's why it's pure idiocy for you to waltz into one of those forums and confront the man."

Without meaning to, he crowded her back until her calves hit the narrow leather bench. Or maybe he'd meant to crowd her. Hell, at this point, Sam wasn't sure of anything except a fierce headache was starting to pound in his temples, only this one had Molly Duncan's name written all over it.

"Look," she began coolly, "I'm not some lieutenant under your command, and I don't respond well to orders cloaked as advice. I appreciate your concern, but..."

"Concern, hell!"

Sam had passed concern the moment she blasted through her damned hedge and tumbled into his arms. He'd passed lust, too, although he didn't quite know when. At this particular moment, he hovered somewhere between irritation and love, which scared the hell out of him. His savage thoughts must have shown in his face. Her eyes narrowing, she issued a warning.

"I think you'd better back off, Henderson."

It was too late for that. It was probably too late the first time she flaked all over him.

"Not this time, Duncan."

"Excuse me?"

"I backed off last night. I'm not retreating again."

"Oh?"

She folded her arms across her chest. Against the superstructure of polished steel, she was all bronze knit and angry female.

"You're treading shaky ground here, Major. Real shaky."

"I got that impression," he drawled.

"Let's get something straight. I left Boston to get away from a man who tried to dictate my choices. I don't want or need another one trying the same thing here in Vegas."

The idea that she would lump him in the same category as the wimp who let her walk out of his life without a backward glance rubbed Sam exactly the wrong way.

"So what are you going to do if I press you too hard or too soon, sweetheart? Run away again?"

The soft taunt cut through the air between them, as alive and explosive as electricity.

Molly sucked in a swift breath. He wasn't talking about Walters now, or her determination to attend one of the congressman's forums. With a seismic movement she'd somehow missed, the ground had suddenly shifted.

This was between her and Sam. About her and Sam. Despite his gruff refusal to back off, he wouldn't force her. Molly knew that, as surely as she sensed that he'd tumble her down onto the leather bench behind her if she so much as blinked.

Still simmering, she tilted her head back. His tanned skin

stretched across his cheekbones. The edge of his jaw could have cut glass. But it wasn't pain that darkened his eyes, she saw with a lurch. It was hunger, raw and primitive, and a fierceness that skidded right past lust into an emotion that made Molly's heart trip.

Her anger fractured, breaking into smaller shards that splintered away. In its place came an answering emotion so strong that she didn't try to fight it anymore.

"No, Sam," she said at last. "I'm not running away. This time I'm standing my ground."

Chapter 11

Molly didn't remain standing for long.

At her soft declaration, Sam's eyes flared with a satisfaction that looked possessive and felt primal. He moved a step closer, still gripping the crossbar, the muscles in his arms bunching.

Molly felt caged by the steel around her. Claimed by the man before her. Trapped in a way that should have panicked her, but didn't. Much. He must have sensed her brief flutter of uncertainty. His voice dropped to a rough cured leather.

"If it makes you feel any better about what's about to happen between us, you can have my couch. I don't use it, anyway."

Her hands trembled with the need to slide them up, over those wide shoulders, around his neck.

"What do you use, Sam?"

He smiled, a slow slash of male amusement that had Molly's nails digging into her palms.

"Upstairs, I use the bed. Downstairs, the easy chair in the corner. The floor. The..."

"Okay, okay, I get the picture."

She drew in a shaky breath. He was so close. Too close. She could feel his heat. See the tendon that corded in his neck like rawhide thongs. She made one last stand before surrendering completely to the desire that raced through her like summer wildfire.

"Just remember that I don't take orders very well, Major."

"I'll keep that in mind."

"No military dictatorships or heavy-handed tactics allowed on either side."

"Got it. Anything else?"

"Not..." Molly dragged her tongue across dry lips. "Not that I can think of."

Who was she kidding? With Sam's mouth only inches from her own, she could barely breathe. Thinking had passed into the realm of the impossible.

"Good."

His knee nudged hers apart, separating them. He edged her backward, until she straddled the narrow, padded bench. Her skirt inched up her thighs with a soft slither. Her breath hitched somewhere in the middle of her throat.

"Why do I get the feeling we're not going to make it upstairs?"

"Molly, sweetheart, you're not going to make it to the floor."

The husky promise sent her stomach into a roll. She stared up at Sam's eyes, unsure where this searing urgency between them was going but in more of a hurry to get there with each passing second.

"Why don't you put your hands over mine?" he suggested in the same, low rumble.

Trembling with anticipation, Molly uncurled her fists and laid her palms over the backs of his hands where they gripped the bar.

"Now lift."

She pulled herself up, just enough for his thighs to slide under hers. Her skirt bunched at her hips. The zipper of his jeans rubbed against her panties.

And still he didn't touch her! They were thigh to thigh, breath to breath, and he didn't let go of the damned crossbar.

It only took one flex of Sam's biceps for Molly to understand why. He pulled downward. The steel cables behind her rattled. The weights clanked upward. The bar lowered, and Molly came down with it. Spread wide now, she pressed even more intimately against the ridge that had formed under Sam's jeans.

He kept her there, straddling his hips, until she turned liquid. Then slowly, so slowly, he let the bar...and Molly... rise. The exquisite, erotic pressure eased. Before she'd steadied her senses, he brought her down again.

Then again.

And again.

"Sam!" she gasped as the molten fire spread from her belly to her breasts to her brain. "We need to...shed some clothes...before I explode."

"No, we don't."

The rough edge to his voice rasped like a file on her jagged senses. That, and the way Sam slid one hand free of hers to unsnap his jeans. She barely heard the sound of his zipper over the thundering of her pulse. Her skin jumped when he tugged her panties sideways across her wet, slick flesh.

Flexing his thighs, he positioned himself under her. Molly slid slowly onto his rigid shaft. The sense of joining was so profound, so complete, that she decided then and there not to waste her money on unnecessary furniture. Instead, she'd invest in a Universal gym for every room of her house. His house. Whichever house they happened to occupy at the moment.

Slowly, Sam pulled her into a seductive rhythm. Down, up, down. The weights rattled. The cables whirred. The leather bench slicked under their hips. Too soon, Molly felt herself start to spin, higher and tighter.

When Sam's thighs flexed under her, she knew she was close to the edge. She couldn't stand the thought of going over without touching him, without tasting him. Abandoning the crossbar, she fumbled with the buttons on his cotton shirt. Three gave. Two popped loose under her frantic hands. When she bared as much of him as she could manage, Molly wrapped her arms around his neck and her legs around his waist.

When her climax came rushing upward, she did a little flexing of her own. Her muscles clenched with a skill that surprised her and wrung a groan out of Sam. He splayed his hands on her hips, driving her down, down. His body thrust up, taking her with it.

She let out a sound somewhere between a sob and a screech. Light and dark together in a kaleidoscope of pure, pulsing pleasure.

Molly drifted back into awareness sometime later. She wasn't sure exactly when she and Sam had abandoned the hard, narrow bench for the hard, flat floor. Or when they'd jettisoned most of their outer clothes. She *was* sure that she'd never, ever, experienced such bone-melting, soul-shattering union.

She propped herself up on one elbow, drinking in the sight of the man sprawled beside her. He looked like some big mountain cat lazing in the sun, those lethal muscles slack under his sleek, tanned hide. His dark hair stood in short spikes. His right shoulder carried two little red crescents where her fingernails had unintentionally gone too deep.

She bent over and touched her mouth to the marks. He

grunted, an indistinguishable male sound that could have been an invitation to continue or a warning that he hadn't recovered full consciousness yet. Molly smiled and decided to test the waters.

"About that couch…?"

"It's yours," he muttered, not opening his eyes.

"Why don't we…?"

She hesitated. She'd never propositioned a man before, much less a man as complex, as aggravating, as intoxicating as Sam Henderson. One of his lids squinched open. Through the screen of his lashes, he squinted up at her.

"Why don't we what, Mol?"

She could do this. She could take the next step. She could tell him that she wanted him in her life. In her bed. In her heart.

"Why don't we share it? The couch, I mean."

"You sure?"

"Yes. Well…" Her fingertip traced a dark swirl. "Yes."

"Okay."

With that, he closed his eye again and gave every appearance of a man whose only concern at that moment was catching a few z's.

Molly's hand stilled. Her ridiculously thumping heart gave a small thud.

That was it? She'd just suggested that they take up joint occupancy for some unspecified period in the near future, and all he had to offer in reply was a single, laconic 'okay'?

Well, what had she expected? A rapture of delight? A passionate declaration of undying love? She hadn't exactly gushed over the idea, either. And, a nagging little voice reminded her, she'd been the one to pull back before, to suggest they take this slow.

Contrarily, she now wanted Sam to press her for a more definite commitment. Or at least show some signs of wanting one. She sat up, giving the curl of dark hair wrapped around her finger an annoyed tweak in the process. That, at least, got both his eyes open.

"Ouch!"

"Sorry," she muttered, groping for the puddle of bronze knit that was her dress. "If you can stay awake long enough to turn on the VCR, I want to watch that video."

"Right. The video."

Sam dragged on his jeans, fighting the resistance that caught at him with the force of a tail hook hitting the arresting barrier. He didn't want to watch the damned tape. More to the point, he didn't want Molly to watch it and follow through with her harebrained scheme of confronting a possible killer.

He'd learned his lesson, though. She'd warned him in her blunt, inimitable style that she didn't respond well to a firm hand on the reins. Hell, to *any* hand on the reins. She'd offered to share an as-yet-undefined part of her life with him in the form of his leather sofa. Sam wasn't going to jeopardize that hesitant offer by pointing out again the idiocy of what she planned to do.

He didn't have to like it, though.

He liked it even less when the color faded from Molly's face as Josh Walters's smooth, cultured voice rolled across the room.

"...the welfare reform bill I introduced last year does guarantee every person's right to a job."

The scene faded. An American flag fluttered. The announcer came on, and a trailer appeared at the bottom of the screen announcing the congressman's upcoming public appearances.

"UNLV," Molly muttered as the printed message flashed by. "Thursday, September eleventh. That's tonight!"

They'd missed that opportunity, Sam thought with grim satisfaction.

Her eyes narrowed on the scrolling words. "Saturday, the

thirteenth, at the Nellis Officers' Club, 8:00 p.m. Tuesday, the sixteenth, at the Cashman Field Center, right before the baseball game...."

She'd seen enough. Spinning around, she pinned Sam with a look that challenged him far more than the mild question that came with it.

"Can I get onto the base without a military ID?"

The cops at the front gate could issue her a pass, but they both knew she wouldn't need one. She wasn't going anywhere without him. Sam conceded with something less than grace.

"My car has a sticker," he said gruffly. "I'll drive. I'll also call out to the base tomorrow and find out whether the appearance is purely political or in conjunction with some official function. You," he instructed, trying not to let it sound too much like an order, "had better call Kaplan and advise him what we're doing."

Molly hugged that "we" to her chest as Sam scooped her up and hugged *her* to his chest. Disagreement was stamped all over his strong, rugged features, but he'd passed the test.

By unspoken agreement, Molly spent the rest of Thursday night in Sam's bed. She then spent most of Friday morning avoiding Davinia's smug glances and unsubtle questions about when she and Sam intended to tear down the oleander hedge and merge their properties.

"We haven't gotten to any discussion of merging yet," Molly finally informed her persistent boss. "We're only at the your-place-or-mine? stage."

Davinia dropped into the chair in front of Molly's desk, kicked off her three-inch heels, and crossed her ankles on top of the desk with a slither of expensive stockings.

"Honey, I'm working on husband number four. You keep

moving at this pace and you might not bag number one before you're forty."

"For heaven's sake, I've only known Sam for a little more than a week. Well, I've known him for longer than that, I suppose but only *known* him for…" She threw up her hands. "Okay, okay, I've known him long enough to recognize that he's special."

"Special." Her boss rolled her eyes. "He's trophy quality, Mol. And I'm not just referring to those awesome abs or preposterous pecs. If it were me, I'd already have him stuffed and mounted."

"I'm sure you would. I'm not the great white hunter you are, though. After my last, disastrous fling with love, I'm taking things more slowly."

"More slowly?" Davinia huffed in derision. "You're moving at the speed of road kill."

"Besides," Molly added, ignoring the gibe, "Sam has a few issues of his own to work through before he lets himself get, uh, stuffed."

The older woman cocked her head. Her shining, blunt-cut platinum hair feathered across one shoulder. "Like what?"

"Like a tendency to issue orders, for one thing."

"And?"

She hesitated, knowing how closemouthed Sam was about his injury but needing to share her own, growing worry for him.

"And a pain that keeps him awake and prowling all night sometimes."

Her boss's feet slid off the desk and hit the floor with a well-mannered thump. Genuine concern filled her turquoise eyes. "What kind of pain?"

Briefly, Molly recounted the few details Sam had told her of his accident.

"He shrugs off any discussion of his headaches, but he

did tell me that he has to meet another medical evaluation board in a few months. I didn't understand all the Air Force jargon. All I know is that he's on some kind of a temporary retirement or suspension list. If his condition doesn't improve, this medical board will put him out to pasture permanently.''

Davinia's legal antennae snapped to attention. ''He can fight a permanent discharge. He's not completely incapacitated. If he can't fly, he can certainly serve in some other capacity.''

Molly shook her head. ''I don't think he'll do that.''

She'd gained enough insight into Sam Henderson in the past week to know he wouldn't put himself back in uniform when those blinding headaches could hit him at any moment.

''Tell him to call me,'' her boss suggested briskly. ''I know an attorney who specializes in worker's comp and on-the-job injury cases. He might know something about the military system. If he doesn't, I'm sure he can find someone who does.''

Molly felt a rush of warm gratitude, remembering how only a few days ago Davinia had offered to involve her ex-husband in a lawsuit on her behalf against her pesky neighbor. Now she was ready to take up that same, pesky neighbor's cause. Her boss was nothing if not generous-hearted.

''Thanks, I'll tell him.''

Davinia got up to leave a few moments later. Sighing, she reported that she was having lunch with Antonio at the health food eatery in the spa where he worked.

''Can you believe it, he's actually got me enjoying bean sprouts?''

Molly could believe it. From the droll expression on her boss's face, she guessed it wouldn't be long until Davinia had the handsome Spaniard stuffed and mounted. Mounted, anyway.

Smiling, she reached for the phone. She'd promised Sam she'd call Detective Kaplan and tell him about Walters's appearance at the Nellis Officers' Club tomorrow night. Might as well get it over with. He'd probably raise the same objections Sam had to Molly's planned expedition.

To her surprise, he didn't. When he called back some hours later, he turned the idea over, examining it from all angles.

"It might work," he said at last. "We'll wire you. If you startle any kind of a reaction out of him, we can move in. What time is this big event?"

"Eight o'clock. Sam called this morning to make sure."

"What kind of function is it?"

"It's a formal banquet in honor of the Air Force's anniversary. Walters is the guest speaker. Supposedly, he's going to use the occasion to unveil the second of his three new strategies for protecting jobs and growing industry in his district, which includes the base."

"Tell you what. I'll bring one of our specialists by your place before you leave for this banquet tomorrow to fit you with the wire, then we'll go to this party with you."

"All right."

"Since we'll be on federal property, I'll have to coordinate my presence with the base. The top cop out there's a pretty cool head. He'll give us whatever backup we need…if we need it."

The grim possibility gave Molly pause. Suddenly, the prospect of going face-to-face with Walters didn't hold quite the same appeal it had before. She hung up a few moments later, alternating between a guilty regret at having started down this road and a determination not to chicken out.

As she'd anticipated, Sam didn't like the idea of Kaplan outfitting Molly with a wire any more than he liked the idea of her confronting Walters. She told him about it later that evening over a candlelit patio dinner of chicken and mush-room crepes, compliments of a French restaurant she'd stopped at on the way home. The bottle of light, fragrant pinot blanc came compliments of Sam's well-stocked assortment of California wine.

Sam, she noticed, had barely touched either the crepes or the wine. The flickering candlelight didn't disguise the lines bracketing his mouth. Nor did Buck Randall's soft lament, which Molly had suggested for background music when she'd taken in Sam's rigid shoulders.

"Kaplan is as crazy as you and your boss if he thinks someone like Josh Walters is going to say anything incriminating in public."

"He's reaching, Sam, just as you and Antonio were last night when you tossed around that impersonator bit."

"That's a lot more plausible than having you waltz into the club and spook Walters into a confession."

"I suggested the possibility of an impersonator standing in for Walters to Kaplan. He's going to nose around, see if any of the actors on the Strip know of an act like that."

"Oh, great." Sam's fork clattered onto his plate. "If Walters didn't know that he's under suspicion before, he soon will. Why not just post a notice on the marquee in front of Caesars?"

They both knew the detective would handle the inquiries discreetly. Molly didn't try to argue the point, however. Her heart ached for the man across the table. Like the fabled character in Robert Louis Stevenson's novel, Sam's darker side was in ascendancy. Unlike Dr. Jekyll, though, he wouldn't let the Mr. Hyde side of his personality win control of his being. He'd fight the stabbing pain with everything he had in him.

Searching desperately for a way to help him with the continuing battle, Molly steered the conversation away from

the contentious issue of tomorrow night into less provoca-
tive channels.

"Speaking of my crazy boss, Davinia mentioned that she
has a friend...an attorney...who specializes in claims for
on-the-job injuries. She offered to get in touch with him for
you if you want representation when you go before this
medical board you told me about."

Sam tipped his head back, studying her through narrowed
eyes.

"Tell her thanks, but no thanks. I'm not going to fight
the board's final decision, Molly."

"I didn't think you would," she replied calmly. "So what
are you going to do, Sam? Besides make love to me two
or three times a day, every day, until we wear each other
or the leather on the bench out completely?"

Her nonchalance startled a surprised look out of him.
Slowly, almost imperceptibly, he relaxed.

"I've had a few offers. Kicked around a few ideas."

Curious, she swirled the pale liquid in her glass. "Like
what?"

"Like starting my own computer-based search service for
classic car parts, for one."

Molly stared at him over the rim of her wineglass, surprised and impressed. She hadn't connected the sophisticated array of computer equipment she'd glimpsed in Sam's
upstairs study with his all-consuming passion for old cars.

"Sounds like a fascinating hobby."

"I wasn't thinking in terms of a hobby, sweetheart. Classic cars are big business. Avid restorers pay thousands of
dollars for original parts."

"You're kidding!"

"No, ma'am. The finders fees alone would keep you in
pinot blanc for the rest of your life...or in enough beer to
eradicate every freckle on your long, luscious body."

"I don't have freckles anywhere but on my nose," she informed him loftily.

A wicked grin tugged at his mouth. "Shows what you know."

Molly caught her breath as he eased his chair back.

"Why don't you bring your wine inside?" he suggested. "You can finish it while I work out. Then...maybe...we can work out together."

Matching her grin to his, she picked up her glass. "Sounds good to me."

Chapter 12

Molly pirouetted slowly in front of the bathroom mirror, studying her image doubtfully.

Was her black dress too much? Or not enough?

Sam had told her that the military would wear their uniforms to the banquet tonight. The civilian men would be in tuxes, and the women would pull out all the stops. With that somewhat nebulous guidance, Molly had debated between her only long gown, a floor-length slide of shimmering gold lamé, and this above-the-knee cocktail dress. The lamé was more formal, but this little number had grabbed her heart and a good chunk of her bank account when she'd spotted it in Saks at Fashion Show Mall. She'd cheerfully delayed her planned furniture purchases for another month in order to possess it.

There wasn't much to it, though, on top or on bottom. Sequined strips of black satin banded her breasts and the mid-thigh hem, without a great deal of black crepe in between. Oh, well, the sinful creation certainly pulled out every stop she had.

Clipping on a pair of square rhinestone-and-jet earrings, Molly gave her upswept hair a final pat, then picked up her black mesh evening bag and headed downstairs. At the sound of her stiletto heels on the oak steps, Sam pushed himself out of the single rattan chair in her living room.

When she caught sight of him standing straight and tall at the bottom of the stairs, she stopped abruptly.

"Wow!"

If her little black dress constituted close to the minimum coverage required by law, just the opposite held true for Sam. What seemed like a half acre of midnight blue uniform molded his broad shoulders and otherwise mouthwatering form. The short, tailored jacket sported silver-edged shoulder boards embroidered with gold oak leaves, shiny silver wings and an array of colorful medals. A snowy white pleated shirt formed a startling contrast. The navy satin bow tie and cummerbund circling his lean waist matched the stripe running down the outsides of his pants' legs. With his neatly trimmed dark hair, gray eyes and tanned skin, he looked like every woman's fantasy come to life...in or out of uniform.

"I'll see that wow and raise you one," Sam murmured, devouring her from neck to knees.

The sudden heat in his eyes sent a prickle of pleasure through Molly. He'd seen her at her worst, with brown mush layered across her cheeks and coffee staining her front. Now he was seeing her at her best, and he certainly seemed to appreciate the view. For a moment she could have sworn she was Cinderella, about to depart for the ball with her handsome prince.

Then a small frown puckered Sam's brow. "I thought you said Kaplan was coming here to wire you?"

Molly slid back into reality with a thud.

"He is." She twisted the gold bracelet watch on her left

wrist to check the time. "He said he'd be here by seven. I wonder where he is?"

"I'm wondering where he's going to plant his listening device."

"Right here," she replied dryly, dangling her little bag by one hand. "I'm not letting this sucker out of my hands for the rest of the night."

"Just so you know, I have the same plans for you." He strolled forward and curled a knuckle to brush it down her cheek. "It's not too late to change your mind about this, Molly."

For a moment, she was tempted. Really tempted. Confronting Congressman Walters in a public forum had seemed like a good idea when she'd first thought about it. Now, with the face-off imminent, she wasn't ashamed to admit she was having second and third thoughts.

If the bell hadn't rung at that moment, she might even have wimped out and saved both herself and Sam the terror that followed. Instead, she merely smiled.

"We're all dressed up. We might as well go to the ball."

Detective Kaplan had dressed for the ball, too. Dark-jowled, dark-eyed and obviously uncomfortable in a tux that strained over his stomach, he greeted both her and Sam, then introduced Detective Sergeant Dee Santos. The short, henna-haired Hispanic, looking more elegant than her partner in pale, oyster-colored satin pants and a matching jacket, skimmed a quick look over Molly's outfit.

"Nice threads."

"Thanks."

"I hope I don't have to try to conceal anything under them."

Pointedly avoiding Sam's sardonic look, Molly held out the black mesh evening bag.

"Will this work?"

"Perfectly!"

Propping her briefcase on the gnarled cypress tree stump that did duty as an end table, Santos snapped open the lid. The bite-sized package of electronics she pulled out looked more like a handheld tape recorder than the high-tech bit of electronics Kaplan had described to Molly. The police officer fiddled with a couple of protruding wires, adjusted an antenna, and flicked a switch. Static screeched through the air, then the tiny black box lapsed into silence.

"This little baby will pick up normal conversation with no problem," Santos said as she clipped the black button inside the lining of the purse. "We'll have a lot of background noise to filter out at the club, though. It'll help if you get as up close and personal with the target as possible."

Target. Molly's skin rippled at the word.

Folding over the mesh flap, Santos handed her back the bag. "Better yet, try to get our boy alone, off to a corner or in one of the anterooms."

"No way," Sam said flatly.

Both detectives looked at him in surprise.

"I don't think that's a good idea," he said with a little less whip. "First, we're dealing with a man suspected of murder here. Second, it's going to look odd, to say the least, if I stand around twiddling my thumbs while another man whisks my woman off to a corner or a private room to huddle."

His blatant use of the possessive caught Molly off guard. Sam, too, if the quick, frowning glance he threw her was any indication. Her independent spirit instantly raised its head, but her objection formed with something less than its usual force. Molly didn't have any great desire to huddle in a corner with Congressman Walters. Even more to the point, a contrary, deeply visceral part of her wanted Sam to claim her, to tell her he was ready to share more than his couch with her.

"I suppose you have a point there," Dee Santos conceded with a shrug. "We'll just have to hope the receiver filters out the background noise enough to keep any conversation between Ms. Duncan and the congressman audible." Flicking the switch once more, she nodded to Molly. "Say something. Anything. I need a voice print."

"A voice print?" Interest flared in Molly's eyes. "Does this device record individual vocal signatures?"

"Not signatures, exactly. The technology isn't that advanced yet. The best we can do is run a print that helps distinguish between speakers when there's a lot of background noise, as there will be tonight." She glanced down at the palm-sized device she held in her hand. "Okay, I've got you. Ready to go?"

Swiping a damp palm down the side of her dress, Molly nodded. Kaplan caught the small movement. His jowls creased in a reassuring smile.

"Don't worry, Ms. Duncan. Detective Santos and I are meeting the base chief of security at the club. We'll have you covered from the moment you walk in the front door."

"So will I," Sam said grimly as he followed Molly and the others to the front door.

Molly had only visited a military post once before. Nellis Air Force Base, she soon discovered, bore little resemblance to ramshackle, WWII-era Fort Devans a few miles outside of Boston. Even in the descending darkness, she noted the professionalism of the guard who saluted and waved them through the gate. As they followed the stream of traffic heading for the Officers' Club, a jet roared down the runway, its engines glowing like twin red suns as it soared into the night. Another followed a few seconds later, adding to the thunder that rolled across the sky.

The military honor guard that snapped to attention and whipped their swords into a flashing arch at the entrance to the Officers' Club impressed her even more. Spit-shined and sharp in their white ascots and blue uniforms, the men and women who formed the honor guard looked young and invincible and proud.

Sam returned their salute, greeting several by name as he escorted Molly up the steps. A square-jawed young sergeant opened the door for them.

"Good to see you back, Major Henderson."

"Good to be back, Brent," Sam answered easily. "I heard that AGS aced the ORI last month. You must have been TDY at the time."

Molly had no idea what the alphabet soup of acronyms meant, but the huge grin that split the young man's face told her it was some kind of inside joke. Taking a moment to simply absorb the unfamiliar sights and sounds, she waited beside a bank of feathery ferns while Sam stepped up to a linen-draped table to confirm the last-minute table reservations he'd wrangled for them.

He was just turning back to Molly when a husky voice floated through the crowded hall.

"Sam? I thought that was you."

A tall, sloe-eyed woman with a sweep of rich auburn hair strolled forward. The side slit in her floor-length uniform skirt showed just enough leg for several men to turn for a second look.

Molly had never seen the stunning officer before, but the husky, dark-as-chocolate voice struck a chord. Memory kicked in when the woman flowed into Sam's arms with a naturalness that said she'd been there before.

This had to be the woman who'd answered Sam's phone the first time Molly called to complain about his music. The one who promised to give him the message when he got out of the shower.

Sam hadn't gotten the message. Observing the expression on the officer's face as she practically fused with Sam in the crowded hallway, Molly wasn't surprised. Obviously, she'd had other things on her mind that night.

Tonight, too.

"You're looking great," she told him. "Better than great. Good enough to eat."

Laughing, Sam disengaged. "You're looking pretty good, too, Janet. How's the intelligence business?"

The redhead wrinkled her nose. "Not very intelligent. We're going through another manpower reduction, just when things are heating up in the Gulf again."

She angled her head, her eyes unreadable, but Molly's keen ear didn't miss the intimate concern that rippled through her voice.

"How are you feeling?"

Lifting his head, Sam met Molly's interested gaze. "Better than I have in a long time," he replied with a slow, private smile. "Come on, I want you to meet someone."

In the few seconds it took for Sam to escort the officer across the hallway, the two women communicated with swift, unerring accuracy. Molly had no difficulty interpreting or answering the silent message that flashed in the slanted, violet eyes.

He was mine first.

Tough. He's mine now.

This time, her independent spirit didn't so much as whisper a protest at the flagrant use of the possessive.

"Captain Green and I have already met," she said when Sam had performed the introductions. "Or rather, we've spoken."

"Have we?"

"I think you answered the phone one night when I called Sam's house to talk to him about Buck Randall."

The redhead's nose wrinkled once again. Obviously, she didn't remember the irate phone message she'd promised to pass on.

"Are you a fan, too?"

"I don't know if I'd go quite that far. Let's just say Sam's encouraging me to develop more of an appreciation for the man's artistry."

Once again, the two women communicated without words. Something that might have been regret shone in the captain's extraordinary eyes for a moment, then her mouth curved in her first genuine smile.

"Better you than me. Good luck."

"Thanks."

She turned to the man at her side. "I'm here with Doc and Mindy and her husband. Would you two like to join us? We can do some quick table shuffling."

"Maybe we'll join you for a drink after dinner," Sam said easily. "We're sitting at one of the 442d tables."

"Uh, oh! You're in for a lively night, Molly. The 442d holds the record for the most trips to the grog bowl. See you later."

"That sounds ominous."

Sam grinned and edged her aside to let another group of officers and their ladies pass.

"Don't worry. They don't go after civilians…much. There are Kaplan and Santos."

With reinforcements, Molly noted. A balding, ramrod straight officer with a glittering array of medals on his chest accompanied the two detectives.

"Good to see you, Sam," he said, thrusting out his hand.

"You, too, sir."

"How's the head?"

"Still there. This is Ms. Duncan. Molly Duncan. Molly, this is Colonel Scott, chief of security for the base."

Flinty blue eyes measured her. Evidently she passed his test. His craggy face creased into a smile.

"Why don't we go into the club manager's office?" he

suggested. "We can go over the security arrangements there and test this equipment you're wearing?"

"Carrying," Sam amended dryly.

The colonel had more sense than to comment on that one.

Fifteen minutes later, Molly and Sam joined the throng slowly filling the club's main ballroom and made their way to their table. They halted frequently while Sam returned greetings and introduced Molly to a host of friends and acquaintances. Halfway across the room, she gave up trying to remember names and faces. There were too many.

Her nerves fluttered even more than the blue-and-silver foil streamers draped from the chandeliers to form a glittering overhead canopy. Hundreds of long, slender blue tapers flickered in glass hurricane lamps. The flickering light added to the festive air, but made it impossible to see much more than a few yards away.

She clutched Sam's arm, skimming the sea of midnight blue that surrounded her. The few civilians in tuxes scattered through the crowd almost got lost amid the colorful glitter of medals and glinting silver shoulder boards.

Almost.

A few stood out. Several of them Molly recognized instantly. One was the mayor of Las Vegas, a portly, red-faced man already sweating profusely. Another was a real estate developer who chaired the Chamber of Commerce, which met regularly with the Tourist Bureau. But it was the tall, distinguished civilian with the shock of prematurely gray hair who riveted her attention. Her fingers dug into Sam's arm as he pulled out her chair.

"There he is," she hissed in his ear.

"I saw him."

"Shouldn't we go over and talk to him?"

"Not now," he said calmly. "Mr. Vice is about to ring

the chimes. We'll have to wait until the smoking lamp is lit."

"Whenever that is," Molly muttered.

A long, lanky major with a white-walled buzz cut and an infectious grin jumped up to assist Sam with the onerous task of pushing in her chair.

"That, sweet thang, is right after the rubber chicken and right before the speeches. I'm Rock, short for Rocket, as in straight up. What in the world is a first-class hottie like you doing with Drac?"

"Drac?" Molly arched a look at Sam. "As in Dracula?"

"As in Dracm," Rock supplied, "a fourteenth-century dragon who owned the skies and belched fire, among other things. Why don't you dump the old man and run away with me?"

Startled, Molly glanced from him to the woman seated on the other side of his empty chair. The laughing mother-to-be folded her hands across her bulging stomach.

"Please! Take him off my hands and I'll give you my firstborn. My second, third, fourth and fifth, too. Heck, I'll even throw in the dog, and run off with the old man you came with as soon as I pop."

"Which we hope won't happen tonight," Sam drawled. "You provided enough entertainment by delivering number five at the squadron picnic." Grinning, he bent over to brush a kiss across her mouth. "Hello, Peg."

"Hello, Drac."

"Got this one named yet? As best I recall, the last one went by 'it' for three months while Rock tried to sell you on 'Falcon.'"

"As a matter of fact, we have a name all picked out." Her hand reached up to curl around his. "How does Samuel Czcynsky sound to you?"

His strong, tanned fingers gripped hers. "Pretty damn good."

She clung to his hand for a moment, sharing what was obviously a vivid memory. Rock shared it with Molly a few moments later, after the flurry of introductions had been completed and Sam turned his attention to the bashful young wife seated on his other side.

"Drac and I participated in some cold weather tests a year or so ago," he told her quietly. "My plane took a bird strike and I had to bail out over some nasty seas. Drac stayed right over me, talking to me, swearing at me, threatening to wring my scrawny neck if I died on him. The rescue chopper arrived and hauled my frozen butt out of the water just before hypothermia took me under for the last time."

He paused, his face seeming to fold in on itself as an icy vision held him in its grip.

"Drac made it back to base on pure fumes, and Peg swore she'd name this one after him whether it was a boy or girl. She thinks a lot of him." His gaze slid past Molly's shoulder to the man at her side. "We all do," he finished softly.

"So I've gathered."

"What about you?"

"Excuse me?"

"What do you think of the Drac Man?"

The seriousness in Rock's homely handsome face told Molly that she'd better give the right answer. It came easy.

"I think a lot of him, too."

"Good."

When someone else at the table claimed the young pilot's attention, Molly leaned back. A small tilt to her head allowed her to study the man with his arm looped along the back of her chair. For all the jokes and banter being tossed around, it was obvious that Sam commanded these officers' respect. Only gradually did she realize that he'd also commanded most of them in battle. Almost all of them were veterans of Desert Storm. A few had also seen some hot action in Bosnia.

Sam belonged here, she thought with an aching sense of loss…for him, for the men and women he once led. He was a warrior at heart. He and the others all shared the same values, the same dangers, the same dedication to their country. Yet as incredible as it seemed, he harbored no bitterness as a result of his accident, no resentment toward an Air Force that would soon put him permanently on the shelf.

He was, as Davinia had said, real trophy quality.

At that moment, the last of Molly's hesitations fell away. Watching his easy smile, seeing his gray eyes light with laughter, feeling the warmth of the arm that circled her bare shoulders, she felt herself sliding the rest of the way down that slippery slope Buck Randall had called love. Her heart opened, and she knew her slide wouldn't stop for a long, long time.

He turned and caught her look. His smile tipped into one of his patented, Sam-only grins. Curling his arm around her shoulders, he drew her closer and bent down to be heard over the noise of the crowd.

"You keep looking at me like that," he murmured, "and we might have to slip out to the car for a few minutes to give those bucket seats one more try."

"You keep blowing in my ear like that and it will take more than a few minutes."

He started to reply, only to be cut off by the squawk of a microphone. Molly jumped, almost hitting Sam in the chin with her head, and shot a quick look at the little black evening bag resting beside her plate. To her profound relief, the noise had come from the center of the room, where a nervous lieutenant on a dais thumped the mike in front of him, raising another squawk.

"Ladies and gentlemen, please take your seats."

A moment later, the sound of a gavel slamming down thundered through the speakers. Molly jumped again and swiveled around to face the head table. A crew-cut colonel surveyed the vast assemblage.

"The mess is called to order. Mr. Vice, you may proceed."

The ceremonies got underway immediately. The honor guard paraded the colors, an astonishing litany of toasts were drunk, Mr. Vice pointed out infractions of the mess rules, intentional or otherwise, and the president sent various miscreants to the alcoholic and nonalcoholic grog bowls placed strategically around the room.

Molly rose when the other civilian women rose, drank when the others lifted their glasses, smiled at the sometimes incomprehensible jargon and inside jokes. Through it all, however, her gaze kept straying back to the couple seated at the head table on either side of the colonel.

Congressman Joshua Walters, and his wife, Jessica MacGiver Walters. One gray and smoothly handsome. The other raven-haired and elegant in rippling silver satin. She smiled out on the crowd with a remote sort of graciousness that could only come with wealth and long years in the spotlight.

Or did that faint, smiling reserve stem from other, darker sources? Did she really know what kind of man she'd married? Could she have any idea that her husband might be a murderer?

Molly was locked so intently on the wife that a few moments passed before she realized that the husband had locked on her.

Her head snapped back. Her heart skipped.

Walters gave no sign that he recognized her. No evidence that he'd noted her reaction. His expression didn't change. His gaze didn't falter. He observed her for another instant or two, then turned his head in response to some comment from the woman at his side.

Molly clenched her hands under the tablecloth to still

their trembling. Cold sweat dewed her back and bare shoulders.

What had she expected? she thought savagely. That his composure would shatter at the sight of her? If he were the killer, he knew her name, but that didn't necessarily mean he knew her face. Even if he did, he might think her presence here tonight just a coincidence.

She was still trying to think of a subtle way to let him know she hadn't arrived at the club by chance when fate, in the shape of a well-endowed young lieutenant, took the matter out of her hands.

Chapter 13

"Ladies and gentlemen, the smoking lamp is lit."

Cheers and whistles greeted Mr. Vice's announcement. Four-hundred-plus chairs scraped back. Replete males stretched out legs and recharged glasses. Brightly gowned women made a general exodus to the ladies' room.

"Would you like to go powder your nose?"

Molly smiled at the shy young captain's wife across from her. "No, thanks."

"This is your last chance before the speeches start," the pregnant Peg chimed in. "Unless that gorgeous creation you're wearing comes equipped with a relief tube, you could be in trouble."

"No relief tube," Molly replied, "but I'm pretty tough."

"I can attest to that," Sam added with a lazy grin. "Why don't we get some fresh air instead? Bring your purse, sweetheart."

The contrast between Sam's casual endearment and his reference to her evening bag jolted Molly. She caught his eye and with it the swift reminder of the reason they'd attended this gathering of eagles.

Her pulse quickening, she glanced past him to the head table. Jessica Walters and the General's wife had already started weaving their way through the crowd. Cigars in hands, their husbands headed for the wall of glass doors that opened onto a patio strung with white lights and silvery blue streamers.

"Fresh air sounds good," Molly got out, her throat tight.

Sam guided her through the crowd, his hand warm and reassuring at the small of her back. She clutched the little mesh bag to her chest and swept the ballroom with a quick, searching look. A flash of pale, oyster-colored satin caught her eye. At a table tucked in a distant corner, Dee Santos nodded imperceptibly. Her shoulder-length sweep of hennaed hair hid all sign of the wire that ran from her earpiece to the recorder in her jacket pocket. Molly didn't see Kaplan or the ramrod straight Colonel Scott amid the forest of men in dark uniforms, but she knew they were somewhere in the vicinity.

The glass patio doors slid open on smooth, silent bearings. A desert breeze, warm after the air-conditioned chill of the huge ballroom, brushed Molly's skin. Glass chinked against glass as bartenders poured drinks at the two small bars set up at either end of the patio. The haunting strains of "Wind Beneath My Wings" drifted through speakers. A few couples swayed to the music, pressed close together by the intimacy of the minuscule, open-air dance floor.

The setting should have been magical. A blending of elegance and pride, of romance and seduction. On any other night, Molly would have melted into Sam's arms and let the sheer beauty of the moment carry her away. Tonight, she absorbed the ambiance through the filter of wire-tight nerves. Her whole being was focused on the man who stood only a few yards away, surrounded by a small clutch of men and women.

Josh Walters was in his element. Urbane, confident, relaxed, he smiled and held court with practiced ease. He hadn't given his speech yet. During introductions of the head table, he and his wife had merely stood and waved in acknowledgment of the warm round of applause they received. Yet Molly could hear his voice in her head. Every well-modulated syllable echoed with the clarity of a bell, punctuated by Joey Bennett's terrified pleas and the splat of gunfire.

With seeming casualness, Sam guided her across the patio. The small crowd around the congressman eddied and flowed. Two couples moved away, heading back to the ballroom. The General turned aside to speak to another officer. A captain hovered at Walters's elbow, then hurried off toward the bar. For probably the first time that night, the congressman stood alone and unattended.

"We're locked on target, Mol." Sam's murmur was a wash of warmth against her cheek. "Let's go get him."

They had taken only another step or two when a woman's voice floated across the night air.

"Major Henderson?"

Sam slowed, turned, muttered a curse under his breath. A vivacious young officer with an hourglass figure that even Mae West would have envied slid the patio doors shut behind her and crossed the flagstones. Molly didn't need an introduction to guess she was Lieutenant Donovitch of liplock fame.

"Captain Green told me you were here. I've been looking for you."

Realizing that she hadn't noticed Walters standing only a few yards away, Sam moved to intercept her. Before he could cut her off, she hurried into speech.

"I won't interrupt your evening. I just wanted to tell you

I've been thinking about that matter we discussed the other day. I was stupid to let myself be intimidated. I'll go to the authorities, if you think it will help.''

Although the lieutenant had lowered her voice, Molly's trained ear picked up every word. So, she saw on a swift indrawn breath, had Josh Walters.

He stood as if cast in stone, his eyes narrowed on Sam and the lieutenant. Suddenly, his gaze whipped to Molly. For an unguarded instant, his handsome mask slipped. She held his stare, her heart crashing like thunder against her ribs.

He knows!

He knows who I am, and now he knows that Sam's made a connection with Lieutenant Donovitch.

Maybe he knows that Kaplan's been asking questions, testing his alibi.

Molly realized she had to act quickly to capitalize on the drama of the moment. Gliding forward, she hooked her arm in Sam's.

"Darling, you promised to introduce me to Congressman Walters. He's right over there. You'll excuse us, won't you, lieutenant?''

The young woman gave Molly a surprised look, then turned a pasty white when she saw the man standing a few yards away. Without another word, she turned and hurried off.

By the time she and Sam stood face-to-face with Joshua Walters, Molly knew they'd missed their window of opportunity. The politician's mask had dropped back into place. His handsome face registered nothing but pleasure as he thrust out his hand.

"Sam! I told Jessie I thought I'd spotted you in the crowd earlier.''

"Congressman.''

"It's good to see you looking so fit…and in such delight-ful company."

If that smooth, educated voice hadn't raised the fine hairs on the back of Molly's neck, Walters's smile might have charmed her completely. It held just the right blend of polite inquiry and appreciation. She didn't doubt that it got terrific results from the female half of the voting population. Sam made the necessary introductions, his voice low and delib-erately neutral.

"This is Molly Duncan. Molly, this is our elected rep-resentative, Congressman Joshua Walters."

With one hand crooked in Sam's arm and the other firmly grasping her black evening bag, Molly neatly avoided any necessity of shaking hands with the man. Not only did she not want to touch him. She didn't want her damp palms to clue him into how nervous she was.

"Not my elected official," she replied coolly. "I haven't been here long enough to vote yet."

"Really?" Walters's blue eyes held hers with the ease of a consummate crowd handler. "What brought you to our wonderful state?"

He'd given her just the opening she needed. "A job, Con-gressman. I'm a translator and tour consultant with the Las Vegas Trade and Convention Center. I speak several lan-guages, and have a good ear for accents" She tilted her head. "Yours, for example, caught my attention the first time I heard it." To her intense disappointment, he didn't rise to the bait.

"I'm not surprised. After a year or two at Harvard, this Wisconsin farm boy sounded strange, even to himself."

Dammit, she couldn't just come out and tell the bastard that he'd sounded more than strange the first time she'd heard him, he'd sounded calm and very, very deadly. Des-perately, Molly sought for some way to shake his composure, to startle him into saying something Kaplan and company would catch on their recorder.

The thought of the recorder triggered an idea. Detective Santos had said that technology hadn't advanced enough to record vocal signatures, but Josh Walters might not know that.

"You're right. Your accent is certainly distinctive. You'd be an excellent candidate for a voice print, using the Hammerstein-Taguchi methodology."

"I beg your pardon?"

Molly improvised wildly. "I studied linguistics before I decided to concentrate on spoken languages instead of the science of speech. One of the professors I studied with at the University of Tokyo helped develop the, uh, phonetic dimensions for vocal signatures."

The congressman's smile didn't lose its easy charm, but his eyes sharpened. So did Sam's. Ignoring the warning press of his arm against hers, Molly plunged ahead.

"Professor Taguchi demonstrated that some languages, like Japanese for instance, use only pitch to accent vowels and the consonants that surround them. Others, like English, use both pitch and loudness to create distinct speech patterns."

Dragging a quick breath, she played her bluff.

"Each voice forms its own, distinct signature. If someone familiar with the Hammerstein-Taguchi methodology had captured yours on a telephone recorder and matched it to, say, one of the campaign ads I recently saw on TV, I think you'd be surprised at the results. Very surprised."

For the space of a single heartbeat, Molly thought she had him. Walters didn't so much as blink, but a sudden, swift stillness stripped some of the attractiveness from his smile.

Almost before she'd noted it, the stillness was gone. Moving with his customary grace, the congressman turned to accept a drink from the captain serving as his official escort.

"Thanks, Pete. Have you met Major Henderson and... Ms. Duncan, wasn't it?"

The bastard. Molly would have wagered her last dollar that her name had been emblazoned on his brain since the night he shot Joey the Horse. He wouldn't admit it now, though. He wouldn't admit anything. The curtain of intimacy surrounding them had ripped apart with the young captain's return.

"It's a pleasure to meet you, sir," he said, pumping Sam's hand. "You, too, ma'am."

Walters sipped the smoky scotch his escort had brought and watched the interchange with a casualness that grated on Molly's nerves like steel wool.

"I've just been selected for Test Pilot School," the captain confided to Sam eagerly. "I know you hold the record for operational test hours in experimental aircraft, but maybe I'll blow it out of the skies one of these days."

"Maybe you will."

The General returned then, greeting Sam with a slap on the back and Molly with a smile. When another couple drifted up, Sam took the opportunity to excuse himself and Molly. He waited until a wall separated them from Walters to spin her around. The easy smile he'd shared with the young captain and the General had disappeared. In its place was a fury all the more fierce for being tightly leashed.

"What in the hell were you doing?"

She didn't understand his anger. Neither did she appreciate it.

"Exactly what I came here to do—trying to shake your friend up a little."

"With that garbage about voice signatures?"

"Hey, he didn't know it was garbage."

"You'd better hope he did, Molly."

"Why? What the heck are you so uptight about, anyway?"

"You little fool. You deliberately gave him the impression you've got something on him. You didn't go to the police with it, so he probably thinks you're setting him up for blackmail."

"Well, I'm not, so..."

"You know that," Sam said savagely. "I know that. But Walters doesn't. If he didn't have a reason to silence you before, woman, you just handed him one on a silver platter."

Molly reared back. "I didn't mean... I didn't think..."

"That's obvious!"

She made up for that deficiency now. Her mind racing, she considered the consequences of her on-the-spot improvisation. None of them particularly appealed to her.

"Okay, maybe I got a little carried away."

"Carried away?" Sam gritted his teeth, controlling himself with an obvious effort. "Look, Walters might walk through that door at any moment. Let's find Kaplan and talk this through."

Clamping a hand around her elbow, he steered her through the crowd. They rendezvoused with Kaplan and retreated to the manager's office. Dee Santos joined them a few minutes later.

"That was some performance, Ms. Duncan," the detective said dryly. "You suckered me in for a while with that Hammerstein-Taguchi bit. Too bad you didn't pull in our target."

"How do we know she didn't?" Sam asked tersely.

Kaplan hitched a hip on the corner of the manager's desk. "You were there, Major. Do you think the congressman believed this voice patterning business?"

"If he did, he didn't show it."

"But we can't discount the possibility," the detective said slowly.

He rubbed his pendulous cheeks, thinking, considering, then turned a sober face to Molly.

"It might not be a bad idea for you stop by the station on the way home, Ms. Duncan. I'll get the supply folks to issue you one of our beepers. All you have to do is depress the button and it sends a silent, coded alarm to central dispatch."

That sounded pretty good to her. "We'll stop by."

"I wish we could dig up something concrete on the man," Kaplan muttered. "This business with the lieutenant bothers me, but..."

"She's here tonight," Sam informed him. "Walters overheard her say that she regretted letting herself be intimidated."

The detective's face brightened considerably. "She said that. Good. Point her out to me and I'll have a private chat with her. Maybe, just maybe, we'll get enough to convince the chief we should haul our congressman downtown for questioning."

When they returned to the ballroom, Sam and Molly both searched the crowd for the shapely young lieutenant. One of her friends informed Sam that she hadn't felt well and decided to slip away early. They relayed that message to Kaplan and got back to their table just as the president of the mess called the room to order. When the noise quieted, the program resumed.

After a lengthy and glowing introduction, Congressman Josh Walters took the podium to a rousing round of applause. Smiling, waving, joking, he finally silenced the room. Molly's skin prickled as the voice that had come to haunt her rolled across the ballroom.

Four hours later, the Mustang tooled through inky darkness, eating up the miles from downtown Vegas. Molly huddled in the passenger seat, fingering the small beeper Kaplan had given her while she chewed over the night's events. Josh Walters's charisma and powerful, passionate speech had added another troubling layer to her image of him as a murderer.

"He could be president," she murmured.

"Unless Kaplan comes up with some hard evidence, he will be."

The prospect made her feel ill. Rolling the beeper around and around in her palm, she let the past hour play and replay in her mind.

"He recognized me tonight, Sam. The moment he saw me with you, and you talking to Lieutenant Donovitch, he made the connection."

"Which makes your attempt to force his hand even more idiotic and dangerous."

Sam's knuckles whitened. He still hadn't worked out the tight knot that had formed in his gut when he saw Walters's glance whip from Pat Donovitch to Molly. Any doubt he might have harbored about the congressman's guilt vanished in that instant.

"I'm beginning to agree with you," Molly replied morosely. "I was tired of sitting back and waiting. I wanted to do something, to end this nerve-wracking, wait-and-see-what-happens game. Instead, I may have dug myself in deeper."

She let out a long, frustrated sigh and slumped down in the bucket seat.

"I pulled you into the hole with me, too, Sam. I'm sorry for that. If Walters gets away with murder, he's not going to forget that you were there with me tonight, or that you talked to Donovitch."

"Do I look worried?"

"Well…yes."

Deliberately, Sam unclenched his fists and forced himself to relax. He wouldn't help matters with any more reminders that Molly had upped the ante considerably tonight. He'd just make damn sure she didn't take a step without that beeper. He'd also make sure she didn't spend an hour alone in the foreseeable future. Davinia could help with that. Antonio, too. They could take the day shift. Sam would handle the nights.

He was debating how best to break it to Molly that she'd be on a short leash for the next few days when the Mustang's headlights picked up the sign for their exit. They left the interstate a moment later. Dark, silent houses and dimly lit shopping centers sped by, then the more developed areas fell behind. The road curved at an angle before cutting through an intersection and straightening for a long, deserted stretch.

It wouldn't remain deserted for long, Sam knew. Not at the rate civilization was eating up the desert. The huge, round concrete culverts waiting beside the road gave mute testimony to that. Earth movers had already chewed up trenches to swallow them. Then...

"Sam! Look out!"

He saw the slash of headlights coming at them from the right at the same instant Molly did. Recklessly, the driver had run the stop sign and now plowed through the intersection.

"He's not stopping!" Molly screeched, bracing both hands on the dash.

Sam wrenched the wheel. Tires screamed in protest. The Mustang skidded sideways. A dark sedan barreled right for them. At that moment, Sam had two alternatives. He could send the Mustang into a full spin and crash it into one of the cement culverts or let the passenger side take the impact of a collision with the oncoming car.

It wasn't a choice.

With the lightning reflexes of a test pilot, he floored the accelerator and spun the wheel full circle.

They almost made it.

The sedan shot by in a blaze of light and squealing brakes. The Mustang skidded in a full circle once, twice, with dizzying speed. Sam barely had time to throw himself sideways as far as his seat belt would allow, straining to protect Molly with his body, before metal slammed into concrete. He heard a sickening crunch. Felt his head slam back against the windshield. Saw the world go white, then black.

After the shattering crash, the sound of silence hit Molly with the force of a blow. She shook her head, dazed, disoriented, barely able to breathe from the weight pinning her to the bucket seat. Her neck ached. Her shoulder screamed where the seat belt had cut into it. When she shifted, slivers of broken glass dropped like confetti from her hair.

With her first, shuddering breath, the world finally stopped spinning. She pushed upright, grabbing at the body crushing down on hers.

"Sam! Oh, God, Sam!"

Sobbing, she scrabbled for a grip. More glass dropped, tinkling when it hit metal.

"Sam, are you all right? Sam!"

She levered him up enough to free one arm. Frantic, she flattened her fingers against the side of his neck and felt for a pulse. She wanted to weep with joy when she found it, beating strong and sure.

With a fervent prayer of thanks, she tried again to shift him. The prayer died on her lips when her hand came away wet with blood.

Fear shot through her once more, paralyzing her for a second or two. Then she groped for the release on the seat belt. It finally gave under her desperate pushing. As gently as she could, Molly scrambled out from under Sam's weight.

"Hang on," she said fiercely. "I can't reach your seat belt from here. The side's all crumpled in and mashed up against the concrete. I'll get you free, though. I promise. Hold on, okay? Just hold on."

Pleading, demanding, cajoling, she scrambled into the back seat and snaked her hand through twisted metal. Sharp edges sliced her skin. A ragged strip stabbed at her palm. It was then that she smelled gasoline. The fumes seeped up through the crumpled floorboards to sear her nostrils. Her heart stopped. All it would take was one spark, one scrape of metal on metal, to incinerate the Mustang and Sam with it. She had to get him out!

Panic choked her. Heedless of the sharp edges, she shoved her hand deeper. When she finally found the belt release, her fingers were so slick with blood that it took a half dozen tries to work it.

"Hang on, Sam. Please, please, hang on."

She scrambled out of the Mustang on the passenger side on all fours. Broken glass crunched under her. Her knee came down on a hard, square object. The pain didn't penetrate her mounting terror, but the shape of the object did. Grabbing it up with bloodied, trembling hands, Molly punched the button Kaplan had demonstrated what seemed like an eternity ago.

Praying that it worked, that Kaplan would send the closest patrol car speeding toward her development, Molly dropped the beeper and wrapped both hands around Sam's arm. She put everything she had into the pull. Her high-heeled sandals slipped in the slick, spreading gasoline. She landed on one hip. Glass and gas scored her skin. Flammable liquid soaked her dress. Disregarding both, she unbuckled the sandals and kicked them aside.

She was reaching for Sam's arm again when light stabbed

the darkness. Molly sobbed with relief. The driver of the other car had come back!

A door thudded. Footsteps crunched on the roadway. Blinded by the bright headlights, Molly saw only a black silhouette.

"Help me!" she screamed. "He's too heavy! I can't move him."

She tugged on Sam's arm, expecting another pair of hands to appear beside hers. When they didn't, she threw a frantic plea at the still figure.

"Please! Help me! We've got to get him out!"

Through the frenzy of her panic for Sam, Molly heard the voice she could identify from the grave.

"On the contrary, Ms. Duncan. I think we'll leave him right where he is."

Chapter 14

Molly's nails dug into Sam's arm. Her throat clogged with horror. Crouching in the light of the other car's beams, she watched Josh Walters take two deliberate steps forward.

For a moment, his face formed a blur above the stark white of his shirtfront, pale and indistinct.

"You surprised me tonight, Ms. Duncan. I thought I was safe."

"I...I don't know what you're talking about," she bluffed desperately. "And I don't care. Just help me get Sam out. Please!"

In answer, he lifted his hand, and Molly saw the gun for the first time. It glinted evilly in the blinding beams, its barrel made hideously long and fat by the silencer.

"You can't shoot us, you bastard!" she cried, abandoning all attempt at pretense. "You can't get away with murder again!"

"I don't have to shoot you," he ground out, his face flat with a terrible determination. "All I need to do is strike a spark, and both you and Sam will perish in the inferno caused by this tragic accident.''

In the midst of her roiling panic, Molly felt Sam stir under her hands. She wanted to sob with relief, and scream with the fear that was spreading like the noxious fuel seeping all around her.

Then Walters raised the gun, and she knew with blinding certainty that she had only an instant to act. She had to get him away from Sam and the spreading fuel, and she had to do it now!

Releasing Sam, she surged up and around, twisting away from the beams thrown by the headlights, lunging for the entrance to the giant culvert only a few feet away. She heard Walters swear viciously, then the sound of his footsteps as he pounded after her.

Like a child in an oversize playground, Molly darted around and through the huge, concrete tubes, one after another, in a dizzying, zigzagging pattern. Her breath tore at her throat. The concrete shredded what was left of her stockings and scraped her elbows.

She plunged out of one dark tunnel and ran for the next. She heard a grunt behind her, another vicious curse. Suddenly, a flash of fire spit through the darkness. A bullet splatted into the concrete a few inches from her hand. Sharp concrete needles flew in all directions, slicing into her arm, her bare shoulder. With a sob of sheer terror, Molly flung herself out of the culvert and made for the desert beyond.

It was darker here, away from the tilting headlights. The moon had disappeared behind scudding clouds. Tall saguaros threw black shadows across the rough, uneven terrain. There was an arroyo to the left, she knew, a gash in the earth that snaked its way toward the distant city. If she could find that in the darkness, she'd have the protection of the jutting angles. Walters couldn't risk letting her get away.

He'd have to come after her, take her down, bring her back to incinerate beside Sam.

She'd lead him through half the desert first, Molly swore savagely, and straight into hell if she could.

She found the arroyo a second later, or it found her. Her foot came down on thin air. The rest of her followed. With a rattle of loose stones, she tumbled headlong to the rocky bottom. Molly sprawled there, stunned, while the moon slid out from behind the black clouds. She'd rolled to one side and had shoved herself up on one knee when she heard the pound of running feet. Instinctively, she flung herself to one side, hoping, praying the shadows would conceal her.

They didn't.

The footsteps slowed. Walters prowled the rim, silhouetted against the moon, listening, searching. Molly could tell the moment he spotted her. He froze, peered into the shallow depths. The gun leveled on Molly. She cringed back, curling into a small, tight ball.

"I didn't want this," he rasped. "I thought... I was sure..."

"You were sure you'd get away with murder."

"I didn't know you were a linguist," he bit out. "I missed that bit of information when I went through your house to find out just who I'd spoken to that night. You're the only link... The only one..."

The gun wavered. For a moment, Molly thought she had a hope. She played every card in her hand.

"If you kill Sam and me, the police will know it was you," she cried. "They were there tonight, at the club, watching you."

"I saw them," he snarled. "I've been keeping tabs on Al Kaplan and his so-called investigation since the night of...the night of the fund-raiser."

"You can't say it, can you? You can do it, but you can't

say it. The night of the murder, Congressman. The night of the murder.''

Desperately, she tried to buy time for Sam, for herself, for the police, praying for the sound of a siren in the distance, terrified Walters would hear it, too.

"How did you do it? How did you duck out of the gala and kill Joey Bennett?"

"I didn't duck out. My wife, the governor, half of Las Vegas will swear I was there the whole time."

"But you weren't."

"I was…except for the few minutes I went to take that phone call from the Speaker of the House."

"A phone call that lasted more than a few minutes," Molly whispered. "It lasted just long enough for you to slip away, kill Joey Bennett, and slip back."

"No one in that mass of humanity would ever be able to say for sure."

"The police can trace the call!"

He smiled then, a thin stretch of his lips that made Molly want to scream.

"It came right on schedule from the Speaker's office, Ms. Duncan. You don't think I'd leave something like that to chance, do you?"

"Why? Why did you kill him?"

The smile faltered. Something that might have been pain flashed across his face.

"I had to," he said with terrifying simplicity. "As I have to kill you and Sam."

The gun rose another few centimeters, centering on Molly. She wanted to uncoil, to gather her muscles for a final, desperate flight, but she knew it was hopeless even before Walters cocked the hammer back.

"I'm sor…"

A shadow lunged out of the darkness. Collided with Walters. The gun spit a ribbon of fire. Molly flung herself sideways just as dirt spouted from the arroyo wall mere inches from her face.

By the time she scrabbled out of the arroyo, Sam and Walters were rolling over and over, locked in a death grip. Even in the darkness, she could see the blood staining Sam's neck and shirtfront.

The gun spit again, a wild shot fired at the sky as the two men grappled for the weapon. Frantically, Molly searched the rim of the arroyo until she found a heavy, flat rock. Gasping, snarling, feral in her need to help Sam, she brought it smashing down on Congressman Josh Walters's head.

"Sam!" She dropped to her knees between the still figures. "Oh, God! Are you all right?"

With her help, he pushed himself up on one knee, his face a mask of blood and agony.

"Get his...gun, Molly. I...can't see..."

She scrabbled in the dirt, her hands so shaky she almost couldn't pry the weapon from Walters's clenched fist.

"If he...moves, shoot...him."

"I will, Sam. I will."

"Kaplan... Wait for Kapl..."

His knee wavered, and Molly scrambled to break his fall as he toppled over. Sobbing, she dragged his head and shoulders into her lap. Holding the gun with one hand, she yanked Sam's shirttails out of his cummerbund with the other. With the wadded material pressed hard against his head to staunch the bleeding, she waited for Kaplan.

Molly had almost decided that she couldn't wait any longer, that she'd have to find something to tie Walters's hands and feet with and go in search of help, when she heard the cry of distant sirens. Relief speared through her, and she was sure she'd never seen anything or anyone as beautiful as the scowling, heavy-jowled detective who came running out of the night in answer to her cries for help.

After the eternity of waiting, it seemed like a matter of only a few more moments until an ambulance arrived. Waving off the EMT who tried to treat her bloodied hands and a cut on her face, Molly climbed in beside the still unconscious Sam.

The ambulance took them to the Nellis hospital, either because of Sam's uniform or because Kaplan told them to. Molly didn't know and didn't care. All that mattered to her was the smooth, practiced professionalism of the Emergency Room personnel when the ambulance pulled into the dock and the way the Air Force gathered to take care of one of its own.

She was sitting in the ER waiting room, her hands and face bandaged, when Rock and his wife appeared. The tall, lanky major had changed out of his dress uniform into jeans and a navy sweatshirt with the logo that Molly remembered from the yellow T-shirt Sam had loaned her.

"We just heard about the accident!"

Gracefully awkward with her pregnancy, Peggy dropped into the chair beside Molly and wrapped an arm around her shoulders.

"Rock said the command post reported that Sam's Mustang was totaled. Thank God you were able to walk away."

"I didn't walk," Molly got out shakily. "I ran."

Before the startled couple could follow up on that one, she turned to Rock.

"The ER physician came out a while ago and told me the preliminary X rays showed Sam fractured his skull, that he might require surgery."

He answered her unspoken plea with a tight nod. "I'll check out his status."

When he returned long moments later, his face was grim. "Evidently the back of Sam's head hit the windshield with enough force to crack both. He's being prepped now and will go into surgery as soon as the team's assembled."

Molly drew in a sharp, stabbing breath.

"We've got good docs here," Peg said, squeezing her shoulders. "Some of the best."

"This is the same team that treated Sam after he crashed through that malfunctioning canopy," Rock assured her. "None of us thought he'd pull through that accident, but he did. Drac Man's got a harder head than anyone I know, Molly. He'll pull through this one, too."

She wanted to believe him. She did believe him. But the thought that Sam might have to live with even worse pain than he'd endured for the past six months made her eyes burn with tears.

The next hours passed in a blur for Molly. Someone draped a hospital bathrobe over her shoulders, Rock she thought. She gathered it around herself gratefully. She'd washed as much of the blood from her face and arms and legs as possible and discarded her shredded panty hose, but large, rust-colored spots still stained her black dress. The medics had treated the cuts on her feet caused by the broken glass and her desperate flight across the desert. The green hospital slippers they'd given her matched the robe she now wore.

When Sam went into surgery, Molly, Rock and Peggy moved from the ER to a surgical waiting room done in soft, soothing desert colors. Peggy took advantage of the comfortable chairs to ease the strain on her back, but Rock paced and Molly stood at the windows, her arms wrapped tight around her, and watched as night flowed into dawn.

Reds, then golds, backlit the mountains to the east.

Worry, then a searing anger coursed through Molly.

Why hadn't she told Sam that she loved him? Why hadn't she admitted it sooner to herself? Why, why had she been so cautious, so damned determined to take things slowly, one step at a time?

Love was a risk, a prize to be snatched up and held onto

for all it was worth. If... *When* Sam recovered, Molly vowed fiercely, she wouldn't let another sun set before telling him that she wanted to share more than a couch with him. She wanted to share Buck Randall and sweaty, steaming workouts and bucket seats and his house or her house or any place they decided to call home.

Slowly, the dawn brightened into day.

More people arrived. The General Molly had met briefly at the banquet. Another couple who greeted Peggy and Rock as old friends and Molly as new ones. Then Davinia and 'Tonio, after a phone call from Molly dragged them from sleep. She barely noticed when the auburn-haired captain Sam had introduced her to last night showed up. Her striking lavender eyes dark with concern, Janet Green huddled with Rock to learn Sam's condition.

He'd been in surgery for two hours when Al Kaplan arrived, red-eyed, unshaven and still wearing his ruffled white dress shirt. He'd been on his way home when he got the call from central dispatch, he told Molly in a private aside. Rubbing a hand wearily over his face, he filled her in on events subsequent to Walters's arrest.

"The congressman gave us a full confession. He admitted shooting Joey, but not for any of the reasons we suspected. Seems his wife has a drug problem. A serious problem. She almost OD'd last year, but the MacGiver family physician covered it up."

"Oh, no!"

If worry for Sam hadn't drained Molly's store of emotions, she might have felt a tug of sympathy for the raven-haired woman who'd smiled and waved to the audience so graciously last night.

"Evidently her dependency caused a rift in their marriage that led the congressman to seek companionship elsewhere on occasion."

"Like with Lieutenant Donovitch."

Kaplan's shoulders lifted under his rumpled, ruffled shirt. "And one or two others, it seems. He claims he loved his wife, though. Enough to try to cut off her supply, anyway. Joey responded by threatening to expose the Missus's coke habit. Walters believed she couldn't take the public humiliation, and he wouldn't let himself be blackmailed by the man he says was killing his wife by keeping her supplied with drugs."

After facing Joshua Walters over the barrel of a gun, Molly didn't quite buy his story. She suspected that the man had been driven as much by his own political ambitions as concern for his wife's addiction. That would be for a jury to decide, though. Right now, her sole focus was the surgeon who walked into the waiting room.

Tugging a green surgical cap off his head, he glanced around the assembled crowd. He nodded to the General, but it was Molly he moved toward. Evidently he didn't have any difficulty identifying the woman wearing a green hospital bathrobe and a stark white face as the one he'd come in search of.

"Major Henderson sent me out to check on you, Ms. Duncan. He came out from under the anesthetic demanding to know how you're doing."

"I'm fine," Molly gasped. "What about Sam?"

The surgeon rubbed the back of his neck. "The man's got the hardest head I ever took a saw to."

When he saw that didn't exactly reassure the group, Molly in particular, he grinned.

"Major Henderson should be back in fighting form soon."

"Thank God!"

A rumble of heartfelt relief rose from the gathered occupants of the waiting room. Never one to show her emotions, Molly nevertheless promptly burst into tears. The surgeon waited until she'd dragged up the lapel of the hospital bathrobe and swiped her nose before continuing.

"Sam sustained a fracture to his occipital…the bone that forms the floor and lower rear wall of the cranium. I had to go in and clean out some glass and bone fragments. It's a miracle none of them cut into the spinal column."

For a moment, nausea threatened to choke Molly. Sam had dragged himself out of the Mustang, followed her across a quarter mile of desert, and thrown himself at Walters with bone and glass grinding at the base of his skull. He could have severed his spine, paralyzed himself for life. She was still fighting down the taste of bile when she caught the tail end of the surgeon's next comment. Her fingers fisted on the bathrobe.

"What did you say?" she demanded, her chest squeezing. "What else did you find in there?"

"A bone fragment so small I almost missed it," he said slowly. "It was lodged right up against the edge of the foramen magnum…the opening the spinal column passes through…and didn't show on the X rays. The calcification makes me think the fragment's from an older injury."

Rock appeared at Molly's side and leveled a hard, hopeful look at the surgeon.

"What are you saying, Doc? Do you think this sliver of bone was left over from Drac Man's collision with that canopy?"

"That's my guess."

"Could that splinter of bone have caused his headaches these past months?"

"It could."

"And you got it out?"

At the surgeon's nod, Rock let out a joyous whoop. "Hot damn!"

Wrapping his arms around Molly's waist, he swung her in a wild arc and planted a kiss on her cheek before dropping her to attempt the same service for his pregnant wife. Laughing, Peggy settled for just a kiss. While the warriors in the room speculated joyfully about when Sam might return to full duty, Molly had more immediate concerns on her mind.

Like touching him.

And telling him she loved him.

And hustling him down to the nearest drive-through wedding chapel on the Strip, if he'd have her.

"Wh…?" She snuffled and took another swipe with the hospital bathrobe at tear-blurred eyes. "When can I see him?"

"Right now," the surgeon replied wryly. "Something tells me the Major won't let us take him into recovery until he sees you with his own eyes. Come on, we'll get you masked and gowned."

If she hadn't been hugging the surgeon's assurances that Sam should fully recover to her heart, Molly might have stopped breathing when she saw him lying on the gurney. As it was, she went decidedly weak at the knees. Bandages swathed his entire head, with only small holes for his eyes, nose and mouth. Bright crimson stained the gauze in spots, and he had so many IV lines and tubes strung from various parts of his body that she was afraid to get too close to him, let alone touch him.

Sam, however, had no such scruples. When he spotted her, he gave a low growl and lifted one hand an inch or so off the gurney.

"Mol…ly. You…okay?"

"Yes." She caught his hand in both of hers and clutched it against her breast. "All I got was a few scratches."

"More…than…a few."

"I'm okay, Sam, honestly. You just rest and get well quickly. We…" She sniffled behind her mask. "We still have to try out that couch you promised to share with me."

His fingers curled around hers with surprising strength for a man who'd just cracked his skull.

"More...than...couch. I love...you."

The tears poured down with a vengeance now. Of all the romantic settings they could have chosen for this moment, a surgical anteroom wasn't the one Molly would have picked.

"I love you, too, Sam."

Chapter 15

The sun blazed a bright arc across an achingly blue sky when Molly woke late in the afternoon. She rolled over in bed, wincing at the ache in her shoulder left over from the crash and let the sunshine pouring in through the windows bathe her in a healing balm.

She hadn't bothered to close the shades when Davinia and Antonio had brought her home just past noon. All she'd managed was a quick sponge bath, made awkward by the bandages on her scraped palms, and a mindless tumble into bed. The few hours of sleep she snatched had taken at least the top layer off her physical and emotional exhaustion.

She stretched languorously, ignoring the sharp stab in her shoulder from the pulled muscle. Despite her various aches, she felt wonderful. Terrific. Filled with the most incredible, delicious joy.

Smiling, she rolled over, dragging the puffy green duvet with her, and reached for the phone sitting atop its upturned cardboard box. Through eyes still sticky with sleep, she squinted at the number she'd scribbled down before leaving the hospital.

A man answered on the second ring.

"Hello."

Brimming with relief at the strong, sure tenor of Sam's sexy drawl, she smiled into the phone.

"Hello yourself."

She cradled the phone against her ear, tingling all over at the sound of his voice.

"I've been lying here thinking about you and what we'll do when you get home. As Buck would say, I've got a bad case of the wants for you, big guy."

A short silence answered her, then the drawl got even deeper.

"That's nice to know, sweetheart."

Molly frowned, catching a hint of an unfamiliar cadence in the reply. She pushed herself up on one elbow, her relief plummeting into worry. Sam must be in pain and trying to disguise it from her. Maybe his headaches had returned. Or the doc...

"Much as I'd like to work on that case of the wants," the speaker said laconically, breaking into her anxious thoughts, "I think you may want to speak to Sam. Hang on, he's right here."

Molly flopped back onto the bed, torn between laughter and mortification. Evidently, she'd just propositioned a complete stranger. She heard a short, pithy conversation, and what sounded like a roomful of males ribbing the helpless patient.

"Molly?"

"Who was that?" she choked out.

"My brother Jake."

"Oh, no!"

Sam's chuckle drifted over the phone. "Don't worry. Jake's too hog-tied by the sixty inches of pure energy he married to take you up on your offer, whatever the heck it was.''

"I'll tell you what it was in person," Molly sputtered. "I'm never calling you again, by the way. Every time I do, I get the wrong man."

His reply was a slow, soft caress. "No, sweetheart, you've got the right man."

Her embarrassment melted, swept away by a rush of love. Sam was right. She had the right man, and she planned to keep him. Sam Henderson didn't know it yet, but she was going to hog-tie him every bit as tight as his brother reportedly was.

"Jake wants to meet you," he told her with another chuckle. "Marsh and Hoss, too. Reece says he doesn't need to. Any woman who can take down a killer like you did has his approval, sight unseen."

"Are all your brothers there?"

"Unfortunately. They're just getting ready to head up to my place, though. The doc says I need sleep more than I need four ugly faces hovering over me right now."

Gulping, Molly realized that she'd soon be facing the four Henderson brothers. She had some serious repair work to do to her face and hair before that traumatic event.

"Get that sleep," she told Sam softly. "I'll see you tomorrow."

Facing the Henderson brothers turned out to be even more traumatic than Molly had anticipated.

Her doorbell rang less than an hour later. Smoothing her bandaged palms down the sides of the cherry red chenille top she wore with her jeans, she pulled in a deep breath and opened the door.

To a man, the Hendersons were tall and rangy and cast in the same ruggedly handsome mold as Sam. The oldest,

Jake, did the honors, tipping his well-worn Stetson to the back of his head as he introduced himself and the others.

Molly showed them in, too overwhelmed by so much blatant masculinity to feel flustered by their quick, appraising glances around her near-empty rooms.

"Sam told us to make ourselves useful while he's stove up, Molly. Are you moving into his place, or do we move his stuff over here?"

She faced the semicircle, blinking. "I beg your pardon?"

"He said to move his stuff," the second brother, Hoss, put in with a grin. "Or your stuff. He wasn't particular which, as long as a certain couch got moved to the exact spot you want it."

"Oh, well..."

Faced with four handsome, shrewdly assessing males, Molly made a lightning decision.

"I don't have as much to move. We'll take my things over to his place."

"Sounds good to me," one of the men said, Reece she thought. "Just tell us when you're ready, and we'll start hauling."

"I guess that depends on when Sam gets out of the hospital."

"Or when you two plan to tie the knot," the fourth brother put in quietly.

Leaner, darker, more intent than the other three, he eyed Molly with a keen, slicing intelligence.

"Sam's had a rough time these past six months," he said slowly. "We knew it was bad when he stayed here to go through physical therapy instead of coming home to Arizona to recuperate. But we didn't know about the headaches...or about the fact that he was getting ready to hang up his uniform for good."

Jake shook his dark head, threaded with just a touch of silver at the temples. "If ever a man was born to fly, Sam was. He could take Pop's little Cessna apart and put it back together again by the time he was six.''

"It must have cut him deep to face losing the Air Force. From what he's told us about you, Molly, it would cut him even deeper to lose you.''

From the grim expressions on their faces, Molly got the impression that no one messed with a Henderson's heart and lived to tell about it.

"If you're asking whether my intentions toward your brother are honorable,'' she replied, duplicating exactly their rich, rolling accents, ''they are. As a matter of fact, Sam and I might hit the drive-by window at the Four Aces Casino and Wedding Chapel on his way home from the hospital.''

Every one of the brothers blanched.

"I hope you'll reconsider that one,'' Jake pleaded. "Mom's the gentlest soul on earth, but I wouldn't want to be within a thousand miles of that woman if she misses her baby's wedding.''

It took a mental leap for Molly to envision the six-feet-plus of solid muscle that was Sam Henderson as anyone's baby, but she managed. Barely.

"Why don't we all wait until Sam has a chance to vote on this?'' she suggested.

For the first time, Reece's face relaxed. A smile every bit as wicked as Sam's tugged at his mouth.

"If we use Jake's marriage as a yardstick, I'd say that's the last vote Sam will have.''

As it turned out, Molly and Sam weren't married at the Four Aces Casino and Wedding Chapel.

They were married at the Nellis chapel, with a weepy-eyed Davinia as maid of honor and four handsome Henderson men ranging beside their brother. Molly's heart swelled with pride at the sight of her groom, standing tall and straight in his dress uniform.

The medical board had returned him to full duty. Just last night, Sam had confessed that the need to drag on his flight suit and climb into a jet pulled at his very soul. But not, he'd whispered, his hands and mouth working magic on Molly, as much as he needed to make love to his green-eyed woman.

Those green eyes misty, she glided down the aisle to the strains of Buck Randall's ode to the slippery slide that was love.

* * * * *

Discover the secrets of

CODE NAME: DANGER

in

MERLINE LOVELACE'S

thrilling duo

DANGEROUS TO KNOW

When tricky situations need a cool head, quick wits and a touch of ruthlessness, Adam Ridgeway, director of the top secret OMEGA agency, sends in his team. Lately, though, his agents have had romantic troubles of their own....

UNDERCOVER MAN & PERFECT DOUBLE

And don't miss
TEXAS HERO
(IM #1165, 8/02)
which features the newest OMEGA adventure!

If you liked this set of stories, be sure to find
DANGEROUS TO HOLD.
Available from your local retailer
or at our online bookstore.

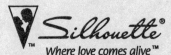

Where love comes alive™

Receive **75¢ off** your next

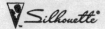 *Silhouette*®

INTIMATE MOMENTS™

book purchase.

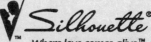

Receive **75¢ off** your next

Silhouette®

INTIMATE MOMENTS™

book purchase.

75¢ OFF!

**Your next Silhouette Intimate Moments™
book purchase.**

**Coupon expires December 31, 2002.
Redeemable at participating retail outlets in Canada only.
Limit one coupon per purchase.**

52604010

Silhouette®
Where love comes alive™

FREE
Gourmet Garden Kit!

With two proofs of purchase from any four Silhouette® special collector's editions.

Special Limited Time Offer

YES! Please send me my FREE Gourmet Garden Kit without cost or obligation, except for shipping and handling. Enclosed are two proofs of purchase from specially marked Silhouette® special collector's editions and $3.50 shipping and handling fee.

Name (PLEASE PRINT)

Address   Apt. #

City   State/Prov.   Zip/Postal Code

IN U.S., mail to:
Silhouette Gourmet Garden Kit Offer
3010 Walden Ave.
P.O. Box 9023
Buffalo, NY 14269-9023

IN CANADA, mail to:
Silhouette Gourmet Garden Kit Offer
P.O. Box 608
Fort Erie, Ontario
L2A 5X3

FREE GOURMET GARDEN KIT OFFER TERMS
To receive your free Gourmet Garden Kit, complete the above order form. Mail it to us with two proofs of purchase, one of which can be found in the upper right-hand corner of this page. Requests must be received no later than December 31, 2002. Your Gourmet Garden Kit costs you only $3.50 for shipping and handling. The free Gourmet Garden Kit has a retail value of $17.00 U.S. All orders subject to approval. Products in kit illustrated on the back inside cover of this book are for illustrative purposes only, and items may vary (retail value of items always as previously indicated). **Please allow 6-8 weeks for delivery. Offer good in Canada and the U.S. only.** Offer good only while quantities last. Offer limited to one per household.

© 2002 Harlequin Enterprises Limited
598 KGJ DNCX